Chapter One

Monday morning, I'm trying to bottle up my nerves about starting my new job. I've managed to succeed in getting the job as the deputy heads' assistant at Bank Croft primary school which is in a small tucked away village where I grew up. This is the first job I've actually ever got, but despite my nerves I'm really excited as the interview I'd had to get in had gone really well.

"Hello, I'm Violet Spring, here for the job interview." I'd introduced myself to a young woman behind a desk. She smiled warmly and led me to a small room down the corridor which had an older woman waiting inside. She got straight to the point and asked me many questions about why I wanted the job; she seemed impressed with my answers and appreciated my honesty.

"Well I'm sure the deputy head will be glad of having a work partner, you can start next week if that's suitable for you." The woman offered me the job there and then so I gladly accepted in surprise, "That would be great, thanks."

Feeling confident now from that uplifting thought I decide to make the ten minute walk across the village to the school. Many people are out and the sun is shining quite high in the light blue sky. I now approach a gate with a bolt on it, which looks newly painted black to hide the rust forming underneath. There is a winding zigzag path leading up to the main school, so I take a deep breath and make my way up to press on the buzzer so someone can let me in.

A young blond woman comes over and opens the door for me; she smiles which calms some of my previous nerves.

"Hello I'm Violet Spring, the new assistant here," I tell her in a quiet voice. Understanding instantly lights her gaze, "I'm Jess, just wait here on one of those red chairs while I get some of the staff to welcome you," she says in a clear and kind voice. While I wait I glance around at all the brightly coloured displays and best work the children have done from all the year groups. The school seems quite friendly with the bird logo on display; there are pictures of different year groups on school trips and staff members raising money for charity. Although proud achievements are clearly being shown I feel like there is a good atmosphere here, and hopefully it's not one of those schools where awards mean everything.

I turn around as I hear footsteps heading my way; six new faces come around the corner along with Jess. They usher me into what must be the staffroom and then we all sit down.

"This is Violet Spring, the deputy heads' assistant," Jess announces to them cheerily. Six pairs of eyes all focus on me and I begin to feel self-conscious.

"I am Miss Collins, the Year Six teacher," a small woman with short, light brown hair tied up in a ponytail and wearing as close to casual clothes as work allows, is the one who is introducing herself to me. I smile timidly; at least she seems nice enough.

"Miss Blake, the Year Five teacher" declares a woman who must be mid-thirties, she's slightly tanned and average height with hazel brown eyes and darker brown hair.

"This is Mrs Parker the Year Four teacher, Miss Thomas for Year Three, Miss Fisher for Year Two and Mrs Green is the Year One teacher," finishes Jess flicking away a blond curl from her face.

They study me and I quietly observe them too, the Year One, Two and Four teachers look like the ones to be most afraid of and who I should steer clear from.

"Well now all the introductions are done I'm sure you'll be quite welcome and settle in here," Jess smiles, turns and then vacates the room leaving me alone with them.

"So Violet, have you met the deputy head yet?" Miss Thomas asks me in a curious tone, I bite my lip feeling rather awkward.

"Not yet, but I guess I will in a few minutes," I reply trying not to show my nerves despite my slight hesitation. Mrs Green's eyes narrow ever so slightly before she huffs an irritated "Yes indeed."

The teachers leave to prepare their lessons for the day while I'm led to a fairly big office which has two huge wooden desks, spin chairs and a flower in a purple vase which has not quite begun to bloom yet. The deputy head's desk is neat but piled high with stacks of work and papers. I marvel at the fact that this is where I will be working from now on, however I won't settle just yet as the person I have to work with will determine whether this job will be suitable for me. I really hope we will get along otherwise this won't be the job I have desired for all this time.

I glance at my watch, surely the deputy head should be arriving by now I think to myself, beginning to let my impatience get the better of me. Seconds later Jess enters looking slightly flustered, "I'm afraid that the deputy head won't be coming in till the afternoon," she stutters a little, seeming rather on edge. "Um, there is this work you can do in his absence; it should take you through till he arrives." Jess now finishes looking worried and tired before excusing herself and stumbling out. I pause for a moment in mild confusion and can't help but let out a long sigh. This day is clearly going to be a stressful one I think to myself before flicking through the work that looks many pages long, deep joy.

Although there is a lot of work it's not as bad as I'd originally thought, I just have to write the school letters and fill out advice forms which is boring but at least passes the time. I was startled when Miss Collins popped her head around the corner and invited me to sit with her for lunch as I didn't recall there being a break time; I must have worked right through it. Even though I still don't know who I'm the assistant of yet I can't help but feel more confident and comfortable now as at least I seem to have made one friend here. Miss Collins leads me to a dry spot under a drooping willow tree outside, "So Violet, I'm Izzie Collins." I feel a wave of relief that I now know her first name, otherwise that would have been inconvenient.

"So how long have you worked here?" I ask curiously, as she can only be a year or two older than me.

"Two and a half years, it's my first job and I quite enjoy it," Izzie answers, happy to tell me all the details and confirming my thoughts. I'm so glad that I have someone who will help me settle here and who I can put any questions that I have to.

"OK, the people you should probably avoid to live longer are Mrs Green, Mrs Parker and possibly Miss Fisher," Izzie half jokes, but I can tell she means it at the same time. Well that is what I'd thought this morning anyway, so no surprise there.

"What's the matter with them?" I enquire anyway and Izzie sighs.

"Mrs Green is one of the worst people you will ever meet, Mrs Parker is a snob and Miss Fisher has very quick mood swings," she explains with a grin.

I cannot help but laugh at that, "I feel so much better now about seeing them every day," I giggle uncontrollably.

Suddenly concluding all conversation the bell rings out loudly signalling that lunchtime has come to an end, that's a shame I had been enjoying our little chat.

"I guess I'll see you later, I have to bring my class in now." Izzie smiles and then we both head off in different directions.

I walk slowly back into my shared office, I'm not really looking forward to meeting who I'm working with now because if they have arrived from being late for whatever reason the chances are they're likely to be in a bad mood. Actually it's probably better if they just don't turn up for the rest of the day as my energy is spent now and I don't know if I can be bothered with any more introductions. Right on cue, an older and clearly confident no-nonsense man strides into the room, he glances me over from my waist long black hair, green eyes and pale skin down to my black boots which are newly polished.

"I'm afraid that the deputy head will not be in today for personal reasons," he spoke boldly, looking me right in the eye. This must be the headmaster I think to myself, whilst also wondering how I am going to survive here.

"Well I'm Michael Lewis the headmaster, and when the deputy head actually turns up..." he grumbles slightly towards the end. He then continues with "I'm sure you'll fit in here well," we both exchange small smiles, not happy about the fact that the deputy head is not here evident on our faces. He turns and walks out without another word, well isn't that great I sarcastically contemplate to myself. Luckily I have finished with my mountain of work from earlier so I opt to get myself a drink in the staffroom as no one can leave until all the children have gone home, and after a staff meeting every night. A staff meeting every night, I scoff to myself, I mean what the hell is the point in that?

So if I'm going to be stuck here then I may as well make a cup of tea and check my phone to pass the evening hours. I soon realise however that checking my phone isn't a very effective way of passing a substantial amount of time; I guess tomorrow I should bring a book for some entertainment.

I glance at my watch for what must be the hundredth time when I notice that Michael has suddenly appeared in the doorway, he registers that I am sitting around doing nothing so he comes over to join me.

"I'm sorry that the deputy head's not here, I'm afraid there's nothing I can give you to do in his absence," he sighs. Michael's clearly irritated by the deputy heads' absence even more than he intended to let on.

"It's OK at least I've met everyone else," I try to reassure him and also I don't want him thinking anything bad about me on my first day. He simply nods and before I can feel any more agitated for the day to be over, I hear all the parents collecting their children and this eases my mood.

Within a matter of minutes the teachers start filing in and allocating themselves seats for the meeting. Izzie sits on my other side and Mrs Green and Mrs Parker seem to purposefully choose the furthest away seats making Miss Blake roll her eyes, which in turn annoys Miss Fisher, great. Michael instantly manages to reduce the tension that had begun to fill the room with his opening line.

"Well it's been a good start to a new week, Violet Spring has joined us and we should hopefully have no more complaints from parents about P.E lessons as new equipment has been bought." Michael proclaims optimistically then gestures for us all to have our say in the daily meeting.

Miss Blake now makes herself heard, "Well I have no complaints about my class, I just feel we may need more whiteboards for lessons, recently we've been doing group work instead which makes it harder to see who is struggling and who is doing all the work."

Michael quickly responds with, "Well Mrs Parker, you don't tend to use yours often so that's that problem solved." He glances between Miss Blake and Mrs Parker as he makes this rather bold decision.

"But what if I need them at the same time as Miss Blake's class?" Mrs Parker practically hisses back at him, she's fairly old with short grey, untidy hair and is wearing her glasses at the end of her nose so she can glare over them at Miss Blake.

"You will have to plan your lessons so that they don't clash then!" Michael thunders back in retort, not prepared to let Mrs Parker shatter his idea. Mrs Green's eyes narrow more than I would have thought possible, however she is clearly intent on holding her tongue. Miss Blake and Miss Thomas direct their gazes resolutely at the floor, Miss Fisher gives the impression that she is completely disinterested and Izzie and I share a loaded look and remain silent.

"Well if nobody's got anything else to add it's time for us to go home." Michael huffs, unimpressed.

I glance at my watch, it's already half four and the school day ended at quarter past three. We all silently grab our bags and walk out after such a dramatic dismissal, Izzie waves to me before I turn the corner and quickly depart.

I feel drained after such a tense and awkward day which seems ridiculous as it's only the first one I've had, but if every day is as dramatic and stressful as this one then I don't know how I'm going to cope. I stop off at a local corner shop to take my mind off everything, but seeing as it's a small shop there isn't much to be said about choice. I settle for a packet of Skittles and a bar of chocolate before deciding to take the longer walk home so I can skip the railway station, and queues of traffic. I feed the ducks which are swimming by in a slow, glittering river where you can see all the shiny, vibrant coloured scales of the fish which dart in and out of the reeds. This is my favourite river in the area as it has much more wildlife around to enjoy than the others.

I return home to my small flat which I've decorated a lot to make it as homely as possible. The main room houses my kitchen, sofas and TV and the other room is my bedroom which has an adjoining en suite near the wardrobe.

Hopefully tomorrow will go better than today did and I'll get the chance to meet the deputy head who I'm hoping will like me. I sigh and let my mind drift to what he'll be like, if he's anything like Michael who is nice but more of a hindrance than a help then I'd rather not bother with the hassle.

Chapter Two

I quickly get drenched as I set off outside; it's pouring down tear drop like rain and I have no umbrella to shield myself with. I rush up to the door where Jess is waiting, expecting my arrival and she immediately opens it for me.

"I knew you'd be here soon so I thought I should probably wait to let you in as its awful weather out there," she smiles despite the fact that her hair's damp too, clearly still not dry even though she arrived here much before me.

"Thanks, is anyone else here yet?" I ask and she hears the nerves colouring my tone of voice.

"Not just yet, but I guess they will be here soon." Jess says and then returns back behind her desk.

I head over to my office and get my comb out so I can try to make it neater and dry over the radiator, which is burning hot. Crap, I think as I hear the gruff voice of Mrs Parker as she storms into the staffroom. So she's already in a bad mood and the day's not even started. My hair is now mostly dry but I put my scarf on around my neck to prevent it from getting damp or cold. I can hear the other teachers gradually beginning to arrive and then Michael also shows up.

"Morning Violet," he greets me cheerily despite the fact that his short brown hair is completely soaked and beginning to curl at the ends. I smile back and continue to dry myself in order to warm up a bit as it's slightly chilly. Izzie also briefly pops in to see me, but she had to go as she has forgotten all her plans for class and therefore quickly needs to form new ones.

Miss Blake and Miss Thomas have now arrived too, they keep me company for a while but have to go and set up their classrooms for the day. Panic races through me as I hear a new, unfamiliar and appealing voice greet Jess outside and then footsteps are heading my way. I tug my scarf off and sling it over the radiator, whilst trying to smooth my now static hair.

He now stands in the doorway, red-brown shoes, smart grey-black trousers and a pale blue shirt with a neat red tie indicating that he's very presentable. He also has pale cream skin, rose pink lips, sea blue eyes and fairly short, dark brown hair which is drenched by the rain. As soon as his eyes meet mine, a smile so welcoming and pure spreads across his flawless face.

"I'm guessing you must be Violet Spring." He speaks in a confident and yet somehow soft voice which has me instantly.

When I nod and smile back he continues with, "I am Tyler Crowther, and it's a pleasure to meet you." We shake hands before we sit down together and I observe him quietly, he's the naturally charming type and clearly very well mannered.

"So how come you weren't in yesterday?" I probe hesitantly, not wanting to invade his privacy. He pauses for a moment before looking me in the eye, his face serious and even cautious.

"My father's very ill, and my parents are split up so..." he trails off and I understand immediately and instantly feel guilty for even asking, a fact that must have somehow shown on my face.

"It's OK, you didn't know," he reassures me gently but it doesn't make me consider my question to have been justified. Only a couple of months ago I lost my mother and a few years before that my father too, I bite my lip which is now wobbling and do my utmost not to cry. It's bad enough to lose your parents, but it's much worse if they were murdered by the same killer. Luckily the killer is locked up; before that I always worried he would hunt down and murder me too.

Seeming to notice my woeful reaction to the topic he holds my hand and gently squeezes it, however he does not question me as he can tell I am in no state to confide in him. Then he gets up and moves over to his paper filled desk, sighing he begins leafing through all the documents. If only he didn't have to go through all the pain soon as well I meditate on regretfully.

"If only I could dump all this in the bin," he jokes to me; I can't help but crack a smile at that, especially when we both realize that Michael's standing in the doorway and has heard.

"Well if you do that Tyler, that's your ticket out of here." Michael comments before turning to me with, "This is who you're working with from now on." I smirk and Michael leaves, rolling his eyes on the way out. Tyler and I look at each other, my smirk quickly leading to my shoulders quaking with laughter and tears streaming down my face until I can no longer contain myself and end up laughing out loud.

"Well isn't that great," Tyler laughs hard too, his face lifting into a smile.

We don't have much chance to talk now though as we are sharing the work out and I can't help but repeatedly glance at the heavy load that we have to get through before lunchtime. Tyler notices me peering at it.

"Bad isn't it?" he mock frowns and shakes his head sadly before continuing and it makes me wonder how much work he's used to. What could only have been five minutes later he was shaking his hand out to get rid of the ache of writing and I hear him quietly cuss to himself. My shoulders begin trembling uncontrollably again and my hand shakes with the effort of attempting to write. Tears begin sliding down my cheeks and I desperately try to suppress my laughter. Despite my best efforts though he picks up on it immediately and throws me a fake scowl which only makes it that much harder to remain silent.

Izzie comes in to discover us both clutching our sides laughing and our unfinished work all over the floor because Tyler has knocked it flying accidentally with his elbow making us chortle harder.

"You've only met a few hours ago and this is how I find you like you've known each other for years," she comments playfully which makes me blush before she continues with, "when Michael sees that paperwork's not finished you're both going to get killed," Izzie grins. Damn it, it's already lunchtime and Tyler was meant to hand Michael the papers now. Surprisingly though he simply shrugs, puts on a bravado face and dumps the not even nearly finished pile on Michael's desk.

"Well I'm out of here because he's going to be really mad and I don't want to be around when it happens," I tell them, Izzie and Tyler agree and we all walk out as fast as we can to escape outside.

"Aww nuts, I was in such a rush to get out of there I left my lunch inside our office," Tyler complains to us once we are a safe distance away.

"Well it's your choice if you actually want to risk going back in there," Izzie answers him, amused.

"Look how much trouble you've got me in on our first day together," Tyler starts laughing again, but we all share our lunch with him to save him from getting an earlier death than if he went inside now. Oh well all my previous nerves about who I would be working for have evaporated, my only concerns are how am I actually going to get any work done with him around? Izzie went to collect her class and me and Tyler are dreading going back to our office so we walk there as slowly as possible. Michael's already there when we arrive and I know we are going to get it now, and now we're actually going to get punished for it, it isn't that amusing.

"Take a seat," he spoke in a quiet voice which immediately alarmed me, I'm not going to be fooled by his calm attitude and facial expression.

"After I was pleased about the first sixteen documents done and ready on my desk, I discovered that all the others were not complete." Michael continues in the same measured voice.

"Violet it's your second day so I guess this can be mostly overlooked, Tyler however you very much know the rules I should think," he says in a harder tone now, losing the calmness. I glance at the floor and refuse to look at Michael, Tyler on the other hand is daring enough to look him straight in the eye.

"Violet your punishment is to finish the remaining the work, and Tyler you can write up the entire school newsletters, calendars and welcome packs by yourself" Michael thunders before striding back to his office.

I can't bear to look at Tyler, the amount of work he has to do is intolerable.

"I thought he was going to decrease my pay, so it could have been much worse," he breathes out exasperatedly and turns on his laptop to get started. I suppose he has a point, we got off very lightly compared to what could have happened. I finish with an aching hand an hour before the school day is due to end, Tyler seems to have done the calendar and welcome packs but is at a loss for what he should do for the newsletters. I go to Michael's office and put my work on his desk, I wonder where he is though because if he's not around I can help Tyler with the newsletter. Jess spots me coming out of his office and informs me that he will be back in roughly twenty minutes.

Not wanting to waste any of the precious time I have to spare I rush back to assist Tyler. I had written half of it when both our heads snap up at the sound of footsteps heading in our direction and I rush away from Tyler and the laptop to make it appear like I have been nowhere near them. I collect the welcome packs and calendars which seriously weigh a tonne so Michael will see me placing them on his desk next to my completed work. He nods to show his approval, checks how far Tyler has gotten with the newsletter and then leaves us in peace. As it's probably too dangerous for me to continue working on the newsletter with Tyler now as Michael can turn up again at any particular time, I get my book out instead. Finally

Tyler finishes and we decide to get a drink in the staffroom while we wait for the meeting.

"Thanks for helping me out, I would've been screwed otherwise." Tyler looks tired and full of relief, there are the beginnings of dark circles forming underneath his eyes from the hard day's work. I relax back into the sofa and finish my drink, now feeling refreshed and revived.

"In a way it was still worth it, being stupid earlier," I admit to him because although we got punished for it it had to be the most fun I've had in ages, also it's proved that I have another firm friend here.

He grins in assent,"Yeah it was very boring before being on my own and it was impossible to get all the work done." Tyler grimaces, remembering what it has been like for him until a couple of days ago. I have to agree, it must really be not that much fun if you can't even talk to anyone else and have a joke.

The school bell peals out then and the teachers commence slowly arriving in a steady stream into the staffroom now that their classes are on the way home. Izzie sits down on my other side and Michael perches on Tyler's other side as if to keep him in check.

"So how has everyone's day gone, is there anything that can be improved upon?" Michael asks in a surprisingly neutral and soft voice. For the first time Mrs Green chooses to voice her complaints which must have built up dramatically since this time yesterday.

"I'd like to bring to your attention that the summer fête is coming up and none of it has been organised yet, my class is getting quite persistent on appealing for details about it." Even her voice sounds what a snake's might sound like if it could speak.

"Tyler has already prepared the newsletter to inform parents of that particular event," Michael slyly returns in a smug voice. Well he wouldn't have if he hadn't been given it as a punishment today I think sarcastically, but obviously he didn't care to mention that little detail. Mrs Green falls silent, stumped that her master plan has failed when she clearly hadn't expected it to.

Me, Tyler and Izzie refuse to speak up because we want to go home as soon as possible and not delay our departure, and the other teachers only have a few simple comments about matters which easily get resolved. I can feel Tyler's desperation to get out of here which only ends up strengthening my own desire to leave. Finally Michael dismisses us and I speed out the room as fast as is physically possible.

"See you tomorrow Violet," Tyler calls to me and I turn and wave to him. His lovely blue eyes hold mine for an immeasurable amount of time before he heads off into the car park to get to his car.

I'm pleased that the day's over and yet I'm already missing the sweet sound of Tyler's laugh and Izzie's quirky comments. I yearn for company as I can't just phone up my parents for support or a simple chat about my day. At least today has been much more enjoyable than its predecessor though and Tyler and Izzie have really cheered me up even though I've only known them both for such a small amount of time. It's going to be hard being alone at the weekend but I can happily anticipate seeing them next week which is nice because I never usually have anything to look forward to. So now I have two new acquaintances and maybe some day I'll tell them all about my parents, but for now it's too soon to burden them with the knowledge and I fear of having a melt down when divulging my secret.

I turn my TV on and start flicking through all the channels, not to my surprise though there's nothing on that takes my fancy and so I put a DVD on instead. Suddenly though I hear music playing from my bedroom, which I now recognise as my ring tone blaring out. Who would be calling me at this time?

"Hello," I answer wearily as the number of the person who is calling is displayed as unknown on my screen, meaning it's not one of my contacts.

"Hi Violet, it's Izzie. I'm really sorry I had to trawl through your paperwork to find your number but this is urgent!" she exclaims loudly and bewilderment ripples through me, what could be so urgent that she needs to call me?

"What's the matter?" I ask fearing something awful now and my voice comes out slightly high.

"Tomorrow morning Mrs Green is planning on making her class do a protest about everyone else," Izzie rushes through her explanation in a panicky voice, which makes my nerves intensify.

"What do you mean? And what can I do about it?" Utter confusion fills my mind.

"If parents find out any one of us could lose our job and I think Tyler will suffer the biggest blows." Following this pronouncement Izzie informs me on everything we need to do tomorrow to prevent this from taking place.

Now that I'm off the phone the pieces fall into place, of course Tyler would be in the most trouble as thanks to Michael mentioning he has prepared the newsletter which stumped Mrs Green's plans she is taking another course of action. It is clear that everyone had been shocked and amazed to discover that the newsletter was ready, which makes me wonder if it's ever been ready on time before which is why she was so confident with her plan. So I could also potentially be in trouble as she's bound to link my arrival to the fact that it's actually been done for once, and may feel that I'm partly responsible. I had thought it was odd that she didn't even consider the fact that her plan could easily have been foiled because the chances of that actually occurring were so minor.

Well I'm determined to shatter her selfish plans before she can implement them tomorrow, me and Izzie are purposefully going in early to make preparations. The only thing I don't understand is why Mrs Green would let us know in advance what she is going to do, does she really think that it will threaten us and scare us into treating her very highly or something? Either way me and Izzie have the perfect plan which will wear hers down until it no longer exists.

Chapter Three

I have just arrived insanely early and rush to Mrs Green's classroom where I find Izzie who has already started on our agreed assault, she smiles at me pleased that I have arrived so soon.

"I've already removed all the paper, pens and whiteboards from her classroom," she cheerily informs me. Luckily we don't need to worry about her taking the other classrooms supplies because as a recent new rule, teachers are forbidden from entering another teacher's classroom in case it's a cause for distraction.

"We still have one problem though, she can easily make her class call out and shout a protest instead." I remind Izzie, as I'm concerned there's nothing we can do about that.

"I've already prepared for that, I've arranged it so that all teachers will be in a meeting for the afternoon while classes are put together for workshops. Also those workshops will only be here in the hall for the week with instructors who can keep all the children out of the way." Izzie slyly confesses how much effort she's put into her plans against Mrs Green's even more devious ones.

So that only leaves the morning to fret about Mrs Green's class protest revolving around the other members of staff. We head off to the staffroom as now there's nothing left we can do to prepare and this way we'll know when she arrives. Almost all of the other teachers have arrived when we get there, funnily enough though with the exception of Mrs Green. As I sit beside Izzie I feel my nerves escalate and suspicions grow, as I wonder what will happen when she discovers the whereabouts of her classroom supplies.

Izzie and the other teachers head to their classrooms while I go to mine and Tyler's office, silently cursing the panicked state I'm now in. Tyler hasn't arrived yet so to ease my mood and mind I decide to do something I know most people would probably frown upon. I seat myself on my office chair and casually start spinning in circles around the room, several times I have to use my hands to stop myself colliding with the desks around me. I'm momentarily completely oblivious to the fact that the door has opened and he is standing there behind me.

"Having fun?" an amused voice enquires from behind me and I instantly spin around and stand up, trying to shove the chair behind me and remove the evidence of what he's already witnessed. Tyler has an extremely pronounced smirk on his face and his eyebrows raise while he shakes his head in mock disbelief. I try really hard not to laugh but it is already too late and a giggle slips through my lips.

"Sorry I was just trying to take my mind off something," I admit, feeling embarrassed. However now I'm just worrying about Mrs Green all over again.

"What's the matter?" he asks me, concern showing on his handsome face which momentarily distracts me from his question. I can't tell him about Mrs Green's plan though when he's the most likely to suffer from it if she succeeds. As soon as I look into his lovely blue eyes I can tell he knows that whatever I am going to say will not be the truth.

So instead he simply changes the topic, after his eyes have tried to no avail to read my face with great effort and scrutiny.

"Did you know that we basically don't have to do any work this afternoon?" he asks me brightly, which catches me off guard.

"Why's that?" I ask him in surprise and he grins.

"The teachers have a meeting so our work can't build up, also I reckon if we work really hard we could even free up some of our morning," Tyler proudly tells me his master plan and it makes me realize how easy it is for him to make me smile.

Tyler was right, we end up working hard enough so that we have nothing left to do before it is even break time. Quickly checking to see that Michael isn't around we head off outside to find a bench to sit on. Suddenly I realise that I have completely forgotten about Mrs Green's plans and this time I really should tell Tyler, especially as it does concern him. Funnily enough though after I explain everything he doesn't seem at all fazed or even surprised about her plan. Even less concerned about her chances of winning, to him it seems to be an impossibility.

"Why doesn't she like you?" I interrogate him in a sensitive voice; I have to know because there surely has to be more to it than the letter being on time.

Tyler lets out an exasperated sigh,"It's because of what my old job was, she wants to know what I did." He seems slightly shaken and stressed now which tugs at my heart strings.

"What did you do?" I ask him quietly, nervous as I am afraid to upset him.

"I had extremely tough areas of work, so I quit." That's his only response to the topic, so although it isn't exactly much of an explanation I accept it, grateful for any answer at all. He reminds me of my parents and how they wouldn't ever give me a straight, direct answer about what they did. So when I had been questioned about them after their deaths I had hardly been able to provide any information. Strangely though this hadn't perturbed the police in the slightest; they behaved as though they had all the information they needed.

I wait in silence for a moment, but as I'd expected he didn't share anything else about his past.

"How's your dad doing?" I quiz him, remembering an earlier conversation we've had regarding his personal life.

"Better than he was, what about your parents?". He asks a perfectly innocent question but it takes my breath away. Obviously he has no reason to know about what happened to them, however I visibly flinch and turn away from him so that he can't see the tears that spill down my cheeks. I would say something but it feels like my throat's closed up, preventing me from speaking. I know my voice will crack and betray how much pain I am in in any case. I feel him stiffen beside me for a second before gently wrapping his arm around me and whispering, "I'm sorry."

We then notice that it is now break time, Izzie had said she would meet me in our office, but for now I feel drained and would much rather stay with Tyler. Weirdly, despite the fact that I hardly know Tyler he seems to be a great cure to my pain, so I can't bear to leave his presence just yet.

Also I like the feel of his arm around my waist,"You remind me of my parents, they were good people just like you so it's a shame you'll never know them." I tell him sadly, I don't know why but it seems necessary and somehow essential for him to know this. He looks at me in surprise and slight doubt, probably thinking the part about him is nonsense as most people don't usually think very highly about themselves. However he doesn't comment, clearly not wanting to dishearten my thoughts but in a way this proves my point, making what I'd said seem more true.

We stay like this for a while quietly sitting side by side, not too long later Tyler coughs as if he is about to say something until we both see Mrs Green and Izzie clearly having an argument. So I never find out what he was going to say because we share a look and before we can get up to make a quick escape, Mrs Green spots us and thunders over. Izzie hurries behind her with a look of clear distress, panic and above all frustration on her face. Oh great, I wonder how Izzie's plans went down with Mrs Green. At the same time though the scene looks really comical, I know it shouldn't be funny but I'm going to have try desperately hard if I don't want to end up laughing in her face, which is going to be made all the more difficult by Tyler who is already smirking at the situation.

Me and Tyler stand up to ready ourselves for the event before us and I take a deep breath as Tyler's arm quickly leaves my waist as they halt in front of us. We both look embarrassed about what that could have looked like but luckily Mrs Green is too busy focusing on the warpath she's paving right now to notice.
"You would never guess what's happened this morning," she half questions and half scowls at us.
Tyler, somehow managing to keep an amazingly straight face replies with "Your classroom equipment mysteriously went walk about, didn't it?". He spoke in a composed voice but I can hear the hints of deep control it's taking him not to crack. I stare at him in shock, why would he mention that he knew what me and Izzie had done? Mrs Green's eyebrows slowly raise while her lips thin and tighten in cold displeasure.
"Well how interesting, more than one culprit is involved I see." She states, observing us all carefully to assess who is the most guilty of the party.
"Actually you're wrong, I'm the one responsible for this but they both found out." Izzie gestures towards us, shouldering all the blame and showing that she wouldn't be intimidated by Mrs Green.

I feel an overwhelming urge to step in as what kind of friend would I be if I let Izzie claim full responsibility? Tyler however gives me a small jerk of his head when he understands that I've been planning on intervening.
So we all remain silent for a moment before I quickly comment with, "Why is it so important that all your equipment disappeared? I'm sure Michael will sort it out so there's no need to be angry," I feign innocence

hoping to steer the attention away from Izzie. Also this way it looks like she's overreacting about nothing which won't support her case against us later.

At that moment break time ends and so Mrs Green simply resorts to glaring at Izzie, giving me and Tyler a swift glance and holding our gazes for a matter of seconds before striding away. I feel myself tremble slightly from the unexpected confrontation and the fact that this definitely isn't over.

"She's been interrogating and threatening me all morning, stupid bitch." Izzie immediately gushes out her frustration which she'd had to momentarily hold back, Tyler laughs and shakes his head not seeming to care or think we're under any threat whatsoever. It's amazing how last week I had no job and nothing to do, whereas now I have two firm friends and a lot of drama going on.

Izzie rushes off to collect her class leaving me and Tyler on our own again, well we still have the staff meeting to look forward to all afternoon now I think dryly. It's weird how I can't think of anything to say to Tyler and yet it doesn't feel awkward at all, for now I can just enjoy the peace. I catch the sweet scent of the roses from behind us and feel the warm rays of sunshine soaking into my pale skin. When I turn around I notice he is watching me, the sleeves of his white shirt now rolled up past his elbows and his tie has been loosened from around his neck, it reminds me of the first time I'd seen him. He had the same red-brown shoes on and grey-black trousers, but he now wears a matching belt which completes his outstanding good looks. His blue eyes study me in a calm, quiet manner whilst his rose-pink lips are set slightly apart and I feel the heat of his warm breath on my cheek. My heart beat quickens and I have to look away due to the embarrassment of where my thoughts are now taking me.

"Strange how you can know someone but as a matter of fact you don't know anything about them, because I do truly know you, I've picked up on a lot of things since we first met." Tyler states a perfectly true but utterly unexpected comment. He has a point, I know him and Izzie in a lot of ways but that doesn't mean that I know anything about their background or what they like, what their hobbies are etc.

"In that case, I know who you are but tell me some random facts about yourself Tyler." I reply smiling as this should be interesting, he grins and then actually appears rather thoughtful taking some real consideration into what I'd asked.

"OK then my favourite colour is green, I have no siblings, I live on my own and my birthday is the 2nd of March." He finishes looking quite proud of himself, if he lives alone I wonder if that means he is single? I don't pry though and then begin my own mini speech for him in return after a moments pause.

"My favourite colours red, I have no siblings either and I also live alone. My birthday is the 22nd of July and I love reading," I thought it was probably necessary to add that last part on the end so I didn't repeat everything he'd said and plus I couldn't think of anything else to say.

Tyler thoughtfully files away everything I've said for further analysis and reference and then we get up.

"I suppose we should grab some lunch now, we can miss out on the rush that way." He suggests to me and I am more than willing to comply to his wishes, I like to do whatever he says as long as it allows me to stay with him. We walk back to our office in silence, both thinking about separate things which somehow involved the other.

"When is the summer fête?" I ask Tyler curiously, I may as well help out as it's not like I have anything better to do. Besides summer fêtes are always good fun with their separate stalls and raffles which bring about a nice atmosphere to attract people.

"This weekend, which is why I think the parents want to know so badly about all the details so they can help out, also I think the children are really excited this time as last year the barbecue kind of failed." Tyler informs me, grinning and shaking his head with deep amusement.

We collect our lunch boxes from our bags and this time head off towards the canteen. Tyler wants to get a drink, so I decide to pick a small round table tucked away in a corner for us to provide privacy. The canteen is quite big considering it's a primary school and there are brightly coloured displays of work on all of the walls. There's also work hanging from the ceiling to make the room more full with vibrant patterns. I am startled when Tyler dumps his lunch beside me on the table, making me draw my eyes away from the beauty of such a simple room.

"I love being a member of staff, it means you get all the food and drink on a major discount," he tells me cheerily and that's when I notice just how much stuff he has brought with him. It almost takes up the entire table.

"How can you eat that much?" I ask him, having already eaten the majority of my average sized lunch.

"Well I thought I'd come prepared you know, especially as we have the staff meeting later." He chuckles to me whilst packing up his snacks and keeping only his main lunch out. I wonder where Izzie is, surely she should be out by now as all the year groups have been dismissed from class.

Suddenly I spot her coming over to join us with Miss Blake and Miss Thomas, they sit down and join our conversation. I can't help but feel a tiny bit nervous though as I haven't talked to either of them properly before. Luckily though after some small talk and the occasional shared piece of gossip we don't have time to talk about much else, ending our conversation as we have to go to the staff meeting together.

The other teachers haven't arrived yet so we get first pick of which seats we want. Tyler sits on my left and Izzie on my right, Miss Blake and Miss Thomas also seat themselves nearby so they can still talk to us. Then Miss Fisher enters alone, she looks surprised to see us all already waiting for the meeting to begin. She goes next to Tyler whilst Mrs Green and Mrs Parker who have just arrived place themselves slightly apart from everyone else. We all wait in an eerie silence for Michael to get here, which is typical when he's the one technically in charge of the meeting. Then right on cue he strides into the room, offers a quick apology about being late even though I can tell being on time to a meeting isn't one of his top priorities and then the meeting begins.

"This meeting revolves mainly around the summer fête," Michael says at a loud volume, making sure he has everyone's full attention.

"I'd like to remind those of you who already know about it, that we will not be having a redo of the episode of a fête that we had last year." He continues sternly and Izzie and Tyler share a look of amusement which Michael decides to ignore.

"Every member of staff is to attend both days of the fête if possible, I want everyone helping out as we have actually successfully ordered all the necessary equipment and parents will also be running stalls." Michael finishes his little rant and has a look of sheer determination on his face, wanting this to work so it doesn't turn out like whatever failure it apparently had been last year.

After a moments pause everyone seems to be considering what they should do.

"I can help out both days," I volunteer up my weekend as nobody else appears willing to speak and to be honest I feel bad seeing Michael struggle underneath so much pressure.

Relief is painted like a picture over his stressed face, "Thank you Violet," he addresses me approvingly and there is a lot of gratitude in his voice towards me.

Tyler glances around at everyone for a moment, checking to see if anyone else is going to take the chance to speak and then he also volunteers up his entire weekend. After that Izzie, Miss Blake, Miss Thomas and Miss Fisher also agree to do both days with us. This leaves Mrs Parker and Mrs Green as the only ones who have not spoken and given up any of their time. They both in the end grudgingly give up their Sunday before we all are granted permission to leave.

Chapter Four

I sigh as I watch the rain trickling outside forming puddles, the weather probably won't be improving any time soon either. Luckily on the news channel it does appear to be more hopeful for the school fête with plenty of sunshine predicted at the weekend.

The next few days at the school everyone will be preparing for the fête and all the stalls that will need thought put in to them, at least for me and Tyler that means we can keep on top of our work load as there's no doubt in my mind that after the fête it won't take long for everything to return to normal. I have to admit though that I am enjoying myself, it feels like I've finally got my life back and can just be the average normal person who gets stressed over the silly daily issues. I can be in control of my life again and be the person I was before all the tragedies I've suffered.

After deciding on what clothes I should wear for tomorrow so I will not be in a disorganised rush in the morning, I take a shower as it's a good way to relieve stress as the hot water is calming and soothing. Not only are you cleaning your body but your mind too. Once I've taken an age on drying and fussing over my long hair I go downstairs to sit in front of the TV in comfortable and snug pyjamas.

It doesn't take me long for my mind to slowly drift off to Tyler, he mesmerises me in more ways than one. Not only his obvious good looks but his charming character and just the way he is in general. It's hard for me to trust people so I can't figure out how Tyler's managed to bypass that barrier and gain my trust as if it can easily be won. I don't think I'll ever really understand that but what's even more confusing about him is the feelings I possess for him, he's my friend and yet why do I feel so close to him, like sometimes it's just me and him in our own distant world. I'm sure he feels it to, but it really is like we share some kind of special bond and moments together where I feel that we're completely in sync, just me and him.

I don't think I'll mention this to him though simply because it could be awkward and if it's only my heart that seems to stop whenever I see him then it wouldn't be good, and could potentially be very embarrassing.

I can't believe it's already a Thursday morning, this has to be the most boring day of the week for me. I grab my bag, a book and some lunch before heading off to the school. Jess smiled, she always waits for me now in the mornings as we're always usually the first ones in. We often like to recommend books to each other as well, but today she already seems to be up to her neck in work so I leave her not wanting to be a cause for distraction. Surprise flashes through me to see Michael already in the staffroom, reading one of the many newspapers that are usually sprawled all over the table. Normally he stays in his office and then goes to the staffroom when everyone else has gone off because they've got work to do.

I greet him as I put my bag down on the seat I usually take, he always seems pleased to see me and I think he's mostly grateful for how much work I've managed to get done since I've arrived. I decide to make us both a cup of tea whilst we wait for everyone else to arrive.

"Oh Violet, you won't be going to your office straight away today. We have assemblies every Thursday morning so we all sit on the benches in the hall." Michael informs me, of course how could I have forgotten. Assemblies were always dull in Primary and Secondary school. Well this is definitely going to be a waste of my time.

Everyone has arrived now, so we all file into assembly and I inwardly sigh. I watch the teachers sort their year groups into rows whilst I sit on one of the long wooden benches with the other teachers. Tyler is talking to Michael so I save him and Izzie a space beside me. Then he catches my eye and gestures with his hand for me to join him. Whilst Michael tries to quiet all the children Tyler quickly whispers in my ear.

"I play the piano in the assemblies, so if you turn the pages of the music over for me it gives you an excuse to be here." He smiles and then pulls up a chair next to the piano for me.

I watch his fingers gently brush over the keys of the piano and then fall still onto the ones he needs to play. Michael gives a quick introduction, the teachers state their notices before Michael gestures towards Tyler to play his piece. I've always loved hearing people play the piano, it's just truly fascinating to me. Tyler's hands move in incredibly fast, smooth and flowing motions. He has clearly learnt to play the piano well as his hands don't falter for a second and the music flows uninterrupted. It quickly snatches my breath away, I have never heard anything so beautiful, so sweet. The phrase music to the ears could never have been so true, to be honest that's saying something as I've been to many piano concerts and none of them could even compare.

The whole room is filling with the melody he plays, then I am startled as I turn the page for him that in his neat hand writing at the bottom it says his name. Tyler has composed this himself, he seems lost in the music, I can tell from just looking at his face that every chord means something to him, every individual note part of a story. His eyes never leave the keys and mine never leave his face, which holds my breath and my heart. He is almost in his own world, a world with only him and his music. Then too soon the notes become quieter and quieter until they trail off leaving an awed silence. Slowly he takes his hands off the keys and sits up away from the piano and there is an immediate response of everyone applauding, I do too but I am still lost in the music and the beauty of the melody. It is almost as if it still hangs in the air, me and Tyler don't move and I am not sure if I can. Michael sends the year groups out one by one with their teachers trailing behind them. Now it is only us and Michael left, I look up across the room at him. Michael holds my eyes before nodding and leaving. He'd had a knowing look in his eyes, clearly everyone would understand if I mentioned it. Tyler's music is something else, something special.

I turn back to look at Tyler, I have always known that behind all the care free humour there is a deep and intriguing character. His blue eyes look up and meet mine, "I've never heard anyone play so beautifully before," it comes out as a whisper as I am still in awe.

He looks at me for a long moment before answering with, "When I was first looking for a job here I considered being a music teacher but with this job I have the best of both worlds. I can be the deputy head but I can still play music," he tells me in a calm, thoughtful voice.

"How much of your music have you written, that are personally yours that you composed?" I ask him and he smiles and pulls out a very heavy folder from the side of the piano, it is overflowing with many sheets of music. They aren't printed though, only hand drawn.

"I don't publish my work," he shrugs. He must have noticed that I have been looking at all the hand drawn notes.

"Why not? It's really good." I tell him, he deserves to be noticed for such an amazing talent.

"I don't know, I just have never really wanted to," Tyler slips the music into one of the many slots of his folder before putting it away.

Thinking of the summer fête this weekend an idea forms in my mind, I just hope Tyler will agree with it.

"Will you do something for me?" I ask him, feeling excited. He looks at me curiously before asking what it was I want him to do.

"Will you play the piano at the summer fête?" I ask him and Tyler looks extremely surprised and unsure.

"Please," I beg him, it would be amazing if he does especially as he's so good.

"Maybe but you have to do something too or it wouldn't be fair," he comments, a smile forming on his lips and his eyes seeming to have an idea dancing within them.

"But I don't have any talents to do at the fête," I reply, feeling nervous now. What if he says something he knows I won't do so he doesn't have to play.

"Look I'll do two things and you only have to do one. I'll play at the fête but in return seeing as it's your birthday soon you have to dance with me," his eyes hold mine, he clearly finds this amusing and I stare at him in bewilderment and don't really know what to think.

He smiles, "Every summer before we break up for the holidays we have a dance," he explains to me, drawing in my reaction.

"So will you be my partner?" he asks this time serious, awaiting my answer. Looking him right in the eye I say yes before blushing the deepest pink and swiftly looking away from his face, avoiding eye contact.

"Are you two planning on doing any work today?" Michael's voice calls out to us, he stands at the other end of the hall clearly waiting for us to head back to our office. As we walk over to him Michael makes a comment directly aimed at Tyler.

"Strange how you two are always talking whenever I see you and yet since Violet's arrived, the work's actually getting done isn't it Tyler?" Tyler simply shrugs in his face before grinning and leading me back to our office. Michael sighs and I bite my lip to hide my smile as he returns to his own office.

It always amazes me how much Tyler appears to get away with, even when Michael openly witnesses it. I sit down on my spin chair and start sifting through all the summer fête work we need to prepare for. Tyler seems to already be getting annoyed with his computer which is refusing to get him logged on to his account, I can't help but snigger considering I'm already logged on and in all the necessary files and documents. I try to hide my amusement as I work hard and finish the first document. Then, noticing that he's managed to log on but can't get onto the documents we're meant to be working on I send him a message saying,'You look like you're enjoying yourself' then clicking back onto my work.

The great part about staff computers is the message icon as it allows you to quickly message anyone. Within a matter of seconds later Tyler replies with 'Very funny (it really isn't)' and I bite my tongue so that I can't laugh, then when he finally gets onto the file I message 'Congratulations'. He turns to me now and gives me a fake glare before answering with 'Thanks a bunch'.

I glance down at my watch which is when I was surprised to discover that it's already break time. However reviewing the amount of work we'd actually done and completed I would feel bad to take a break now. Tyler gets up to give Michael the only papers we have done and so I don't notice at first when Izzie comes in as I am concentrating hard to make up for our lapse earlier.

"How's it going?" she asks me and smiles when I look up in surprise to see her standing beside me.

"Really dull, but I haven't done much and it could be a lot worse." I reply still typing furiously hard but then me and Izzie look at each other questionably, is that arguing we can hear coming from the staffroom?

Saving my work, we then both head off and press our ears against the staffroom door.

"It's none of your business, if you keep bothering me about it you could end up in serious trouble." Tyler seems to be threatening someone, hearing his voice like that admittedly does sound intimidating. Whoever it is obviously must have replied as Tyler now continued.

"Leave her alone you sad witch. Do you really have nothing else to do other than irritate and interrogate people? But don't you dare..." He trails off, it is mostly being muffled by the door but of what we can make out it doesn't sound at all good. Tyler's voice has gone fearfully quiet towards the end which in a way is more threatening than hearing him shout.

"What's going on?" Michael thunders a bark from behind us which makes Izzie give a small scream of shock as we hadn't expected to see him and had no idea he was even there. He huffs with annoyance before barging into the staffroom interrupting the commotion.

Me and Izzie flee back to my office but just before we get to the door we see Mrs Green and Mrs Parker exit the staffroom briskly. Luckily they don't have time to notice us standing there and the bell rings signalling the end of break. Izzie rushes off to retrieve her class whilst casting me a concerned look on her way out. Through the small crack of my unclosed office door I spot Michael leading Tyler into his office and I sigh as the door shuts behind them.

After that I quickly finish the work by myself, before laying my head down on the desk and closing my eyes to take myself away from here momentarily. I am startled when I see how much time has passed, sometimes when I find anything really stressful my mind shuts down and I sleep away my worries for a while. I gently rub the sleep away from my eyes before getting an even bigger shock, Michael is sitting in Tyler's chair and he looks up upon hearing my movement. He smiles his kind smile that always tells me he's only smiling for me as he really is under a lot of pressure and a greater deal of stress than me.

"I thought I'd check on you and when I realized you were asleep I stayed with you as Tyler quite firmly insisted that I should stay with you, that you shouldn't be alone." He informs me, sighing slightly.

"What happened?" I ask him hesitantly.

"Tyler and those two, they've never seen eye to eye. Sometimes when too many comments are made Tyler can't handle it and so outright explodes at them," Michael concedes, but I cannot help but notice he had been steering clear away from mentioning what the actual argument had been about. Also something Tyler had said before is bothering me, the 'leave her alone' part. Who is he referring to and why have they used this person as a weakness against Tyler?

Michael gets up and exits back to his own office, obviously not wanting to discuss the matter any further. I wonder where Tyler is as he's definitely no longer with Michael now and he can't have been when I was out of it either as Michael stayed with me. Although members of staff technically aren't allowed to go wondering around the premises I need to find Tyler who's gone off on his own accord as well.

It doesn't take me long, it would have been impossible to miss the sound of the piano playing and so I go straight to the hall. Even from this distance I can tell it looked like he is trying to rid his pain and anger through his music. I watch him for a while before slowly approaching him, this time he simply budges up a bit on the stool so I can sit beside him and his music continues uninterrupted from this action. I sit next to him and feel his angry, violent trembles vibrate through me. The next time I see Mrs Green and Mrs Parker they're going to get it, I think feeling a wave of burning hatred towards them. His music is soothing though and I let it calm me down and soften my mood, Tyler also seems visibly less upset now. I press gently against him and a few silent tears scatter and escape down my cheeks, I never want to let them get the chance to do this to Tyler again, they have no right.

Finally he stops before taking a deep breath and turning to face me, that is when I see that he too appears as if he has recently been crying. Quickly with his thumb he flicks away the tears that had been pooled around his devastatingly perfect blue eyes. Then his eyes don't leave mine when one of his warm fingers gently brush away the streak of tears that I can feel hot on my cheeks, the soft touch of his finger however leaves my face burning a bright pink. A sad, timid smile creeps up on the features of his face and I love the way that his eyes seem to smile at the same time.

I honestly can say that nothing much happens at lunch time and the afternoon also passes in a blur of which most of my thoughts revolve around Tyler as usual.

On Friday I can't resist casting a resentful look at Mrs Green and Mrs Parker. I know that Izzie's noticed I'm being much quieter and reserved today but I'm in no mood or state of mind to talk right now. I usually prefer to deal with issues alone, or at least that's what I've always had to do in the past. As we work me and Tyler don't mention the inevitable topic of the summer fête. I can tell though that that's what we are both thinking about and I'm worried about what might happen.

I say goodbye to Tyler on my way out, we have to meet at ten o'clock tomorrow morning to help prepare and set up for the fête. His brown hair is unaffected by the light breeze and his lovely blue eyes gaze at me, his pink lips set in a warm smile and I take in the sight of him unconsciously wishing he could be mine. Now my only option is to wait at home for the event I've lost the desire to attend, but everything has to play its course.

Chapter Five

I am running a bit late already, knowing I don't have to go in till later today has made me oversleep. Grabbing a jacket, my bag and a couple of sweets I rush off to the school. I decide to head up the back way to get to the school so that I will get straight onto the playground where we will be setting up.

The only thing I can see on the playground is a giant bouncy castle, to my astonishment Tyler is mucking around inside it whilst Michael is trying to inflate it. He's fighting a fight he can't win, but instead of looking angry with Tyler he's simply smiling.

I grin as I approach them, "Need any help?" I ask whilst Michael now gives Tyler a fake disapproving look seeing as I am here and he is pretending he actually has some authority but I'm not fooled. So then Michael simply shakes his head in answer to my question and smiles, we both look at Tyler who now stands on the edge of the bouncy castle looking proud and pleased with himself. I can't resist smiling at him and the sight of him makes me sigh in a good way, Michael studies me curiously for a second before pulling up a chair and practically falling into it with exhaustion from all his hard work.

I look back at Tyler again, his perfect smile and his sea blue eyes. Then he holds out his hand for me to take and pulls me up beside him.

"You have to do some work you know, none of the stalls are set up yet." Michael tells us before heading off to make preparations even though he hasn't fully recovered yet.

"We can't set up the stalls until the parents arrive, so we may as well have fun at the moment." Tyler simply shrugs, not bothered by Michael's comment.

We hold each others' hands whilst bouncing as high as we can actually manage without bashing our heads on the top part of the castle. I giggle when he nearly loses his balance and he purposefully rocks the whole castle so I lose mine, but his arms save me before I can fall and we stay in this embrace. Neither of us notice when Izzie and Miss Blake approach us, so when we do see them me and Tyler quickly jump apart and off the bouncy castle.

We exchange a sheepish glance full of embarrassment and I can't look any of them in the eye. However I can see Izzie clearly trying to tame her amusement whilst Miss Blake simply raises her eyebrows at us.

"The parents will be arriving now, we can help set up if you're not busy," Izzie comments and then Miss Blake begins trying desperately to control her shaking shoulders. For once Tyler seems to be at a loss for words and looks at me, willing me to cover up for the both of us.

"Yeah let's get on with it and set up," I stammer slightly, knowing that it was the lamest cover up ever and so I rush off to help Michael.

I feel all of their eyes following me as I went and begin sorting out the raffle tickets onto different prizes, out of the corner of my eye I spot Tyler begin welcoming the parents with their children who will be running the stalls. He appears confident to the untrained eye but even from here I can sense his unease and it doesn't help that his face is still tinged red from embarrassment. I jump when Michael informs me on what I have to do next as I haven't been paying attention for once; it is unusual to catch me out. He follows my gaze which lands upon Tyler, we share a long look which causes my heart to flutter with panic, I dread what Michael might say but luckily he just sighs and hands me the next of my delegated assignments.

I swiftly walk away from him and begin putting out tables and chairs where the barbecue will take place, that's not the first time Michael's noticed that I've been unobservant and less efficient because of Tyler. I hope it doesn't happen again otherwise he'll notice a pattern forming and me and Tyler will both be in trouble. Miss Blake comes over and helps me arrange the tables, we don't talk much as I still don't know her particularly well and there's no doubt in my mind that her and Izzie have contributed to getting me and Tyler in trouble. She quickly picks up on my unease and discomfort about being alone with her, so when we have finished she leaves without a word. I feel a bit bad afterwards seeing as me and Tyler had been the ones fooling around in the first place, I decide to wait for Tyler or Izzie to finish before carrying on as there isn't much left that I can set up by myself.

"Would you mind helping me set up the stationery stall Violet?" Miss Thomas asks me, noticing I am waiting around and resolves my previous thoughts for me.

I look up and smile at her before replying with,"Sure, of course."

We work hard, opening up boxes and displaying all the stationery. When we have finally organised the stall for people to come and buy from it we decide to take a break by sitting behind it in case any one does come over.

"This has got to be the most well prepared summer fête so far," she comments to me, I look around us and am surprised by how many stalls are now up. We have been working so hard on our own stall that we haven't noticed the other ones being set up, there are raffles, games, gifts and sweets. It looks like a proper summer fête, definitely one worth attending and it reminds me of the ones from my own childhood.

"I know this is a bit late to tell you but, I'm Jacqueline Thomas. I feel I know you better now and so that we can be friends I thought it was time for you to know my first name," she smiles. Her blue eyes shine bright and her brown-blond hair flows around her face due to the calm breeze, I smile and we shake hands whilst I feel a great sense of relief to now know her name and that she wants to be friends. I glance around the fête until my eyes catch Izzie's mischievous but apologetic ones. Well at least she is sorry for getting me in trouble, but I know I would of forgiven her any way.

Then I remember Tyler's promise, he had said he would play the piano for me today. However I don't have time to go and find him as it is now time for everyone to arrive, children from all the different year groups come running in, tugging their parents along. Me and Jacqueline share a look and take a deep breath to ready ourselves for the hours ahead.

All the scented rubbers and highlighters are bought immediately from our stall, I am not really surprised as they were probably the coolest and most popular item on our stall.

Jacqueline has gone to help out others as most of our items have already been bought meaning we don't have many pupils coming over any more, so I can easily manage by myself but others are struggling.

I watch the fête with a quiet happiness, it isn't often I spend my weekends around people so I'm glad for the distraction and welcome it. The raffles have already been won now and the barbecue is dwindling and losing popularity, after the sweets are handed out the fête is going to draw to a close. I spin around in surprise when I feel a warm hand touch my arm.

"I thought you would want to watch me fulfil my promise," Tyler spoke calmly, in a sweet pleasant voice.

He leads me through the crowds of people and into the hall where the piano waits, I sit beside him on the stool whilst he begins flicking through his music to choose a composition he wants to play.

"Aren't you going to make an announcement that you're going to play?" I ask him, gesturing towards the crowds of parents and children. Tyler shakes his head, I can detect a trace of embarrassment in his eyes and a shy smile forms on his lips.

His cream-pale hands begin swiftly playing the beautiful notes he has composed, yet again I experience awe as I watch him. He becomes completely absorbed and lost in his music, the unbearably sweet and beautiful melody fills the room despite all the conversation in the air. I notice parents turn to look in our direction and their children begin pointing excitedly at us, the room quickly begins to get reasonably quiet as everyone watches and listens to Tyler's performance.

I watch his hands moving impossibly fast, his eyes held and brimmed with emotion whilst his lips quivered and trembled. I've had to turn over four pages of music for him already, I feel captivated and locked in the moment. The last note hangs in the air, Tyler takes a slightly shaky breath before standing up and bowing to his audience. There isn't a single person in the room that doesn't clap for his spectacular performance, everyone seems to have momentarily lost the ability to speak from their awe.

Eventually people begin moving on and going home, clouds have now begun to cover up the glorious sky and rays of sunshine like a blanket. Me and Tyler hold one another's gazes before we both break into smiles and I give him my own little round of applause as well, I also thank him appreciatively for keeping his promise to me.

"You need to keep your part of the deal though," he softly reminds me and I nod before we get up and leave the hall. Now we're going to ask Michael if we can go home, he stands in the doorway waiting for us.

He observes us distantly for a moment before telling us we can go, "Why didn't you tell me you were going to play today?" he asks us just before we leave.

"That would ruin the surprise," I tell him, then we exit the school together in a calm, peaceful silence. It makes me think though, Tyler clearly hasn't played before and Michael must have asked him to.

Tyler walks over to his silver-blue car before turning around to smile and wave at me, I wave back before I leave and walk home.

Now it is the second and final day of the fête, most of the stalls are only half as full, considering that yesterday had been the main day of events. There's a quiet atmosphere in the crisp air today, unlike yesterday when everyone had been filled with excitement and anticipation. It is a typical relaxing Sunday, but then again that is when I see Mrs Green and Mrs Parker arrive together. Mrs Parker is clearly having a hard time setting up her stall, well just because I don't like her doesn't mean I can't get in her good books. Mentally preparing myself, I walk over to her and in the most positive voice I can muster I ask "Would you like some help setting up?". She turns around and looks at me in surprise.

Then in a wondrous tone says "Yes, thank you."

I work hard to get the job done as fast as is physically possible, "There we've done a good job of that fast," I smile at her whilst really thinking about how she'd basically left me to do the whole lot.

However just as I am about to leave she turns to me and thanks me properly for my help.

"No problem" I answer truthfully, satisfied before walking away, feeling less manipulative as it has benefited the pair of us and now I've done it I'm actually glad I did. Also hopefully now I've given her less reason to plot against me for the time being, this can potentially be an advantage in the future and make her think twice about plotting against me with Mrs Green.

Then I see Izzie come rushing over to me and then stopping, gasping for air. I raise an amused eyebrow whilst waiting for her to regain her breath. "Violet I'm really sorry about yesterday," Izzie begins begging me for forgiveness until I cut her off and simply grin.

We exchange a hug before she has to rush off again, that's when I notice a figure sitting on a bench tucked away under a willow tree. With his hand he gestures for me to join him, "I wondered when you would notice me over here." His voice is soft, but quiet.

I duck under the willow and make my way over to Tyler, he is wearing his usual red-brown shoes but now with matching trousers, a pale blue top which isn't completely buttoned up showing his neck which then flows down to the beginning of his chest.

"I wouldn't go near Mrs Parker if I were you," he says in an unsure, somewhat cautious voice now.

"I thought I should give her a reason to leave me be, that's all" I tell him, feeling slightly startled by his prickly comment, "besides it's not doing any harm."

I'm not sure what else to say and I don't feel like I should own up and answer to Tyler about what I say to other members of staff.

"It will if she uses you to get to me though," he answers within a sigh and it sets me off.

"You know Tyler, I don't know what your old job was but if you keep bringing it up or think it's so amazing then what's the point in mentioning it and not explaining. I want you to either tell me or never speak of it again, you can choose!" I end up snapping at him. Just because he has a grudge against certain members of staff does not mean I should, she hasn't personally done anything to me therefore I shouldn't judge her over something I have no knowledge of.

I stand there fuming in silence, waiting for his answer to my confrontation. Minutes pass by and he refuses to move or speak, I feel my throat tighten before I turn and walk away leaving him behind. I can't care less about the fête now and so walking as fast as I can manage without tripping up I rush to the toilets and lock myself in a cubicle. I let the tears stream until they flow no more, drying my eyes and cheeks I exit the cubicle and go to one of the mirrors. I brush my long black hair and put on some lip palm before leaving so I can pass as composed.

As I navigate my way back to my office, I quietly and on my own wait out the last hours that I have to be here and my thoughts drift to my parents. I touch the ring I wear on my finger gently, caressing it. It had been my mother's and I treasure it dearly. I spin around in dread when I see the shadow of a figure standing in the doorway, it turns out to be only Michael though.

"Do you know where Tyler is?" he asks me in a completely unaware voice.

"Outside," I reply stiffly, feeling stung and tormented by his question.

"Are you OK?" he questions me, concern and worry now colouring his tone and features.

"I'm fine, but I'm sure Tyler needs you." I respond bitterly and instant suspicion was clear in his mind, Michael knows that I've always defended Tyler and so to hear a remark like that clearly meant trouble.

"Has he said anything to you, anything to do with his past?", Michael is on the verge of getting worked up now.

I tremble slightly with nerves before quickly lashing out with, "He didn't say anything and we all have our pasts Michael, some of us however are too deeply affected by them and get no credit for pulling through it though." I'd chosen my words carefully but I partly regret them considering how much trouble I've got myself in for. I don't dare look at his face as I leg it out the door and off the premises.

The whole way home I wonder if I've lost my job, not too long after I get back home my phone starts ringing. Should I dare answer it? I decide to take the call, silently praying whilst doing so for it to just be one of those waste of time phone calls that everybody gets. It is Jess, she tells me that I'm to see Michael tomorrow at ten o'clock in the morning. Uh-oh, now I'm in for it, proper doomed. I head to bed early and bury my face underneath the duvet covers and my pillow, wanting nothing more than to escape the situation I'm now in.

Chapter Six

My tactics of delaying myself as much as possible from leaving to go to the school are already failing. I have still somehow managed to get everything ready early, I begin the small walk to work and try to get there late by stopping off at every single shop down the high street. The school gates quickly loom up in front of me, I take a minute to control my nerves before slowly walking up to the door. Jess as per usual is there waiting for me and she looks as nervous as I feel, after she lets me in I can tell she is burning to ask the question I really don't want to answer. Luckily she keeps quiet as my hands and fingers twine and untwist from each other as a distraction, Jess returns back behind her desk leaving me to make my own choices.

I don't dare go to my office in dread that Tyler will already be in there, I can't face him yet. I visit the staffroom and make myself a cup of tea so I have a reason to be in here when everyone else arrives. Mrs Parker and Mrs Green arrive first just to brighten my mood, but this time Mrs Parker smiles and nods at me proving there had been some point in what had happened yesterday. As I want to keep this up I make both of them a cup of tea as well before sitting in my usual space. Luckily before I'd rushed off yesterday I had taken some work with me, therefore I have something to do to help me delay going to my office even more. Izzie comes in with Miss Blake however we still feel awkward around each other so when Jacqueline enters I seize the chance to talk to her so that the icy and tense atmosphere can't be discussed.

I glance at my watch and sigh, all the teachers have to go off to their classes now leaving me alone to await my fate. I have just under an hour to get this work done before I'm due to see Michael at ten o'clock, I work hard but slow. I hadn't realised how much work I'd actually taken, luckily though it helps occupy my mind leaving no room for any nerves to enter and torment me. I have ten minutes left. I clear everything up and pack away my work into a folder so that the sheets won't get disorganised or lost as I speculate over what will happen. Finally the clock ticks onto exactly ten o'clock, slowly I rise from my seat and try to compose myself before heading off to Michael's office down the corridor. I stand in front of the door for a few moments before lifting my hand up from my side to knock on it, instantly Michael's voice answers for me to enter.

Slowly I push the door open, keeping my eyes down as I close it behind me before turning around to face him. My heart plummets and stops when I see Tyler in one of the chairs, I hadn't expected him to be in the room as well and I feel an overwhelming urge to go back through the door.

"Please take a seat," Michael orders, guessing my intentions, I notice Tyler's hands firmly holding onto the arms of his chair in a sign of distress as he was venting his nerves into it.

"I'm guessing you know why you're here," Michael confirms with me and I simply scowl and nod in affirmation.

"Well then let's begin. We need to get something sorted out fast, don't we?" Michael is clearly not in a good mood, especially as he's obviously already been trying to break Tyler's barrier unsuccessfully before I got here.

"I know what I said was out of line, but it's not entirely my fault" I decide to begin, Tyler looks at me in surprise now and then I understand that Michael hasn't told him about what happened after I had left him. Well it isn't my job to tell him, so Michael may as well get on with it and tell me off.

"I never said it was which is exactly why you are also here Tyler," Michael's unimpressed with the both of us then, well at least I'm not completely on my own.

"Violet I understand why you lashed out the way you did. After this meeting it will be forgotten and put behind us, but you have to understand that Tyler's past is none of your business." He observes my response to his new rule before looking away from my gaze.

"Well my past is none of his business either," I proclaim in a cold, distant voice and Michael nods before turning to Tyler.

"You however need to keep your thoughts to yourself, you know nobody is allowed to find out!" Michael snaps at him and me and Tyler both visibly flinch.

"With respect Michael I was only trying to keep her out of harms way," Tyler glares directly at Michael and has spoken in a dangerously quiet voice, which is far worse than if he'd shouted. In just that moment the whole atmosphere turns dark as if clouds of mist swirl around us, Tyler stands up and shoves his chair out of the way before exiting the room without being dismissed. Then surprising myself and Michael I get up and rush after him down the corridor and out the building.

He walks extremely fast and I'm finding it difficult to keep up with him, so I decide to run after him and my hand reaches out and grabs his arm which instantly makes him spin around causing our faces to be only a few inches apart. I tremble for a moment, we both stare at each other trying to anticipate the others' next move. However then I let my defences go down and I burst into tears,"I'm sorry," I whisper. His arms pull me up against him and I rest my head against his chest, and his chin presses against my head. I feel his arms on my waist and back and my hands cling to his shirt, I wasn't going to let him go.

"You don't have anything to apologise for," he murmurs softly but I shake my head in disagreement.

Too soon his arms leave my waist and he withdraws a bit, I gaze into his eyes and know as a gut feeling that Tyler's someone that I cannot lose and I must never let him go. We share a moment where we both understand how much we mean to one another.

"It's my fault, I was trying to protect you. Now I've probably just made it worse though," he looks upset with himself.

"I shouldn't have mentioned your past, if you ever want to tell me it I'll be here for you but if not then it's fine." I tell him honestly.

"If I tell anyone it will be you. I really care about you Violet, which is why I told you to stay away from Mrs Parker, I wasn't trying to boss you around." He looks me right in the eye.

"It's fine, don't worry about it. Come on let's go inside, I'm sure Michael's not pleased." We head back into the building,

"Don't worry about Michael." Tyler smirks, recovering some of his usual humour.

Michael is so mad that he actually can't speak, instead he goes back to his office and slams the door in our faces, forgetting the professionalism rule completely. Tyler bites his lip and has a look on his face which shows that he finds the situation really funny, I put my hand over my mouth in case I accidentally start laughing. We share an amused look before rushing back to our office in hysterics, the only reason I'm not scared of losing my job is because I have made the whole place more organised and up to scratch. Many teachers have commented on how everything is actually getting done on time now, whereas before the summer fête wouldn't have been anywhere near as big a success. Also Tyler isn't worried as he has his own reasons for job security so we are in no position to be concerned to be honest.

What really makes us laugh is that Michael hasn't given us the work for the day, and there's no way I'm going to bother risking my life to ask him for it.

"Don't worry about getting into trouble, I can easily prevent that from happening." Tyler says to me in a confident and very sure of himself voice. I smile, whatever power Tyler has it sure is useful in circumstances like this. Then surprising us both the bell rings out loudly signalling break time which only ever means good news.

We walk out onto the playground without a care in the world. I'm really no longer bothered any more, I have Tyler back and that's all that matters to me.

"Things are much better now that you're here Violet," Tyler regards me in an odd way for a moment, I can detect a huge depth of emotion in his eyes. "Well I'm glad, its nice to feel wanted or needed for a change." I reply truthfully as my life really wouldn't be much to speak of if I hadn't met him and got this job. We walk in a peaceful silence around the playground together, both lost in separate thoughts as we watch the children play from a distance.

We both turn around when we hear echoing footsteps heading our way, Michael seems to be reassessing the situation before him as he comes towards us. I look to Tyler for some reassurance and he bends down and quietly whispers in my ear that everything will be all right. He notices my hand is still shaking in panic and so he takes it firmly within his own. The calm warmth which radiates out of his hand and into mine helps soothe me nearly instantly, Michael now stands in front of us looking at me, then Tyler and finally our hands linked together.

"Made up already have we?" he asks in a stern voice which neither of us responds to except from I hold onto Tyler even tighter.

"It would be safer for the both of you if you weren't so comfortable in each others company," Michael continues, getting slightly agitated now with our lack of concern and interest.

"I'm his assistant," I say in a calm and unwavering voice which holds a hint of a challenge. This also shows that we have to be together and that he can't split us up.

"Well that's odd because I'm seeing something more than a mere work partner relationship here," Michael easily throws back the challenge, meeting it head on as he yet again glances at our hands. I feel my skin prickle red and get flushed in panic, but above all the deepest and purest form of embarrassment is clear on my face.

"We're together in this, a team." Tyler sharply replies in a cutting tone, he's desperate for this conversation to not turn into an awkward and yet honest one. I really hope Michael isn't suggesting this because of he keeps catching me looking at Tyler...

However then we share a glance and a knowing look. So he does know after all; great I'm actually done for now.

"You both need to control your behaviour and actions, but if you can convince me that nothing else is happening here then that will do for now." He confirms with us looking directly at me as Tyler doesn't seem to have a clue before walking off back to the building.

"What was that about?" Tyler huffs but then however he picks up on how guilty and embarrassed I must look and he quickly catches on.

"You don't think that he was suggesting that we-" I cut him off and simply nod, unable to hear him say it.

"Oh..." is all he could think of to say making us both extremely uncomfortable.

I have been trying really hard to not let myself think about the fact that I am developing other feelings for Tyler, so when Michael comes along already suggesting exactly that when I've only really just noticed myself what am I supposed to do? Seriously though, I haven't been doing anything stupid or obvious so maybe Michael just gave a fake warning and is being typically annoying. Well that's not the real issue here, I have to hide any feelings that I have from Michael but most importantly from Tyler himself.

"I think the reason Michael mentioned that was because the dance is on Friday, he wanted to know if I'd be doing it as I've never bothered to before." Tyler reminds and explains his theory to me, it makes sense to arouse suspicion of Tyler doing it for the first time since I arrive.

"So why now, what made you do the dance this time compared to the other times?" I ask him and deep down I want it to be for reasons I will never admit.

"Because very recently my priorities and personal order of interests have changed dramatically," he answers in a voice which implies that he wants to say more, however he's no longer looking me in the eye and his lovely pale cheeks are now the shade of roses.

I feel my heart beat quicken and pick up the pace, I know that there is nobody else in this world that I would rather have this dance with. We finish our walk around the playground holding hands the entire time before returning to our office.

The rest of the day passes fast, Izzie and Jacqueline notice that I am more shy around Tyler at lunchtime which secretly torments me. Then our afternoon proceeds with us sharing looks and smiles, at this rate he's going to discover my secret before the dance even takes place.

Chapter Seven

Tuesday, a quiet peaceful day for long as I can remember anyway, for the first time Tyler has arrived before me and he smiles his sweetest smile whilst heading over to me with a cup of tea.

"For you," he says softly and already my cheeks begin staining into a light pink.

"You're here early," I compliment him and he smiles brighter and nods.

"Thought I should probably try to make amends with Michael," he grins and I can't help but smirk, I'd love to know what he'd said and how Tyler had tried to weasel out of it.

Then Izzie comes in, when she sees me and Tyler she simply smiles to herself enjoying a private joke. Well it was meant to be a private joke but me and Tyler share a look which confirms what I had also thought. The worst part is that I don't know how to act in front of other people when I'm with Tyler, it always feels like it's just me and him so I let down my guard and then it shows how strongly I actually do feel for him.

"Can I talk to you later?" Izzie asks me, uh-oh this isn't going to be good. "Um... yeah OK," I reply trying to suss out what she's going to say and more importantly how far she's planning on taking it. She looks at Tyler before smirking and walking off, luckily when the other teachers arrive they don't think anything odd about how much time me and Tyler spend together, just as they shouldn't.

Jacqueline waves but doesn't join us, Mrs Green's eyes narrow and Mrs Parker looks at Tyler, lingers on him for a moment before she nods at me. We all sit together in the staffroom biding our time, me and Tyler sit next to each other; so close we're practically touching. Jacqueline's nearby and everyone else keeps a small distance away from our private bubble, nobody daring to burst it. It isn't too long later though that we are left alone as the teachers always have to go early, "Well I think I know what Izzie's going to be asking you later." Tyler lets out an exasperated sigh, before looking at me.

"Why does everyone seem to think me and you are..." I trail off unable to finish my own question due to how embarrassing the topic is. We gaze at one another for a moment, wrapped in our own world.

"I don't know but Michael accidentally started it," his face doesn't display a trace of anger, however in my opinion it does show something else. Hope and despair, if it's possible for both feelings to occur at the same time.

As we work I keep catching myself watching Tyler and observing his face, it's like I have no control though and I can't resist the temptation and urge that fights within me. Three times he's already caught me looking at him, every time I have swiftly looked away afterwards.

"How are we getting on?" Michael's stuck his head around the door, surprising us both.

"Quite good actually, we've done all this." I hand him a folder full of work and papers and he smiles pleased, checks on Tyler and gives me a reminding glance on his way out back to his office. It is clearly going to take a lot of convincing before I get Michael off my case, that's just what I need and want to know. I let a sigh slip out, I really don't know what I can do to make him convinced when I can't even convince myself. It especially doesn't help that I am always with Tyler so I don't have much to use to put up a fight on my behalf as all the evidence can be turned against me.

Tyler looks how I feel.

"What should we do?" I ask him as I have officially run out of any good ideas long ago.

"Well to be honest the only reason he got the wrong idea in the first place is because we held hands, if we avoid that when in others' presence then we should be fine." Tyler half suggests and half comments to himself thoughtfully, however I'm concentrating more on the fact that he'd only said in others' presence not, not at all. Oh God, I have to stop thinking like this it's going to make it so much harder to prove a point against Michael in my defence if I've given myself less points to say in my defence than I've already got in the first place.

"Don't worry about it, it's not like he can really do anything without hard evidence which he won't get." Tyler shrugs the situation off, not worried as he has no reason to expect why there would be any evidence as he obviously doesn't feel the same way and so thinks that this will blow over as in his case it isn't true.

I feel crushed inside, I'll never know how he can be so relaxed about the amount of trouble we can potentially get ourselves into but on this occasion it's because he has nothing to fear as it isn't true. This is one of those times where I really want to tell Tyler what's really on my mind and what I think, but I hold my tongue as I can think of nothing worse than bringing the unnecessary pain and embarrassment of him discovering my feelings on myself. Tyler also appears as if he wants to say something but decides against it, at this rate both of us aren't going to be convincing anyone of anything apart from the wrong idea. We're both tongue tied and finding it harder and harder to act like friends as time goes on because even if he doesn't like me the way I like him, something is definitely going on.

There has to be a way to show Michael that I don't have these feelings for Tyler, but if I try too hard it might become apparent that I am actually pretending. The other problem with this situation is it isn't just a mere crush or some kind of phase that I can potentially get out of, I have never felt such a strong tie and pull towards someone else before. Never experienced such a deep confusion of emotions and forever had someone in my mind for so long, every waking moment he consumes my time. Imagining he's with me and what he would be saying, I want to share everything with him and spend all my time with him. He only has to say a few words to brighten my day and that can take me through all the hours just glad I saw him or what he'd said. It almost feels like I can no longer breathe normally, he catches my breath and holds it like I can't function properly without him. My eyes forever linger on his perfect handsome face, my body numbs from staying still so long as I gaze at his glory. Everything ceases to exist or pales in comparison as he captivates all my attention, and all he has to do is look at me and smile to double and intensify those feelings.

Tyler is honestly like no one else I have ever met before and the words both beautiful inside and out spring to mind, the truth behind that is unbelievable. His amazing patience, listening for ages without an interruption, looking people in the eye when speaking to them. Those are just a few examples of how he attracts me to him, he's always interested in any gossip someone has to share, he's respectful, humorous, generous and heart stopping.

When you fall in love with someone you love all the qualities about them and you become attracted to them in the other ways afterwards, there are no faults or flaws to the person in your eyes. I knew a short while ago that my feelings were deep and pure and that nothing can be done about it, how can you hate the feelings that make you happiest of all and give you the greatest pleasure? It leaves you defenceless and powerless, so in other words it leaves the best part of you untainted and true, the part that brings out the best in yourself is the then the part others see.

"Come on let's go, it's break time now but maybe I can help delay Izzie's chat with you if we go now." Tyler voices his plan, then he looks at me and realizes that he has just interrupted a very serious line of thought. Before he can say anything though I get up and we walk out of our office together.

"If people ask you about the rumour about us, what are you going to say?" I ask him curiously.

"I'll say that you're my assistant therefore I have a right to be able to be with you, also how would they like a rumour set up about them? Believe me I could easily make that happen," he answers without hardly a pause and a spark within his eye. I feel a hundred percent better and secure with him more than usual within a matter of minutes.

"Have you chosen a dress yet for the dance?" Tyler asks, now in a shy voice which takes me by surprise. I haven't actually thought of that though, but I really should as time is ebbing away fast.

"No not yet,"I tell him whilst looking away to hide my blushing, luckily though he appears so nervous that he doesn't notice for once.

"Then would you mind if I help you choose," Tyler looks up and we both hold our breath.

"N-no problem, that would be nice. I'd like that." I stammer in disbelief as I can't believe my luck that he wants to plan to go out with me.

"Are you free today?" he continues, sounding hopeful and it lifts my spirits up.

"Yeah, um..." I feel slightly flustered now though as I'm embarrassed about this fact but he needs to know.

"What's the matter?" he asks, his voice taking on a panicked shaky edge. "Oh it's not that it's just...I can't drive, so I don't know how I'll be able to meet up with you." I confess feeling awkward, I don't have a car as I'm too afraid of learning how to drive which is why I chose a job just down the road to me.

The atmosphere immediately lightens up and is no longer tense, he smiles in relief that he had been jumping to stupid conclusions on why I couldn't go.

"Oh well that's OK, God you really had me worried for a second. I didn't know that though," he says in a rush trying to cover up the fact that he had genuinely been panicked that I didn't want to go with him which makes me smile, he's so sweet.

"Can you not afford driving lessons?" he asks me curiously.

"Oh no I probably could just about, but I'm really not keen on learning." I may as well be honest, so although he's surprised he doesn't question it any further.

"Well that's fine, we can go to my place after work to drop off our bags." Tyler confirms with me, pleased and satisfied with the plans we'd made.

I smile glad that I have something to look forward to after work for a change, the fact that Tyler is eager to be with me makes me feel special inside. I'll get the chance to go round his house and enjoy time with him as just the two of us, away from work and worries so I will have a chance to bond with him more. We head back to our office, both feeling high and elated about our plans. This part of our work is the hardest, working before lunch time so you feel hungry and now me and Tyler have another reason for being even more desperate to go.

Michael pops in when it's nearing lunch time, he always seems to catch us when we look at our most comfortable with each other. I've finished my work and so am helping Tyler on the computer, and as it's only going to take a few minutes he let me perch on his seat next to him. Michael however clearly isn't going to be seeing the situation that way though and doesn't look pleased especially when my hand accidentally brushes against Tyler's, so much to both of our embarrassment I swiftly move afterwards.

Izzie comes in announcing that it's lunchtime, so I seize the opportunity to get away from Michael before thinking through the fact that she wants to interrogate me. Tyler subtly mentions that he'll catch up with us later so Izzie will have time for her questioning or bothering in other words first, Michael simply scowls at the lot of us and leaves us to our plans. We select one of the many benches outside and then Izzie begins, in full swing.

"How are things going with Tyler?" Izzie starts off basic and so that is how I'm going to reply by feigning innocence.

"Good, we're managing with all our work at the moment." I answer as if I have no idea what she is getting at, she looks at me for a moment but can't decide if I am just good at acting or being genuine.

"Are you going to the dance on Friday?" she continues, trying to hint closer to the point now as her first target has failed and missed to strike a reaction.

"Probably, it should be fun." I try to avoid saying anything that will give me away or can sound awkward.

"Are you going to go?" I ask her, attempting to worm my way out of the spotlight.

At that exact moment I spot Tyler heading over to us after Michael quickly mutters something in his ear, looking directly at me, subtle. It certainly gives Izzie more reason to be suspicious.

"What's up?" Tyler asks as he sits beside me and places his bags down, Izzie notes the fact that there had been more space next to her than me to sit down and I avoid looking at her smirk.

"We were just talking about the dance, I don't know whether to go though as there's no point if there's no one to dance with." Izzie informs him and Tyler grins, a smile forms on his face making his lips curve up which shows he's thinking about something he probably shouldn't.

"Why don't you ask Michael, I'm sure he doesn't have a partner." Tyler chuckles, finding his own suggestion particularly funny, however me and Izzie also crack up at the thought. It would certainly be a sight to see.

"It should be a dare, ask him and see what happens." I carry on, eager for her to do it now.

"Thanks you guys, really appreciate it." Izzie giggles but even she has to admit it would be hilarious, but I'm so glad that Tyler has offered this one to Izzie as it's a pretty hard dare. Luckily for me he only teases me when we're alone in our office so it only stays between the two of us, but he has no problem teasing Izzie openly.

"If you do it you'll be the ultimate champion of dares," I tell her, hoping to add an appeal to do it and encourage her.

"Sorry but Tyler's got that position covered, last year he managed to explode the toilet system with a bottle of Michael's health drinks." Izzie laughs whilst high-fiving Tyler who's looking pretty pleased with himself.

"Even Michael found that funny." Tyler comments on his moment of genius.

"Well he didn't when he found out how much it would cost to fix the system," Izzie giggles. I feel bewildered, how had he managed that? It does explain though why Michael keeps his health drinks away from the staffroom fridge.

We eat our lunch in a calm silence, my thoughts don't take long to drift back to the dance though. When I dance with Tyler the suspicions are only going to rise, it's bad enough that some of my own friends have these superstitions, but they're my friends so hopefully this problem won't get much worse. Michael still doesn't actually know for definite yet that we're dancing together either, he's only implied that he suspects this a few times. I feel Tyler watching me, his blue eyes resting on my face so I turn to meet his gaze. We stare silently at each other for a moment and I know that he has also been following the same train of thought, his eyes read the concern and yet longing on my face which I try to conceal. I have really gotten myself into a mess now, but what can I really do about it?

Izzie leaves us together and looks at me for a moment, she seems to mostly find it amusing about me and Tyler. At the same time though there is a kindness and feeling for my situation shown in her eyes. She can see the peace I get from Tyler, the way the world only seems to fit and function properly when he's there. I know she can also see the longing and desire though, the endless depth of love that I can't surrender to and give in because if I do I could lose everything. However she only thinks that's because of it's against the rules for us to be together, not because Tyler doesn't share my passionate feelings. So in some respects I'm still alone in this after all. After she has gone we don't speak for a while; I wonder where he will take me out today, where exactly he lives and what his home will be like inside.

"Do you have any particular shops that you want to look in?" Tyler asks me, he's deep in thought trying to organise and prepare well ahead for later. "No not really, and what about you, you need something nice to wear as well." I point out and he shakes his head smiling.
"I already have my suit sorted, one of my most expensive ones to be precise." He informs me, I'm sure Tyler can wear anything and look handsome. He does tend to usually wear smart clothes anyway though and he always looks good in them, even his more casual clothes are nice and make him look well dressed. It's strange because whenever I've asked the prices have always been affordable and not rich, Tyler has said he would

never spend too much money on clothes as long as he can buy something cheaper with quality.

"In that case then I know a few shops near where I live, they usually have decent clothes suiting every occasion." Tyler offers and it sounds like a perfectly good plan as we haven't thought of anything else. After we have eaten and our lunch break is drawing to an end we decide to go back into our office and wait for the bell to go. I begin tidying and organising my desk in our spare time as I'm surprised to see how quickly it has gotten cluttered and clustered, everything is taking up unnecessary amounts of space from just the short while I have been here.

Michael briefly pops in again to inspect us and what we're up to, honestly when is he going to give us a break? Sometimes I think he's expecting to walk in and find us kissing or something, not that that would be a bad thing but it's not going to happen and I can't believe he acts like it's only a matter of time. He only gives us a small load for the afternoon which I'm grateful for as I don't think Tyler has the energy to do any more either. We work slowly as there's no reason to rush, we still have the staff meeting later to attend anyway. The work has been easy with only a few tricky problems which Tyler manages to research our way around, so we finish with half an hour to spare.

Tyler makes us sit in our usual seats in the staffroom early so that we will be settled for the meeting before anyone else even arrives, I wish we can just go and get on with our evening.

"I don't see why the staff meeting can't just be at the end of the week, do we really need one everyday?" I ask Tyler as this is something that I've found rather irritating for a while. He sighs and shrugs, not really satisfied with the arrangement either but he obviously doesn't want to push his luck by questioning Michael's authority even further.

The teachers all file in, Michael hard on their heels before heading over to his usual place to begin the meeting.

"Well I hope everyone's had a good day, now if there's anything you feel is necessary to be sorted out or others should be aware of then now is the time to share it." Michael gives his opening line to the discussion as usual, it's the same every day, like being on repeat except that there are only one or two minor changes. Everything mostly revolves around preparations in classes to do with equipment, and other typical petty complaints that I really don't have the patience for.

Literally the second the words of dismissal escape from Michael's lips me and Tyler bolt and make a swift exit out the door, we're down the zigzag path and past the gate leading into the car park quicker than should be physically possible. His striking silver-blue car waits for us in its space, where it gleams and shines as if it's brand new and has just left the garage selling it.

Chapter Eight

He opens the door and holds it for me to get in like the perfect gentleman he is, before heading around the car so he can get in and join me. The seats are a light grey colour and smooth and cold to the touch with a nice silky feel to them, they're mainly leather with a design neatly styled on them. Tyler quickly buckles his seat belt and starts up the engine which purrs to life as he withdraws his pale, pianists fingers onto the wheel instead. He drives just under the speed limit and so when we get off the main roads it doesn't take long to reach the long winding lanes. On either side of the car there are the most beautiful, spectacular countryside views and landscapes I've ever seen, nearest the edge of the road grow dozens upon dozens of flowers of all colours, shapes and varieties. Then behind them leading as far as the eye can see are fields which are glittering green, fresh and vibrant. However when he turns into one of the many narrower lanes which leads to the routes up to peoples homes I'm at a loss for words.

He pulls up on the gravel which lies before the most striking and breathtaking house, the gravel also turns out to be a path which leads right up to the front door. Around us I fully observe and appreciate the sight before me, a garden which spreads out across more space than you can imagine and contains a huge willow tree which is draped over on one side. It's huge leaves and arm-like structure blow and sway gently in the mild breeze, a small bench is positioned slightly away from the path on the other side of the tree in the direct location of where the sun shines rays down onto it. I spot a selection of fruit trees lined up along the edge of the garden so that they don't quite reach the grass which is spiked up and a dazzling emerald green.

"This is amazing," I just about manage to say, afraid that if I blink and turn to look at him then it will all vanish and disappear to only be a memory.

"It is beautiful, but the back garden is the real treasure." Tyler tells me, seemingly at peace now that he's back in his own comfortable surroundings. He takes my hand in his and leads me around the side of the house where his back garden leaves me in awe.

Tyler has a stream running through the full length of his garden and it passes into the neighbours' as well. It has to be the exact shade of blue as his eyes and it flows in swirling waves, creating a bubbling music. I watch the way the water pours and trickles over the small jagged rocks, on an endless journey towards the sea. However that isn't all, scattered all around the stream in patches are thousands of bluebells. I love bluebells, when I was younger with my parents we used to always visit the bluebell woods. "I can't believe this is your garden, it's just so amazing." I tell him and he smiles, pleased and delighted that I like his home.

We go back to the front of the house and whilst Tyler unlocks the door with a small silver key I glance up at his home. It is a beautiful and pleasant white cottage which looks like something you will only find in a fairytale or in a painting. From the inside I notice that the windows don't have locks but a black handle which fits into slots to prevent the window being opened, also there is a small curl at the end. The roof is a dull red which looks like it was previously one with bright colours and patterned tiles, the soft white of the walls are rendered and the porch keeps the wooden brown door hidden by the growing vines hanging down on either side. When the door clicks I pass over the mat outside and follow Tyler into his home as I put my bags down next to his.

I manage to get a quick peek of all the downstairs rooms which all have the walls and carpets as soft, bright colours which let in the light such as cream, pale yellow and peach. The layout is one massive living room which leads into a huge kitchen with the typical round wooden table and chairs set out. I smile as I see how neatly arranged everything is before following him out again and shutting the door.

We set off to go to the shops Tyler had decided would give us the best deals and yet maintain decent levels of quality. There is a long row of shops lined up against either side of the high-street and to our luck there are few people around, so we park quickly and Tyler gestures which shop should be most suited to our needs. He tentatively takes my hand and we head inside the store which is fairly big and has special occasion clothes hanging up everywhere. A young woman with swishing brown hair who had been standing near the door instantly smiles and beckons us into the shop, her ID card informing me that she's an assistant to customer needs.

There are racks of dresses, suits, skirts and other fashionable high quality clothes dotted all around the store. I bend to look at the price tag on one of the dresses closest to me and am astonished by how affordable it is for its regal,glamorous design. My lips curve and flicker up into a smile as

I gently start sifting through the silky materials and choosing colours with Tyler.

We both stop when we come across two particular dresses, the same style but in different colours. There's a perfect white one with ruffles which end just above the knee, the material is smooth to the touch and it looks pretty against my pale ivory skin. Then there is the indigo violet coloured one which also has the ruffles before the knee.

"Well there's a dressing room just over there, so you can try them both on." Tyler suggests in an eager, excitable tone. I decide to try the white one on first and as soon as I glimpse myself in the mirror wearing it I know that I want it, my black hair flows down my back which adds to making me look pretty and stylish in it as the two bold colours contrast and compliment each other nicely. I draw back the curtain and step out next to Tyler, anticipating his reaction.

He turns around to face me and instantly a winning and charming smile spreads across his handsome face, I smile in return as it's the exact response I'd wanted and more.

"Y-you look beautiful," he stammers from being impressed, his eyes captivated on me. I hold the other dress up against me, but I think we both know there is no point trying it on considering the sight of this one. Tyler returns the other dress back to its rack whilst I change into my normal clothes, then collecting the dress approach the counter where a man is waiting behind the till. When Tyler notices me pay I can tell he feels uncomfortable, however the prices are so reasonable that I can't possibly let him pay for me.

Once the man has packaged it up for me I return to Tyler's side and we leave the store and go back to his car. I'm surprised by how much time has just evaporated since the whole process hasn't felt that long, Tyler's going to have to take me straight back home when I've collected my bags from his. When we get there I don't ask to see his suit despite how curious I am as I want it to be a surprise on the day, after I've given him the instructions to get to my flat I feel sad that I have to say goodbye to him. Thankfully though there's only this night and then I'll be able to rejoin him tomorrow.

*

Now it is a Wednesday morning and everything is dull, tired and quiet after the excitement of yesterday. I head off to the school slightly early as there isn't anything I can occupy my mind with at home, I watch all the people around me in their morning rush. I don't feel part of it though, I feel disconnected from everyone else and like everything has slowed down at an exaggerated pace. When I arrive Jess also seems to share my mood, the feeling that the day is going to considerably boring when in fact its hardly even begun. I don't bother going to the staffroom first today, I'd rather get on with the work and have a quiet afternoon undisturbed. Michael doesn't appear to be in yet so I head over to his office and select the work I want for myself, today's just going to be a slow productive one.

It doesn't take too long before Tyler arrives; we share out the pile of work and I try to get through it as fast as possible. Tyler on the other hand is noticeably struggling and as I watch he ends up getting so frustrated that he eventually gives up after receiving a hand cramp from all his efforts. I leave to put my work on Michael's desk who must be running late as he still hasn't turned up yet, and when I return Tyler has gone, well it's nothing to worry about as he'll be back in a minute I reassure myself. It's beginning to get annoying how much everything Tyler does affects me, it sure does make simple things difficult at least and interrupts my level of concentration.

In his absence though I may as well check what it is that he's actually stuck on, if I'm lucky I might be able to do it for him. To my relief it's only the lists that need to be sorted out, Tyler often does the hard work I can't get my head around and then finds the simple work complicated so I shouldn't have been surprised. I hadn't realized Tyler had returned so it startles me when he exclaims "How have you already done most of it?" from behind me. Tyler stares at me in shock and I know it would've taken him a lot longer to get this far with it, I shrug and smile as it's hardly a big deal.
"Just thought I'd help you out," I address him kindly and continue as I may as well. I can probably finish it without much more effort, also it is my job to assist him in any way I can.

The last part is fairly hard though so I base it mainly on guess work, I suppose I'm going to have to hope Michael doesn't mind as I don't have a clue. After leaving that on Michael's desk we decide to have a rest in the staffroom from doing all the work load at once, also we'll have it to ourselves as all the teachers have gone off to their lessons now. Tyler makes us both some tea and I settle down on my usual chair, letting myself sink into its familiar embrace as he comes to join me.

"What kind of dance is it on Friday?" I ask him as I don't actually know half the details on what's supposed to be happening.

"I think we can choose, we turn up in our usual clothes then at lunch time we change and the dance takes up the entire afternoon." Tyler informs me, looking particularly pleased with the last part of what he'd said.

"Do you know who else is taking part?" I ask him curiously as it should be interesting to see who else is participating.

"Well Jacqueline usually does, Miss Blake and Miss Fisher. Oh and of course Izzie will be asking Michael..." Tyler snickers, his eyes dance at that thought. Well it's no surprise that Mrs Green and Mrs Parker won't be taking part, but I'm glad that Jacqueline is as it gives me someone else to enjoy the amusement over Izzie and Michael with. It's going to be nice to see what everyone else wears at the dance too.

We chat about the dance until break time, then Izzie comes over and I bring up the topic of whether she's asked Michael yet.

"Should I ask him at lunchtime?" she jokes, but me and Tyler are deadly serious. I'm desperate to see her ask him and even more intrigued into what his answer will be. Izzie leaves again to go bring in her class from the playground, but we have arranged to meet up so that we can be there to witness the big moment.

Michael comes in then as he's noticed that we haven't returned to our office after everyone has gone and break time has technically ended. "Shouldn't you be working?" he questions us with an unsure frown on his face.

"Actually no, we've done all the days work already and you'll find it on your desk." Tyler informs him, his voice nearly being sarcastic but he's mainly just pleased that we have a valid reason to say no to work for once. Michael's impressed that we have done all the work, it means that he can carry on with his own and stay on top of everything.

He doesn't seem to know what else to say to us and so leaves shortly afterwards so it won't be awkward. To pass time me and Tyler decide to complete all the puzzles in the newspapers and magazines which are scattered over a small brown table. However I think we are both still tired from yesterdays events and so give up pretty quickly. I rest my head back against the chair and close my eyes so I can no longer see the bright lights which make me more tired, Tyler plugs his phone into the speakers which I know are on the table. He begins playing soft, gentle music at a background volume, but that is too much for me and so I fall asleep within a matter of seconds.

What seems like only minutes later I feel a gentle warmth brush against my cheek, my eyes flutter open instantly and I see Tyler's hand withdrawing from my face. His face is close to mine, leaning over me and he smiles at my disorientation.

"I thought I should wake you just before lunchtime, you deserved a rest." He says calmly, I notice that he hasn't been sleeping as there are now slightly visible shadows under his eyes indicating how long he's gone without a proper rest. I sit up feeling embarrassed, this is the second time now that I've drifted off for a long period of time at work. He watches me in a quiet and thoughtful way, making me wonder how long exactly he's been watching me for before waking me up. He withdraws from me and gathers all his belongings up for lunch and then I follow him out.

Izzie quickly navigates her way over to us and then we rush through our lunch, we are eager to find Michael as soon as possible. We have to wait around for a while though outside his office as Michael must be still eating, so while we wait I ask Izzie about her day. It sounds like she's taught her class an awful lot recently considering in Primary school it's meant to be more of a relaxed atmosphere.

Michael hasn't been expecting to go back to his office and find us all waiting outside, however he doesn't appear bothered or concerned about the peculiar situation. Instead we all go in and take a seat before he asks us to discuss whatever matter we wish to.

"Izzie's here to ask you something and me and Violet are here to witness your answer." Tyler says cheerily, his voice full of enthusiasm and Michael doesn't look like he knows how to respond to such a bold statement. So instead he simply turns to Izzie and we hold our breath waiting for her to fulfil her dare.

"Michael you know it's the dance on Friday..." Izzie begins basic, she is desperately trying to tame her silent laughter.

"Yes," Michael replies with a hint of suspicion entering his voice.

"Well I was just wondering as everybody who participates needs a partner..." she trails off again trying to shake off the fit of giggles that nearly consume her. My shoulders also begin shaking and I quickly wipe a tear from my eye, I can't give it away.

"Do you have a partner?" Izzie asks him trying to bring herself to look him in the eye, Michael looks very uncomfortable for a moment then which is utterly priceless.

"I don't actually," he replies looking away, clearly feeling embarrassed by that fact.

Tyler gives Izzie a glance to remind her that she has to ask him properly, "Then would you be my dance partner?" she asks him and me and Tyler try to contain our amusement.

Michael looks startled and then suddenly becomes quite shy, "Y-yes if you're sure you want to go with me." He stutters and stammers before looking away and avoiding all eye contact from any of us, Izzie nods and we quickly dash out of his office.

However me and Tyler run out a bit too fast and end up tripping over and colliding with each other, we land hard in a heap on the floor together. I feel winded from the fall and so can't move as I lie on my back struggling to breathe, the impact has been hard and has completely left me in a daze. Tyler quickly disentangles himself from me and rushes behind me so he can pull me up into his arms on the floor, I rest my head on his chest and let him support me as I can't support myself.

"What happened?" Izzie asks, shocked to see me in Tyler's arms as he kneels on the floor, my back pressed against his legs and my head still resting on his chest.

"We tripped over one another, but Violet landed hard on her back." Tyler's voice has taken on a panicky edge, but there's no need for his concern as I no longer feel like I can't get enough air. It always scares me though when I feel like I can't breathe properly, I try to get up but my whole body refuses and feels too weak.

"It's all right, I've got you just lean against me for a while, you don't need to move until you're ready." Tyler murmurs softly in my ear, like a whisper.

After a few moments I try again and Tyler wraps his arms firmly around my waist pulling me into his lap, in a more secure embrace. I feel a bit wobbly at first when he helps me stand up, but otherwise I'm fine. Tyler however keeps his arms securely around my waist, not convinced I am OK and I don't object to having him hold me, the side of his cheek pressed against my face where I can feel his warm breath tickle my skin and make me blush.

"You should probably go and get your class," Tyler instructs Izzie, sounding authoritative and actually playing his role as the deputy head for once.

"I'm fine Tyler honestly, you can let me go now." I tell him shyly and his arms slowly let go of my waist after I feel something gently caress my cheek, his lips? The rest of the day he constantly checks on me but I never ask if it had been his lips on me, I know I haven't imagined it but I'm too nervous to bring it up.

Thursday also passes quickly with everyone discussing the dance.

Chapter Nine

I carefully pack my dress into my bag and prepare myself for the day ahead, my mind in a jumble of confusion mostly concentrated around Tyler. I decide to take a hot shower so that I'll be clean and fragrant for the dance, also to calm some of my nagging thoughts. If it had been Tyler's lips brushing against me that day then does that mean he shares my feelings, or I am over thinking everything and it was just a caring gesture? I select a posh pair of shoes to match the dress and then shove my hairbrush into my bag, knowing it's best to get going now so I won't be late. I smile, excited about what the day will bring and so arrive at the school in an exceptionally good mood this morning.

Jess instantly picks up on my excitement to do with this afternoon. "Who will you be going with?" I ask as I can't think of another man around besides Tyler and Michael who are both taken.

"The technician, he's really good looking." Jess giggles, embarrassed but secretly thrilled, well I haven't seen the technician yet but if she's pleased then that's what matters. "Have fun with Tyler, you're going to look so sweet together!" Jess calls after me as I'm already heading off to my office. I stop dead, how does she know I'm going with Tyler? Also that last comment, I really hope she's not getting at what I think she is but even so how would word of that rumour spread even to the receptionist?

Michael greets me cheerfully, he seems to share the bright vibe going around in the air at the moment as well. Everyone's spirits appear to be lifted for now, as if some unknown weight has been taken off our shoulders for the day. Tyler also obviously is no exception to the rule, I hear him call out greetings to Jess and Michael the second he is through the door.

He smiles a dazzling and charming smile at me as soon as he stands in the doorway, "Hello dance partner," he greets me happily. I rise up from my seat and do a small twirl in front of him, his eyes gleam and shine the lovely blue that make my green ones sparkle with unspoken joy, we're both anticipating this afternoons event to be a good one.

Michael doesn't give us much work today so that we will get everything done before this afternoon, however I know this means it will all pile up over the weekend. It doesn't help that me and Tyler are doing a particularly poor job of getting it done as we can't stop chatting either.

"What music do you think will be played?" I ask him intrigued, seeing as he will have more of an idea than me as he's had to attend before despite the fact he's never taken part.

"Usually there's a selection, so there are songs everyone can have a laugh at but there's also more romantic ones to dance to as well." Tyler raises an eyebrow at me and grins, his eyes teasing and taunting me slightly.

"Well Izzie better watch out when she dances with Michael then," I comment to wheedle myself out of the limelight and Tyler clearly enjoys the joke.

"Yes very funny Violet, but I don't see an awful lot of work being done here." Michael's voice suddenly comes from behind us and me and Tyler stare at each other in shock, where had he come from and how long has he been standing there?

Then Tyler cracks up laughing at my idiocy and that Michael has heard me say it, but I feel too surprised and embarrassed to even speak. Michael smiles though, also enjoying the joke before shaking his head in mock anger and leaving to go back to his office. We both can't stop laughing, if I had known he had been anywhere nearby then there's no way I would've risked saying that. I can't believe he overheard and doesn't even care about my tactless comment, Izzie joins us at break time and when she finds out what happened she also cracks up and congratulates me on my stupidity.

We mess around for the rest of the day and although Izzie has gone back to her class I message her through the computer and quickly receive a sarcastic reply, it was to do with if she was looking forward to dancing with Michael. In truth though I reckon she is excited, me and Tyler ignore Michael's warning over how much work is being completed and stare at the clock instead, time seems to be dragging and we're willing it forward.

The exact second the bell rings signalling lunchtime me and Tyler head straight over to Michael to ask if we can get changed for the dance; he looks quite distracted and nervous so quickly waves us away and says we can. Me and Tyler share a look saying 'what was that about?' before heading off to the toilets to change. It doesn't take long to change into the beautiful white dress which fits snugly on me, I get my brush from my bag and do my hair until it's impeccably straight down my back and over my shoulders. After changing into my other shoes and applying some pale pink lip gloss I exit the toilets to find Tyler already waiting for me.

He's dressed in smart black clothes, from shiny black shoes, black trousers to a posh black jacket which has a neat, white collared shirt underneath. The tie fits precisely with the collar and it is a dark blue colour which hangs down his front. He smiles angelically when he sees me and gently grasps my hand, however we decide to stay and eat in our office today as this way nobody will see us and it will be a surprise what we look like at the dance. We feel like we're trapped waiting around forever so it comes as a great relief when the speakers announce that everybody including the students have to have a dance partner and make their way to the hall.

Tyler smiles but for a first appears nervous as he takes my hand in his, so I hold his hand tightly so we can reassure one another. I take a deep, uneven breath as we link arms in the correct way for dancing before heading down the corridor and into the hall. Michael is already there looking at his best with Izzie by his side in a purple dress, she's trying to make her class partner up and Michael is glancing around the room nervously. Jacqueline stands with Jess as they wait for the technician to arrive I'm guessing and all the year groups present are having a hard time choosing who to partner up with, probably due to feeling awkward about it.

Instantly as we come into view my friends hush slightly with awe and smile and beckon for us to join them. At that point all my previous nerves evaporate and are replaced by excitement, I pull Tyler along with me to join them. My sudden display of confidence seems to work on him as well, we begin blending in and chatting with everyone else just as usual. I feel very comfortable and secure as I hold firmly onto Tyler's arm, my hand clutching his sleeve in a gentle grasp and he stays linked to me. When the other teachers arrive and join our conversations even the ones I hardly know yet compliment me on my dress, for once I'm not the only one blushing as even though Tyler's more used to dealing with attention than me it seems like he's holding me for as much support from me that I need from him.

Tyler begins discussing songs with Michael whilst I stay by his side, occasionally adding my opinion but I'm more interested in spotting the fact that me and Tyler look like a couple more than anyone else as they aren't linking arms. I gaze at Tyler's open and happy face, his pale cheeks still slightly flushed pink and his blue eyes shining. His darker brown hair compared to Michael's looks soft and it would be nice to fiddle with the part on the back of his neck, his face newly shaven and fresh... I get a grip on myself, I can't allow myself to swoon over him so openly. Finally all the year groups gather and partner up leaving only the teachers to sort themselves out, simple party music starts playing which sets the dance off on a role.

Me and Tyler stay on the side lines to begin with, but when the music becomes more romantic and less party styled most of the pupils give up to get refreshments leaving the floor mostly empty.

"Well then, will you dance with me Miss Spring?" Tyler implores me, whilst bowing and I give him my hand. He smiles to himself as he leads me into the middle of the hall, he places one hand on my back and the other on my waist. I put my hand on his shoulder and the other rests on his chest before we begin. It turns out that Tyler knows his fair share of dance moves, however we mostly keep it basic at an average speed in his arms.

I feel myself blushing as I dance with him and as the dance progresses I find it harder and harder to look him in the eye, his soft hand gently brushes against my cheek to make me look up into his eyes. We become lost to everyone else, just in our own world with the fluent movements of the dance together. Out of the corner of my eye I notice Izzie beginning to dance with Michael, I smile encouragement at her and she rolls her eyes at me.

"I can't even remember the last time I danced," I inform him as I twirl beneath his arm.

"Well that's hard to believe considering how well you're doing," he compliments me, his lips in a perfect smile.

We take a break to get a drink together and enjoy the once in a life time view of Michael dancing awkwardly with Izzie, Michael is focusing too hard on getting the moves right to enjoy himself whilst Izzie is failing to teach him.

"I never knew you were both so good at dancing," Jacqueline has joined us, she's pleased with how the event is going. Then I spot Jess dancing with the technician, well I don't know what all the fuss was about over him but it sure is amusing to watch.

"Well it's hard to say who the couple of the dance will be, Izzie and Michael will undoubtedly be popular as it's the headmaster and a teacher. On the other hand though Tyler, everyone loves you and Violet you're new, so who knows." Jacqueline continues feeling in her element before leaving us alone. I turn to Tyler.

"I wasn't aware there would be a 'couple of the dance'," I question him teasingly.

Tyler shrugs, "It hasn't happened before but Jacqueline is right, Michael and Izzie will be the big hit." He tries to reassure me, confident as per usual. Still, I'm glad Jacqueline is pleased that more people are taking part this year especially as it's also Tyler's first time.

"That doesn't mean you can slack off though, I've been looking forward to this." Tyler lets me know cheerily, well at least I've fulfilled my part of the deal and I've been looking forward to it too.

He wraps his arm back around my waist and draws me close to him, we don't talk much as we dance but instead salvage the perfect moment and I gaze into his eyes. No matter how he feels about me I know my feelings are soaring and will soon become uncontrollable and unbearable, he's irresistible and just for now it really feels like I belong to him and he is mine. Michael and Izzie have given up, although they still keep their arms linked as they watch everyone else delight in the successful event. Tyler gently pulls me aside so we are no longer near the spotlight on the dance floor, then we join them. Izzie is unable to look me in the eye, but she does smirk at how close me and Tyler must look. Considering her and Michael though is a much bigger scandal, I'm going to be the one getting the last laugh when I tease on her.

Michael however is being specifically observant of us and quietly notes Tyler's arm around my waist, Tyler being Tyler though returns this by flat out staring at him and Izzie in general. None of us no longer look comfortable in each others presence and so me and Tyler swiftly move on to talk to others. We share a long look of confusion though, why would Michael and Izzie seem so uncomfortable about Tyler's back chat when it had been a dare for her in the first place?

"We can't get into trouble, they look much worse than we do. I'm the deputy head and you're my assistant, so nothing weird should be thought about it." Tyler sounds like he's trying to convince himself, never mind me as well. So that may be true but they're not the ones with a rumour going around about them, I don't mention this though as it will only stress him out further.

Jacqueline now stands on the stage to make the announcements.

"Now it is time for everyone to cast their vote for who will be the 'couple of the dance'." She begins excitedly before continuing, "Then that couple will dance one last time to finish the evening." Everyone begins moving excitedly to stand near the couple they wish to win, it becomes obvious that there is a definite tie between us and Michael and Izzie.

"As it's a tie both couples will dance and then there has to be a clear winner!" Jacqueline announces and then gestures for us to get back into the middle of the hall, or the spotlight in other words.

"Lets make it dramatic, it'll be funny." Tyler suggests to me, whispering in my ear as we stand waiting for the music to start.

Tyler bows to me and I give him my hand, then he lifts his arm up high and I twirl underneath it into his arms so we're ready to dance. Everyone's eyes are fixed on us now, oh well it's a once in a life time chance so we should make the most of it. Michael and Izzie stand awkwardly together, clearly embarrassed but me and Tyler are all for it and begin to show off a variety of moves. Soon all the classes are cheering for us and we end the dance with a simple but winning move, my back pressed against his chest and his arms holding me in a warm embrace. We are both smiling and grinning, although it hadn't been as romantic and memorable as our other dance it had been light and fun and was more appropriate for everyone to see. Izzie and Michael give up and the dance comes to an end.

"Well now everyone please vote," Jacqueline says, gesturing to the pupils to get up and stand in front of us again. The majority of them move in front of us including the teachers.

"Mr Crowther and Miss Spring are the 'couple of the dance' everyone." She finishes and the teachers clap and smile, the pupils cheer and Michael and Izzie make a quick exit from the spotlight. We are handed a certificate made by one of the year groups which Tyler tells me he wants to stick up onto our office wall.

I spin on my chair in our office while waiting for him to display our achievement.

"Are you doing anything later?" Tyler asks me once he's finished.

"I don't think so, why?" I ask, standing up and getting ready to leave.

He smiles at me like he has all afternoon, "Then would you like to go to dinner with me?".

This surprises me, I hadn't been expecting that at all. "Yes of course, I'd like that." I turn away from him as I answer, silently screaming with joy inside.

We head back out and wait until all the parents have collected their children and then we are finally dismissed, when I head over to Tyler's car I notice Izzie waiting to get into Michael's. I rush into Tyler's car so that neither of them will see me, I don't want to arouse more suspicion and cause us more trouble. It doesn't explain why Izzie is attempting to be secretive and subtle about getting into Michael's car though. I decide not to tell Tyler, I don't want him to look around and make it obvious as we're also technically breaking the rules. This way they can't question us and regrettably we can't question them either, but it's the only way we can avoid getting into a worse situation.

Tyler drives me to his house so we can stay there until we eat out at a restaurant later, I put my bag near the front door so that I won't forget it and then go into his living room to join him. I sit beside him on the sofa, it's nice to be here again and enjoy his company as last time I only got a glimpse of his home. I watch his quiet happiness, it makes me feel complete whenever I'm near him as he gives me unexplainable hope and something worth living for considering the situation I'm currently in.

"Do you want me to call up and book a table for a nearby restaurant?" Tyler asks me, his eyes intently fixed on my face awaiting my answer. I nod, it's a good idea as we might not be able to get in anywhere otherwise.

I feel myself sink into a quiet and slightly distant mood, I have a few problems that need deep concentration and thought put into them to solve and sort out. Tyler gets up to make the call whilst I sit there feeling indecisive about what I ought to do, how am I going to stop Tyler from noticing and encouraging my feelings towards him?

"I've booked a table for six o'clock, is that OK?" he asks, I hadn't even realized he'd gotten off the phone. He picks up on the fact that he has pulled me from a deep train of thought but I hastily reply so that he won't question it.

"That's fine, yeah that's OK." I lamely try to cover up for myself, feeling increasingly awkward because of what I'd been thinking about before he'd distracted me.

We flick through television programmes, but as there isn't much on we settle for some board games instead on the table which Tyler moves next to the sofa. It turns out Tyler is a master of chess and I completely fail, embarrassing myself with my petty attempt against him. He seems to always somehow avoid getting his chess pieces in danger of mine whilst eliminating them one by one, in the end I surrender and give up, relaxing into the sofa next to him. Time has passed faster than either of us had anticipated, and so now I'm already getting into his car again ready to go to the restaurant. It's a short drive and then we pull up in front of a well lit, but cosy restaurant which appears to be rather full so it's a good thing he did call. Being a typical gentleman he holds my door open for me and takes my hand as we walk up to the door where a man waits.

He is nicely dressed and politely greets us on our way in before showing us to a table a short distance away from everyone else, this means we get the vibe from the good atmosphere and the privacy. There's a huge variety and selection of dishes on the menu, but I settle for a simple lasagne whilst Tyler decides on a steak. Whilst we wait for the food to be prepared I fill Tyler in on what I'd witnessed earlier in the car park about Michael and Izzie. He looks bewildered which is rare as usually Tyler has an explanation for my wonders, but this time he's just as sceptic and puzzled as me.

"So she didn't want to be seen getting into his car?" Tyler quizzes me, that seems to be the main issue he's bothered about, I however am following a different train of thought.

"No she didn't, but I didn't want to get caught getting into your car either." I point out as a reminder to him.

I can tell as the food and drink is delivered and we eat that we're both thinking the same thing, neither of us are brave enough to voice it though. What if Michael and Izzie are playing the same game we are? Izzie has expressed some emotion over Michael, but she has also observed that my feelings are much deeper for Tyler than I'm willing to let on. I'm beginning to worry and get paranoid that Tyler's starting to understand how much I care about him, I still have the vain hope though that he won't find out that I love him as otherwise it could ruin everything.

After we've eaten Tyler gives me a lift home remembering the route from last time, he looks so desperate to say something to me but instead he just says goodnight. I watch his car disappear around the corner before I go inside and decide to go straight to bed, however sleep refuses to come as my head is so full of everything that happened today. Dancing in Tyler's arms had been like a taster of heaven, and him inviting me to dinner had been splendid. I know deep down though that it's only a matter of time before my secret will no longer be a secret, the problem is I have no control over how much I show it. Every day it's like my invisible pull towards him is being strengthened.

I have a lie-in now that it's the weekend, my phone however begins ringing, disturbing and breaking the silence.
"Hello," I answer it before the ringtone drives me insane.
"Hi Violet, it's Michael." Alarm bells start ringing in my head. "I'm calling to make sure you remember our agreement?" he interrogates me and a thousand different swear words rush through my mind at this point.
I gulp before answering with, "Y-yes I do remember." I stutter this out fretfully.
"Well if that's the case then why can I not see any improvement? It seems to have gotten worse since our last little chat", he rightly claims to me, how can I possibly defend myself when everything he has just said is true?
So instead I do something unthinkable, "You and Izzie had better watch your own actions, I dread to think what would happen if that got out." I smack my hand over my mouth, I can't think of anything worse I could have said.
There's a sharp intake of breath before he responds with, "This conversation isn't getting anywhere so I'll see you on Monday." His voice falters before he hangs up and the phone goes dead. I can hardly breathe, what should I do? I dial Tyler's number and in a panicky voice explain everything that has happened. We are both in undeniable shock over what I've said, he takes a different approach to the situation though and starts laughing. Great, so Tyler isn't even taking this seriously, after a short chat we hang up and I get up unable to rest at a time like this.

I have to do something though, Tyler might not care but Michael isn't going to get off my case ever now. My weekend is dreary and bleak as I fret over what I'm going to do.

I choose to arrive early on Monday, best to get it out of the way before the work days start.

Michael's in so I go straight to his office and hover outside the door, "Ah Violet, take a seat." Michael says as soon as he sees me, after I sit down I wait for him to begin as words can't describe what I'm feeling right now. "Violet I'll make it simple for you, I need to know if something is going on between you and Tyler."

He patronizes me slightly but it's evident he wants a truthful answer, "Nothing is going on, I can't help it if I'm always with him as I am his assistant." I try to escape the situation and his eyes pick up on it.

"That's not why you're here though, this is about why you're always watching him and when you danced on Friday you really did look like the 'couple of the dance'." His voice has a dark note to it, and I don't fail to understand the meaning behind his words, he means 'couple' literally.

"We are not together, I know everything you said is true but it's not like that for him." I attempt to explain miserably, I can't believe I'm confessing this to Michael.

He raises his eyebrows now, "So what you're saying is you do love him, but don't think he shares those feelings and so you're not together?" he questions me, intrigued.

I sigh "That's right, but don't repeat it to anyone."

Michael watches me with sympathy, "Don't worry I won't, but I just needed to be aware of this Violet." He is expressing concern now whilst pitying my unfortunate situation.

"If you ever need any support Violet I'm here, OK?".

I nod and stand up, but before I leave I have to ask him something.

"Do you have feelings for Izzie?".

We lock gazes and Michael sighs. "Yes, so if I keep your secret then you must keep mine."

I nod, "So we're in the same boat then; both love someone we cannot be with." I confirm with him and a friendship now forms between us over a secret only we know, it's against the rules to get with people you work with in our Primary school but both of us wish that isn't the case.

Chapter Ten

I leave him and make my way to my own office, glancing at the calendar which hangs limply on the wall. Not too long now and then it will be my birthday, before breaking up for the summer holidays. I'm worried about that though, how am I going to earn enough money if we're off for six weeks?

"Oh Violet, if you're interested in the summer holidays we have a special Year Six trip before they leave. It's just I know it will help you with how much I can pay you..." Michael informs me, sometimes I swear he can actually read minds.

"Yeah, I'll probably do that." I smile in relief; he had just in some respects saved my life. He writes up the dates on the calendar for me in his neat script whilst adding my name onto the list of staff who will also be going, I notice that my birthday clashes with the trip. Oh well, at least this way I'll be with friends on my birthday.

Tyler arrives not long after Michael has left, when I first see him in the morning is one of the hardest times for me, he always looks so perfect and unbearably attractive.

"What?" Tyler asks when he noticed me staring at him.

"Oh I was just wondering if you were going to go on the Year Six trip?" I ask him, Michael shares a look with me from his office, he has clearly seen through my cover up.

"Well I haven't got anything else to do in the summer, so I may as well." He tells me, completely oblivious to my lack and lapse of control for once. I inwardly sigh, but how am I going to keep this up? I'm not always going to be able to cover up my mistakes forever.

"What are you going to do about Michael?" Tyler asks me, I'd forgotten that he doesn't know as I'm used to telling him everything.

"I've already seen him today, it's fine and sorted." I tell him dodging the question, I'm more interested in his point of view on what is going on between us, that's what really matters. I'm beginning to get frustrated and angry with myself, I seem to be getting even worse at controlling my actions and reactions when I'm with Tyler or thinking about him. To be honest though that's basically all the time. Tyler notices I am losing my concentration, me who never loses concentration.

"I'll be back in a minute; just need to go to the bathroom." I give him the quick excuse and then rush out of our office.

Instead I just want the chance to pull myself together and get a grip, Michael spots me trying in vain to calm myself and he smiles a sad smile. "Take as long as you need Violet, just don't let him know."
I nod but I really feel like giving up, how can I hide my secret from Tyler when it's about him? When I return to our office Tyler eases some of my nerves by his easy conversation, it helps me forget to constantly be careful around him and I can just be myself. It's soon break time and I go to find Izzie, we chat the whole time and yet although we want to be with each other, we both silently yearn to be with a certain someone else as well. However I can't say anything with Tyler being there, my eyes mostly hold his and a flirtatious grin creeps up on his face from time to time. Whereas other times we will be distantly looking at one another in our own world; Izzie has to snap me back to attention which amuses Tyler. However she doesn't embarrass me and we share a moment where we understand perfectly what the other is going through.
"Meet me at lunchtime, I think we both know why." Izzie tells me, urgency in her voice and after I agree she heads back to class.

Tyler openly places his arms around my waist as Izzie leaves before leading me into our office.
I stare at him in surprise, "Are you trying to make Izzie have even more gossip?" I ask him in shock, he has been listening to our whole conversation in our office as we've talked outside it.
"Is that what you were talking about?" he teases me as he asks it in a perfectly innocent voice.
I mock glare at him and he laughs, "It seems to me that when you're not even with me you think about me," his tone of voice abruptly softens and almost melts my heart as I blush so bad I have to look away.
"Don't worry Violet, Tyler's always asking about you when you're not around, you're honestly all he talks about!" Michael calls out to us, eavesdropping and we both spin around in shock.
"I...I-" Tyler breaks off and burns so bright a red from embarrassment that it stuns me; Tyler has never looked so vulnerable and inwardly tortured. We both look the colour of tomatoes, I try to figure Tyler's reaction out to what Michael has said. He wouldn't be so embarrassed if it isn't true, right? Michael raises an eyebrow at the pair of us before leaving

us alone to sort out the strange events occurring between us. We both look like we clearly want to deny the situation and the facts before us, but neither of us say a word and finally the penny drops for the both of us.

We both stare at each other in a ridiculous and unbearable silence, so now not only have we noticed the feelings that we have for one another but that the other possesses those feelings in return. This isn't allowed though, we can't be together Michael has stated that much himself. I slowly back away from Tyler, turn and then run as fast as possible out of our office and out the door. This time Tyler is the one running after me, we fall down together on a patch of wild flowers a small way away from the school building. He lies his head back on the grass and stares up at the sky, whilst I gently rest my hand on his smooth chest and my hands hold firmly onto his shirt.

I can't help but cry, we are a perfect match so why should a stupid rule prevent us from being together? Tyler feels my warm salty tears soak his shirt, he wraps his arm around me and delicately with his tender lips kisses the top of my forehead as a gesture of comfort.

"Forget the rule, Michael may know now but he has no evidence of us actually being together." He says firmly, I sit up and we gaze at one another for an immeasurable moment. His pale hand brushes my cheek, then cupping my face up in his hands he leans towards me. I lay one of my hands on his shoulder whilst the other gently runs through his rich dark brown hair. When his lips meet mine I let my eyes slide closed so I can truly take in the moment. His touch is soft and yet rough at the same time from the range of emotions flooding through us, the actual kissing is soft and the roughness comes from the desire of craving more.

When we do finally pull apart I'm gasping for air and from shock, I have never experienced anything so satisfying. Such a pure and beautiful feeling to have and we break out into wide smiles, we feel as if we have had a taste of freedom and an amazing sense of release, real love and enjoyment. We hold hands and stand up slightly shakily from the unbelievable moment, then the lunch bell rings out and I tell Tyler how I am supposed to find Izzie. He nods in understanding, still in a daze and says he'll wait for me in our office.

Me and Izzie both appear to be very nervous as the time has come to discuss this very significant topic.

"Violet, this is obviously about Tyler... it's just because at first I wasn't sure but now...well how high are your feelings for him?" she asks me in a hesitant voice.

If I lie to her she'll only see through it anyway, "I really like him." That's an understatement, but enough to make me blush and confirm what she wants to know. "What about Michael?" I ask her as it's only fair and now it is her time to be embarrassed.

"I've only liked him for awhile and so when you gave me that dare..." she trails off and hides her face from me.

We start laughing about the absurdity of the mess we're in, I like the deputy head and she likes the headmaster.

Although her situation is admittedly worse than mine, "Oh well at least we're not alone and can help each other." I decide to point that fact out, so we both feel considerably better about all of this. We join Tyler then so we can go to the canteen and have our lunch, however everything feels weird now as although nothing much has actually changed it's almost as if everything has. It feels amazing to know that Tyler feels the same way and that I no longer have to worry about him finding out my secret and hiding my emotions, although somehow a lot of other people know. I still haven't gotten over the kiss from earlier, there is no way I can forget how it felt at that priceless moment with his lips on mine.

We say goodbye to Izzie at the end of lunch and intend to call each other later if anything interesting happens. I collect the work off Michael's desk and share it out with Tyler as we sit next to each other. Our hands and elbows occasionally brush, but now I don't have to be embarrassed as Tyler has basically said that we're together now so instead it feels natural. I have never been so close to someone before, I obviously loved my parents but in a way I hadn't actually known them that well and didn't have the urge to share everything with them. I try to lift myself out of those thoughts as it only saddens me in the deepest way possible.

Tyler notices my unusual silence, the silence he knows only overcomes me if my parents are mentioned. He looks at me in such a way that I feel compelled to finally tell him for the first time about why I react the way I do, I take a deep breath as I've never told anyone about my parents before and he patiently waits.

"A few years ago I lost my father and only a few months ago now I lost my mother too, the reasons I've booked random days off in the year is because I need to follow the trial and everything that's being said about the case." I speak in a very quiet voice, well aware I haven't really explained things properly but for now it's the best I can do. He doesn't speak although I can tell he's clearly confused about some of the things I've said, instead he simply pulls me close and does his best to comfort me.

"If you ever want to tell me more about it then I'm here for you," Tyler makes sure that I know that, that I can trust and rely on him.

"Same for you for whatever reason," I tell him and we gradually pull apart so I can wipe away my glistening tears.

"We've suffered more than most just in different ways." Tyler says quietly to himself, I wonder if he's referring back to his old job?

"It's weird because as soon as I met you I knew that I could trust you, I don't trust people easily either." I confess to him thoughtfully, glad I have him beside me. Michael comes in then; he observes us for a moment thoughtfully.

"I thought I'd just remind you that you both have days off soon," he informs us, well as if I'd forget. Tyler knows what my days off are for, but I wonder what his are for? Maybe he's planning on visiting his father, I haven't asked recently how he's been doing. Michael doesn't actually know why I need my days off, however he's watching Tyler carefully to see if he is all right.

There is definitely something big going on here and eventually I will figure it out, Tyler seems to be silently communicating with Michael so that he won't say anything. It seems like he wants to protect me from something, something like knowing a secret about him.

The day is already drawing to a close so Michael leaves to go to the staffroom and we decide that we may as well go after him, as we also still have the staff meeting to attend. I sit next to Tyler as always, his leg brushing against mine as I study Michael; I am going to get to the bottom of this at some point. Everyone else is arriving now, Izzie sits on my other side and I can tell she is still thinking of our conversation from earlier. She notices however that I'm thinking down a very serious line of thought, she knows that if I want to figure something out I will eventually succeed no matter what the consequences are. Ever since my parents have died I've been very good at finding out all the information I possibly can.

Michael now grasps everyone's attention for the meeting, "This meeting will be about discussing the year six trip. I will inform everyone on who is on the lists to go," Michael tells us, observing everyone as he does so.

"Miss Collins, Miss Thomas, Miss Spring, Mr Crowther and myself." It sounds weird to hear our names said out loud like that, Tyler also looks like he isn't used to being addressed so formally.

"Is anyone else planning on going?" Michael asks looking at the other teachers with a flicker of hope that more of them will participate in such an important event. As expected nobody else volunteers, "OK if you're not going you are allowed to leave this meeting." Michael makes it clear that he wishes more members of staff will help out, but if not then there's no point being here and so are dismissed.

After they leave it's only my friends in the room and so the atmosphere abruptly lightens up and relaxes.

"Now we have got one slight issue, rooms have to be shared except from mine..." Michael informs us and we all look at him like 'well what's wrong with that?' The penny drops in my head first though, Izzie and Jacqueline will go together leaving me and Tyler. Michael sighs slightly when he realizes what is going to happen without a doubt, the other two both look at me to go with Tyler seeing as I'm closest to him. Obviously I have no problem with that, but that's exactly the reason why there is a problem as Michael knows my feelings for him.

Nobody clearly wants to be the one to state this fact though, "Izzie and Jacqueline you'll be together and Tyler and Violet you'll be together." Michael announces, however he then lets Izzie and Jacqueline go leaving us alone with him.

"Now I've made this arrangement as it suits the other two, I trust that as Violet is your assistant nobody will view this situation the way I do." Michael looks directly at Tyler to make sure he understands that he still suspects us, "You both know the rules so I would appreciate it if you'd stick to them." Michael and me now share a look, but at least he is also talking about himself now as well. Tyler is dismissed next and then I turn to Michael.

"Why can't members of staff get together?" I ask him timidly.

"It just seems inappropriate if different year teachers share the same name, also in your situation it can be off putting and distracting to work with your lover." He sighs and I blush, "Also it would create all sorts of gossip." Well as much as I hate to admit it that part is definitely true.

"You Violet are in a better position than I am, however this should be controlled if at all possible." Michael tells me, strange how he's acting like I'm with Tyler when he shouldn't know that and yet he's acting like he's stopping us from being together when in his mind Tyler doesn't feel that way for me. I leave confused and slightly angry, Tyler's waited for me outside.

As I'm saying goodbye to Tyler outside his car we both share opinions and strategies, "We'll just have to keep it secret, but if we're sharing a room together for the trip we already have an excuse lined up." Tyler mentions pleased, it always makes me happy when he expresses the fact he wants to be with me. He takes my hands in his and gives me a quick but satisfying kiss before he gets into his car. I wave him off before heading home myself, well only a few seconds after Michael tells me to control myself I've ended up kissing him, aren't I off to a good start.

So much has happened today that it's got me excited and eager for what tomorrow will bring, I can't wait to be with Tyler again and for the time when his lips on mine will become natural from doing it all the time.

Chapter Eleven

Tuesday morning, I can't get past my excitement for the school trip but as it's a few weeks off yet I'm going to try to think of other things so that the next few weeks won't drag by because I have my heart set on one event. After carefully choosing one of my favourite dresses; a dark blue one as it will look good on such a warm sunny day like this one, I set out the door with my bags and make the small walk through the village to get to the school.

Tyler pulls up in the car park at the same time I arrive so I decide to wait for him, my heart almost stopping as he walks towards me out of his car. His adoring smile, the gleam in his blue eyes and the handsome way he looks in general. Tyler's dressed smartly, when he stops in front of me there is only one thought going through my mind. How can this attractive gentleman be mine? He gently brushes his slender fingers across my cheek before embracing me.

Taking my hand Tyler walks with me up to the door and Jess comes over to let us in and greet us as usual. Jess doesn't seem at all bothered about how close we look with our hands clearly linked which I blush about as it is so openly obvious. The technician smiles at her when he walks past and me and Tyler cannot resist sharing a look, Tyler also can't hide his grin. Jess now blushes embarrassed and returns back behind her desk quickly afterwards.

"How are you both this morning?" Michael asks as he comes out of his office, his eyes bright and a smile on his lips. He observes Tyler's neat clothes and my dress with a satisfied nod and luckily we're no longer holding hands.

"Good thank you," I reply brightly optimistic, I feel really uplifted and happy today for no particular reason. Tyler also smiles and nods at Michael to show he agrees with me. After we have just settled into our office for the day we hear Michael speaking on the phone in a agitated voice. A moment later he sighs and inevitably enters our office, "I need advice, what do we do about the fact that Miss Fisher isn't in today and I can't get hold of any supply teachers?" Michael asks us in an exasperated voice full of stress.

"You ask Mr Crowther the deputy head, and Miss Spring his assistant to take over the year group for the day." Tyler rallies without even having to think about his answer first. Surprise flashes across mine and Michael's faces and I smile as it's a great idea that I wish I'd thought of. Tyler will make a great teacher and I would love to help him with it, Michael also visibly perks up at the suggestion.

"Well if you're both happy with that arrangement then that sure would solve a lot of hassle," Michael says and we all grin.

"Well then I'd better prepare for my class; meaning making everything up on the spot." Tyler notifies Michael before we set off to the Year Two classroom.

It's a fairly small classroom which is decorated with many displays of the classes achievements and work, Tyler grabs a board pen and writes up our names on the main whiteboard which is situated in the middle of the classroom. I don't bother taming my smirk as Tyler writes up rubbish on the board, this is clearly going to be a unique lesson for this class.

"Very inspirational Tyler," I comment on his teaching skills and methods seeing as the children haven't arrived yet and we should probably get our act together before they do.

"Why thank you for your support Violet, I couldn't ask for a better assistant." Tyler replies, his voice dripping with sarcasm before we both start laughing about it uncontrollably.

We spot the children lining up outside and can't help but exchange excited smiles, we still have five minutes however before we can let them in.

"So what are we actually going to teach them today Tyler?" I ask him as otherwise we're going to be in a spot of trouble.

"English; we will read stories to them and get certain pupils to read parts back to us. This way we can test who is the most confident in the subject and who needs help." Tyler shrugs as if it should have been obvious. Well it is a pretty good idea considering our options and I have no problem reading to them, I will never understand though how Tyler can have these moments that really do remind me of a teacher.

"You know you really do impress me sometimes," I compliment him in an off hand tone to suggest that I'm not making a big deal about it. He looks at me in surprise and then smiles pleased as he saw through my attempt of covering up how impressed I really am.

"I have my fair share of talents it's true, but it's you who is truly impressive." He confesses honestly, but before I have the chance to ask him what he means by that remark it's time to let our class in.

Tyler heads off to open the door, his voice instantly greeting them in an irresistible and appealing tone. I smile, it's like whenever he's confident it gives me a boost as well and I've never been a self assured type of person so it's nice how much more secure I feel around him. They all come rushing into their seats excitedly talking about having me and Tyler as their teachers for the day.

"OK class, as you've probably already guessed you're teacher's not in today, so for that reason me and Miss Spring will be your teachers instead." Tyler announces to them but he's grinning at me, he clearly is going to enjoy today and make the most of it. When Tyler tells the class that we will be reading a story everyone cheers and begins bringing their chairs up to the front, they gather around us and call out the stories they want us to read to them.

"We will be reading but you also need to read some pages as well as obviously we need to observe your skills. Anyone who we think is reading particularly well will be rewarded," Tyler engages with the children in a motivating voice; he clearly hopes that the class will be more cooperative if there's a prize involved.

After taking suggestions from the pupils Tyler finally decides on which story we should read, "Well class let's begin." Tyler opens the book and carefully flicks through the pages to the first chapter with his graceful pianists fingers. When Tyler reads he captivates my full attention, his voice is charming and irresistible helping me lose myself in the story by the way he expresses the words and enhances the meaning behind them. His voice helps describe the story in a way I've never experienced before, words cannot describe Tyler's voice. It is alluring, smooth and you can truly hear his thoughts and emotions by the way he expresses himself when he speaks so you get his interpretation of it. When it's my turn to read aloud I get nervous, however once I've started I let myself become absorbed into it and speak in the way I feel the story should be told. Mine and Tyler's versions of the story put together sure do make an interesting contrast and we've certainly kept everyone listening, they've been holding their breath the entire time.

Then the bell rings out for break time, Tyler smiles and places a bookmark in between the pages to save our place.

"After break you will start reading," Tyler informs them and then dismisses them whilst holding open the door politely in his gentlemanly manner. Once the last pupil has left Tyler turns to me, "I think that went rather well." He states to me looking satisfied, however that isn't what is really on his mind. "You look very pretty in that dress," Tyler compliments me in suddenly a very quiet and almost shy voice. I blush as per usual and then smile, "Well you look very attractive yourself." I admit, looking away from his perfect face.

He gently presses me up against him, our cheeks brush before his tender lips meet mine causing delighted tingles to shiver up my spine. Every time we kiss it feels like something magical is occurring, which in a way I suppose it is.

We pull apart smiling, "We really need to control ourselves; if we keep this up we'll get caught in the act." I whisper softly in his ear, but at the same time I don't want him to stop at all, his endearing face is inches from mine. "You invite me in though, I have never been so tempted." It's his turn to whisper in my ear now, he caresses my face then with his pale delicate fingers. My hands lie limp on his chest and he holds me tightly against him, just as our lips were meeting a second time we hear footsteps coming our way. We swiftly jump apart but it isn't quite fast enough, Izzie comes in and looks us over in surprise.

"So you're doing the lesson," she comments mischievously.

"Is there a problem with that Miss Collins?" Tyler addresses her in a formal way to show he disapproves of her comment, however she simply ignores him.

"You both look so guilty," Izzie giggles at us, so maybe she didn't just see us being so intimate a second ago? Tyler flushes pink so to cover up for him I simply raise my eyebrow at Izzie as she seems to have not noticed us as she was covering up for herself in the process.

"Enjoying your break time?" I ask suspicious. She shares a look with me understanding what I'm getting at with ease, however it is time to collect our class.

"I'll be late at lunch; I have a meeting." She quickly tells us and then we walk in silence out onto the playground. I sigh to myself, it seems the closer we get to the one we want to be with the more tensions there are in our friendship. The class is lining up by the time we arrive and Izzie leaves us without another word.

We lead our class back inside and wait for them to get comfortable in their seats and settle down.

"OK, who would like to read first?" Tyler asks them and everyone in the class manages to end up getting a turn. I write down the names of the children who struggle and those who perform best so as to distract myself from Izzie.

"All right I want you to get your books out and see if you can write a short story." Tyler instructs them whilst writing a title up on the board and handing me a piece of paper and a pen, I guess we'll be taking part in this activity too. Then I realise that he has done this to take my mind off Izzie, but it only causes me to think of him then and how passionate we've gotten which is probably worse. I draw in a deep breath and avert my eyes from him as in my neatest hand writing I write the title at the top of my page 'The Meadow'.

The long grass gently swayed and swished in the summer breeze, birdsong drifted harmlessly through the air and throughout the meadow. The trickling music of a stream bubbled by and filled my ears with its sweet melody. Golden rays of glorious sunshine shone through the leaves of the trees and rested upon the flowers. The wild flowers are scattered randomly filling the meadow with their sweet perfume scents and vibrant colours, the soft sea blues colour the sky perfectly like a splash of paint which holds the clean white clouds which slowly chug by. All of these features are of which only belong to the meadow.

I could have written much better however this class is year Two after all and so I decide to leave it at that. Tyler and I swap and read each others', Tyler has also purposefully kept his basic. After making a few pupils read theirs aloud it's time for lunch, I collect in all the work and put them in Miss Fisher's drawer for English. After the pupils have gone we head back to our office to collect our lunch.

"Oh you two, Miss Fisher has arrived now." Michael calls to us and Miss Fisher emerges from his office behind him. I can't help but feel slightly disappointed, I've enjoyed this morning. Tyler fills Miss Fisher in on everything we have done with her class, where she can find the work and the list of pupils I've written down. She appears pleased and grateful for what we've done so we leave soon after to find a decent spot to eat together outside.

Tyler picks a bench surrounded by flowers, it's well out of the way from anyone else guaranteeing our privacy. This way we won't be disturbed and can enjoy each others' company in peace. We eat in a comfortable silence, I love the way the sun feels as it soaks into my pale skin warming me up. Tyler undoes the first few buttons of his shirt and he looks like he's feeling the heat, as I watch him I feel complete as basking in his presence is enough to satisfy me.

"After we've eaten will you go with me to the music room?" Tyler requests, I hadn't realized when his eyes had met mine. It is then it occurs to me that I haven't actually been to the music room before as it's linked to the nursery.

"Sure," I answer, but I don't see what's wrong with just going to the piano in the hall? We finish quickly and Tyler leads me to the music room.

"I figured that it would be better to take you here than the hall as this is more private, just you and me." He confides in me and takes out a sheet of music from his bag and then gestures for me to sit beside him on the stall.

He carefully props the sheet up against the piano and I see that it's title is 'My time with you'.

"I finished this one last night, it's for the both of us." Tyler spoke softly and emotionally, his voice getting shy again.

"Well let's hear it, our song." I encourage him and smiles spread across both our faces as this is going to be something special. He takes a deep breath before he focuses and begins to play, his music takes me through a journey. The beginning when we meet, developing feelings and then all the way to the stage that we're at now. The song is beautiful and I know I'll never forget it. However I'm always going to want Tyler to play this now, it melts my heart and gives me the happiness only one can feel if they have a special someone. When he has finished I let my hands rest where he's undone his shirt, exposing his neck and his hands hold my waist on the silky dress as his lips meet mine for an immeasurable amount of time.

Only when we pull apart do I notice the time, Izzie is meant to have met us by now but she hasn't showed up anywhere. Guilt washes over me like a wave, I really hope she isn't too mad at me as she's my best friend.

"What's the matter?" Tyler asks me, worried about my sudden silence, I'd forgotten he can read me as easily as a book.

"It's Izzie, I hope she's all right that's all." I answer him truthfully and he frowns for a moment.

"Why don't we go check the staffroom she might be in there?" Tyler suggests but I mostly get the feeling that he's just trying to make me feel better.

My doubts unfortunately prove correct though, Izzie isn't in there and the other teachers haven't seen her around either. I decide to ask Michael, he's alone in his office and looks surprised to see us.
"Sorry to bother you Michael, it's just I was wondering if you've seen Izzie?" I question him hesitantly.
"Yes I just had a meeting with her, I don't think she'll want to be disturbed at the moment though as she has a lot of work to do." Michael informs me, it doesn't seem right though as Izzie always lets me be around when she has work to do. I would have gone and found Izzie anyway but lunchtime is drawing to a close so we have to go back to our office.
    Tyler also doesn't buy Michael's story about work seeing as he's known her even longer than I have, I need to know what her meeting was about as that's probably the reason I'm forbidden to see her.
"Do you have Izzie's mobile number?" Tyler suddenly asks me.
"Yeah why?" I query with him as it's not like we can ring her up now. Tyler however does just that and dials her number into his phone whilst withholding his own, it goes straight to voice mail though as expected.
"It was worth a shot, I thought if she didn't know who was calling she might pick up." Tyler shrugs but I know that he's annoyed that his plan has failed, we both sigh in unison. What did Michael say to her?

Me and Tyler mostly talk about Izzie and Michael in the afternoon, neither of us are able to conclude what could possibly have happened though.
"Look can you promise me that you'll never repeat this?" I ask him making sure he knows I'm being deadly serious. He nods, I have his full attention trained onto me now.
"Michael and Izzie really like each other but they don't know the other has those feelings, at different times they've both told me." I rush through my explanation, "So do you think something has gone wrong as members of staff can't be together!" Once I've finished we both agree we are finally putting the pieces of the puzzle together.
"I thought Michael might... but Izzie, I thought she was joking." Tyler seems bewildered, but then utterly out of character he completely snaps and becomes absurdly angry and aggressive. "And he's the one giving us a

hard time!" Tyler shouts leaving me totally stunned, Michael comes in now clearly wanting to know what the fuss is about, he can't have worse timing even if he tries.

Tyler spins around, his hands shake with violent trembles and he openly and outwardly glares at Michael. He strides up to him and I fear he might do something dangerous he'll regret later, instead he tries to pull himself together a bit. He stands away from the shocked Michael who quickly manages to sort himself out too and then comes right up to me slowly, he closes his eyes and whispers "I'm sorry," to me before opening them again. Michael shares a look with me, he's checking to see I'm all right and I nod, he's clearly seen Tyler like this before but still it must be rare considering Michael's reaction. As soon as Michael has gone I pull Tyler close to me "It's OK, it's OK." I try my best to comfort him, especially as I can tell he's only really just understood what he's done and is beginning to get embarrassed about his outburst. I know how it feels, it's happened to me on many occasions and usually with Michael. I always feel like telling myself to get a grip afterwards.

For the first time neither of us give a damn about being caught any more, I begin to kiss him my hands holding onto his hair, ruffling it. His mouth fights for mine with a passion that is very deep and very satisfying. I feel him calm down in my arms, his lips become more tender and soft and his grip on me less tight. I rest my head against his chest and let him hold me in his arms.

"Whenever I'm feeling low remind me that you're the most perfect and best gift I could have, that you are my greatest prize." Tyler whispers softly and treasures me in his arms, after kissing him one final time we pull apart. "Come on we should probably get ready for the staff meeting," I tell him gently and we take our usual seats and make ourselves comfortable.

When Izzie comes in she rushes towards us despite the fact that Michael openly displays his disapproval, we hug quickly and she sits on my other side.

"I'm so sorry I didn't turn up at lunch," Izzie gushes out to me apologetic, I smile.

"You know you're my best friend right?" I ask her pleased that we're fine. She grins realizing she hasn't needed to worry, the meeting passes quickly and I wave goodbye to Izzie. I turn to Tyler who I'm still concerned about and he kisses me goodbye in full view if anyone happens to walk past. Luckily I don't think anyone sees, it's a nice goodbye though.

Chapter Twelve

This Wednesday seems to be a promising one, I'm fine with Izzie despite Michael's strange behaviour and I personally usually get on with Michael and obviously everything is perfect with Tyler. I feel reasonably in control of everything now, it feels nice to have some power over what goes on in your life. As I get myself ready for the day I let my thoughts take me to hopes that I will get the chance to question Izzie about why Michael has been acting so odd lately. My views on the matter have changed since my conversation with Tyler yesterday; I don't think there is a problem between the two of them. To be honest I have suspicions that Izzie is upset over an agreement about me and Tyler, what the agreement is though I have no idea but it must be that considering her reaction when she witnessed us jump apart yesterday.

I force my thoughts to take me to a lighter and more care free world; one with no problems and where I can be with Tyler. Tyler literally means everything to me now, I have no family or anyone else who really cares about me and I for them. So finding Tyler has changed and altered my whole life, he's probably the best thing that's ever happened to me. Tyler also seems much happier now compared to when I first met him, he has obviously been his charming and gentlemanly self but I've noticed that many great burdens and haunts of his past have been lifted from his shoulders now. It makes me glad that I've managed to help heal and restore him from some of his inner pain.

I gather all my necessary possessions such as my phone and then leave to go to the school. We will be receiving more information about the school trip today, I'm excited about the extra time I'll get to spend with Tyler and on my birthday. However today I need to focus on what's bothering Michael recently, Izzie's my best friend so she's also my best hope of giving me any answers. If I can just get the chance to talk to her alone then maybe I'll get somewhere... After I have greeted Jess I check to see if Michael is already in, thankfully he isn't there so I go to Izzie's classroom. "Izzie?" I call out, hoping she'll find me. Then she and Michael come around the corner, great so he's already managed to get to her before me. "Ah Violet, Izzie's busy so I suggest we leave her be for now." Michael asserts to me, blocking my path to her.

"Well it won't take a moment," I confront him holding his gaze, Izzie looks uncomfortable as me and Michael attempt to stare the other down.

"This has gotten far more complicated than I originally anticipated, I tell you what, after the end of day meeting I want you two to stay behind." Michael spoke in an authoritative voice and I can tell Izzie doesn't appreciate being treated like that, so when Michael departs neither of us make an effort to stop him.

"Izzie what's going on?" I quiz her, annoyed and in confusion as I hope for an explanation. However she then starts crying over Michael's attitude and peculiar behaviour, so I don't dare ask anything else and simply hug her as I guess if we have to stay behind later I'll find out then.

"It's all right if anyone's going to be in trouble later it's going to be me, I'm sure he didn't mean to upset you." I tell her whilst wishfully thinking that Tyler hasn't arrived yet to make matters with Michael worse.

"I'm sorry Violet, I don't want you to be mad at me. I did it because I didn't want you to get in trouble." She cries to me, but what did she do?

After she has calmed down I leave her feeling even more confused than I'd started.

"Why do I have to stay behind later? I don't even know what's going on!" I hear Tyler's voice coming from Michael's office, well now we're all in trouble. As soon as I come around the corner I try to sneak past them unnoticed into my office, but immediately Michael spots me.

"Well don't worry Tyler, Violet and Izzie will be keeping you company there too" Michael comments, stopping me in my tracks.

"You're staying behind as well?" Tyler asks, even more confusion colouring his tone.

"For a reason I have no knowledge of," I sarcastically retort. No, I think I know what's going on here now, I'm beginning to get the gist of this.

I glare at Michael, hating him for what he's done as not only has he upset Izzie but I can tell now that he's doing everything in his power to stop me and Tyler from being together. There shouldn't be a problem with it though, so is it really because he can't be with Izzie? Does that mean that just for that reason me and Tyler can't be together?

I rush into my office and slam the door behind me as hard as possible, vibrating all the walls around me. I quietly curse a few words of specific choice in Michael's general direction before I try to calm myself.

"What's the matter with you recently? You always tell me to cheer up and find something special that makes me happy, so when I do why do you try to prevent me from being with her?" Tyler argues with him in a low attractive voice. However I hear no reply or response and a matter of seconds later Tyler opens the door and closes it after he's joined me to maintain privacy.

"I've seen Izzie, he's upset her probably more than us." I inform Tyler loudly in the hope that Michael will also hear. "I'm so glad I fell in love with you instead of that selfish grump." I mutter, feeling bitter after everything that's happened.

"When I realized that I was in love, I couldn't cope at first as I knew of the rules. Falling in love with you though is the best thing that's ever happened to me." Tyler breathes in my ear and the look in his eyes makes my heart ache. His lips trail across my cheek and then he pulls away trying to control himself, "I'm sorry but I think I basically told Michael that we love each other. He knew from you earlier on and after what I just said he must know...". His voice aches with pain about how he's basically admitted his feelings for me.

"I don't care, he can deal with it now it's not our problem." I kiss him silencing his worries and embracing him into the passion we share. "I think it's mostly my fault, all of this," I sigh as we stop, he looks at me startled. "Why?" he queries, baffled.

"Well you and Izzie had no problems before I came, now I've gotten you in trouble over me and Izzie well..." I trail off caught up in the guilt.

"Listen to me, it's not your fault I fell in love with you. Also it's been me making most of the actions in front of Michael, and Izzie... well her feelings have nothing to do with us." Tyler attempts to convince me, yet I remain unable to completely rid myself of the guilt.

I wonder how Izzie is coping though, also Michael, why would he purposefully hurt her feelings? The annoying thing is if we all fall out with Michael, he's the one in charge and has control over everything. However that's another thing that confuses me, Tyler has said before that he doesn't need to worry about losing his job. No matter what Tyler's old job was though why should he have that guaranteed? I guess there'll always be some things I'm never going to get my head around though.

"Come on we should probably get some work done." Tyler points out and I work as hard as I possibly can and Tyler also pushes himself exceptionally hard. Before break time we have managed to send all fifteen documents to Michael completed and I have also filled out an additional ten piles of work. I turn around when I hear Tyler moan, he's trying to stretch his fingers out after putting his pen down. I smile in sympathy but it has been worth it as we've been falling behind on work for weeks.

"All this work is making my head hurt." Tyler complains and I have to admit it's taking its toll on me too.

We get up and decide to take a rest on one of the sofas in the staffroom, Tyler's repeatedly holding his hand to his head and I start to get concerned so give him a tablet and order him to stay there and take a break. I continue the work alone and yet I find it hard to concentrate knowing he's unwell, also it's too quiet without him and so after I've finished another set of work meaning we're now on top of everything I resolve to check on him. I find him with his eyes closed and his breathing slower, he's asleep and it's probably for the best as the circles underneath his eyes haven't completely vanished yet. I sit next to him and read my book for awhile, just before lunchtime I wake him up. His eyes flicker open and hold mine for a few moments.

"Are you all right?" I question him hoping that he's recovered a bit. He sits up in a daze clearly wondering how time has flown so fast, "You should have woken me up, now you've done most of the work by yourself." Tyler looks embarrassed and ashamed of himself.

"It's fine, I thought I should let you get some rest so that you'd be OK in the afternoon." I reassure him gently, besides he'd looked so sweet whilst he'd been asleep.

We grab our lunch and head outside, I think the mild air helps wake him up and refresh him a bit. I smile when I spot Izzie, I'm glad she'll be joining us this lunchtime. After we have eaten the majority of our lunch Tyler asks Izzie what she knows about Michael's behaviour, which I'm also dying to hear the answer to.

"He asked me to keep an eye on you and to make sure you weren't actually together. I was meant to keep him updated on your situation" she sighs. "I only did it because I thought I could prevent you from getting into any more trouble, and I was right to do so after how you were yesterday break time..." Izzie finishes miserably distressed and displeased by what she's done.

Me and Tyler are in shock, firstly I thought Izzie hadn't seen us that time and secondly I can't believe how far Michael has taken this to do that. "So why has he been mean to you?" I ask, curious as it doesn't make sense. "Well I think he found out that I've been supporting you and lying about stuff to stop you getting in trouble," she admits gloomily. "Also I think he wants me to keep my distance as he doesn't want to love me or me to love him as it's forbidden." She gulps now, her body is racked with trembles and tears, Tyler tries to comfort her whilst I feel devastated and destroyed by what she has said. So we are all suffering due to the same rule, me, Tyler and Izzie and Michael.

"We need to have a proper good talk with him later," I voice my idea so everyone knows what I am planning on doing.

"There's nothing we can say though, although I don't like the facts it is the truth that none of us should be together." Izzie says the thing that we all know and have all denied up until now.

"I guess I'll see you guys later," is all she says before she departs. So now it's time to face up to the facts and the truth, Tyler also remains silent as even he doesn't know how we are going to get around this one. To be honest it's about time everything gets put out in the open, everyone's heard different things or suspected a multitude of others. I'm not prepared for this but it can't be delayed any longer, "I think the entire truth has to be revealed today, and if it is then maybe we can find a way forward." I speak slowly, I don't want it to happen but obviously it has to. Tyler looks uncomfortable about this but agrees eventually.

We go back inside and I grab a pen and some paper, we need to write down everything that needs to be confessed. The list has gotten quite long, varying from flirting and up to going around his house. There are some things we neglect to write down though, there's no way we want Michael to know how many times we've kissed. Other things Tyler crosses out as he doesn't want us to look too bad, however writing everything out like that causes me to realize just how much we've done. Tyler smirks as he glances at how much we've omitted.

"Totally being truthful and honest." He grins in complete amusement, I can't help but smirk as well because at this rate we won't be owning up to anything that we'd originally put on our list.

"There is no way he is going to believe that that is all that's happened between us," Tyler chuckles wiping away a tear from his eye whilst his shoulders shake. I smile to myself despite the outrageous situation as somehow Tyler can always turn everything around and make me laugh.

It's hard to accept and deal with this situation as whenever I'm with him all I want is to kiss him, Tyler catches me gazing at him and smiles.
"Does my presence really affect you that much?", enjoyment shines in his eyes over my embarrassment.
"I can't help it if I enjoy my time with you," I remark and we both smile as it's the name of our song. Tyler gently hums the tune as we work and when it finishes he moves onto another one, this time though there are lyrics that accompany it. I have never heard him sing before and his voice surprises me, hearing him play the piano and the guitar on one occasion had been mesmerizing so this rare moment where I get to hear him sing lifts my heart.

I carefully file away all the work that we've done, when I open the drawer though to collect the next piece of work I am stunned to see we have completed everything. This means we have not only gotten on top of our work but we don't have any left either which is a great relief. So that leaves only the meeting to worry about, another thing I'm concerned about though is if everything goes wrong then what will happen on the school trip? Michael's already arranged whom is sharing a room with who and it will be a bit difficult and obvious if he changes that now.
"You know Michael's already sorted out the room situation on the school trip?" I mention to Tyler; he looks to me to continue. "Well he hasn't sorted out which teachers will be leading each activity or group," I point out, if me and Tyler are in a different group we won't be together all day.

He cusses under his breath as he registers what I've said and what Michael will undoubtedly do, but there's nothing we can do to stop him. I glance at the clock on the wall, we still have a few minutes but we may as well go to the staffroom now. Whilst we wait we discuss what we should do, however when the other teachers arrive it's going to be hard to express the main issues and our opinion on the matter. Jacqueline and Izzie enter then, breaking up the conversation. I'm surprised the other teachers haven't turned up yet, Michael strides in then and sits in his usual place.
"The other teachers won't be joining us in this meeting as the school trip needs to be our main focus." He announces, answering my unspoken question and then the meeting begins.

Chapter Thirteen

"OK so far we have only sorted out who is sharing which room, but we have a lot more to do." Michael begins as he takes out a few documents relevant to the school trip, "There are quite a few activities that we need to get through per day and for that reason we need to sort the year out into groups so as to get everyone around each activity. Also some activities can only have a certain number of people there at each time," Michael tells us, watching our reactions carefully as he reviews the situation.

"I have worked out from the information we have been given that we need to split the year into three groups, so red, blue and green for example." He continues and I glance at Tyler as we both know what's going to happen now.

"So I've decided that Izzie you will have the green group, they're your year so I decided it would be easiest if you were the one on your own." Michael actually has the guts to look her in the eye after he's just isolated her.

"Jacqueline you'll be going with Tyler, so you will have the blue group and Violet you and me will have the red group." Michael finishes watching me in particular, he knows that that won't go down well, talk about drawing the short straw though. So he finds it necessary to keep an eye on me the most, Tyler can't cause trouble if he's with Jacqueline as she's the only one who isn't involved in our awkward situation. Also if Izzie is on her own she can't talk to me or Tyler, and obviously if I'm with Michael then there's nothing I can do. He's worked it out to suit him perfectly, but why did it have to be me with Michael?

After sorting through a few other arrangements such as the coach journey and the children's rooms our meeting pretty much has drawn to an end, Michael then dismisses Jacqueline pretending we're only going to be finishing up arrangements that don't concern her. As soon as she's gone me and Izzie share a long look, now we're in trouble. Michael looks at me clearly daring me to speak first, however none of us utter a sound waiting for him to start.

"Awhile ago I gave Izzie a job concerning you both, she was meant to make sure you weren't actually together and to report back to me. That idea however backfired," Michael assesses Izzie shrewdly before his gaze rests upon us.

"You know why I've arranged the school trip to be this way don't you?" Michael asks us knowing we know the answer.

"So that Izzie will be separated from us, me and Tyler can't be together and Jacqueline will therefore notice nothing." I take the liberty of answering him, I may as well show him that I have no intention of planning to cooperate with him on this trip if I can help it.

"Also Violet, this way I can keep an eye on you. I know Izzie's not going to try anything that's not smart, Tyler won't have the chance unless he wants to give his secret away to Jacqueline. You though, you're exceptionally good at getting around situations like this. Therefore I want you with me, we can also have a catch up." Michael looks directly at me as he speaks and only once he's finished does he look at Tyler. "We all know the rules, if we're too tempted then shouldn't we remove temptation from our path?" Michael asks us all and I don't appreciate his version of being smart.

"Don't worry, you've been too harsh to make me desire your company." Izzie glares at him and I hold my breath, I think we all know though that that's the biggest lie she could have said. However she's clearly deeply upset by his actions, "If you don't mind I'd like to go home now." She continues and I can see the tears shining and glistening behind her eyes, obviously she wants to leave before they spill over and give away how upset she is. Michael nods and then she rushes from the room leaving us behind.

"Well I hope you're happy now, got what you wanted?" Tyler snaps at him angrily.

"She really loves you and that's how you treat her." I support Tyler.

"Look I didn't do it because I wanted to, I can't be with her and I'm only saving her from all sorts of trouble and pain later." Michael lashes back now, he isn't going to let us gang up on him over a decision he's found hard to make.

"This is exactly why I need you with me, you've already caused so much trouble." Michael stares at me before turning away, he can no longer bear to look at us, that last comment really hits home and stings.

Tyler grabs his bags and prepares to leave although we aren't actually allowed to go yet.

"How involved are you?" Michael's question surprises both of us and we look at each other sceptic on what to say.

"Don't look at me like that, I know you're in love with each other. I got the truth out of Violet ages ago and you Tyler, well your actions and comments are a give away!" Michael snaps at us losing his control completely for a moment.

"I really don't think my feelings for her are your concern Michael," Tyler replies acidly and he's chosen his wording carefully.

"It is my business to know if my members of staff are hitting on one another though!" Michael retorts, displeased that this isn't getting anywhere.

"I don't think we're your main problem, Izzie loves you and you love her. Well it's fine if you're avoiding one another but even so it might not be enough if gossip spreads, think about it you're always watching her and checking she's all right. Guess what she's concerned about you too and I would worry if people are going to notice that," I slyly comment back, however I'm not happy about some of his previous comments either.

Well the tables have turned now, it's not just him using threatening little comments. We're all shocked by how out of control this little meeting has gotten, also we are stunned to notice that we have been here for nearly two hours. I sigh, I should probably leave before I get myself into even more trouble. I collect my bags and walk to the door, just when my hand is about to reach the handle I feel his hand on my arm, trying to prevent me from leaving. However he swiftly pulls it away and I leave.

Tyler catches up to me outside, "Are you all right?" he asks looking overwhelmed by what's just happened. There's no way I'm OK after that reality check, I let him hold me there in the car park. I see Michael's figure watching us from the window, so I turn to Tyler and begin to kiss him right on the lips. His hands find my waist whilst my fingers are locked in his hair, I close my eyes to take in the victory fully before we finally pull apart. "Stay with me tonight, stay around my house." Tyler invites me desperate to satisfy his hunger and passion for my company whilst having no idea what I've just done. I smile, I like the sound of that plan a lot. Tyler holds the car door for me whilst I get in and then we're ready to go.

"Can we stop off at my flat first? It's just that I should probably get some clothes for tomorrow," Tyler is fine with my suggestion and so we drive there first leaving Michael behind.

Tyler waits in the car whilst I rush up to my room and grab all my necessary belongings, I decide to put everything in a bag to make it easier to carry downstairs again. I pick some pyjamas, my clothes for the next day, toothbrush and hairbrush and my handbag containing my phone and purse. Tyler takes my stuff and puts it in the boot of the car for me before we set off to his house.

"Tyler," I say his name in a guilty way as I contemplate whether to tell him about my rebellious act in front of Michael.

"What?" he asks, not taking his eyes off the road ahead.

"Michael's going to kill us tomorrow," I reveal to him seriously however he smirks and grins, not understanding what I mean. I bite my lip indecisive, should I tell him? He turns to me now though and instantly senses that I'm not telling him something, his eyes are too good at reading my face.

"What's wrong?" his tone is curious, I can't bear to look at him.

"Well it's just... oh god dammit it's just that Michael saw us in the car park." It comes flooding out, my voice has gone strangely high at the end as I feel like I've been strangled to get the words out.

"What!" Tyler exclaims as he pulls up outside his house, I hadn't realized we've already arrived due to the nerves of telling him.

"I'm sorry, it's just I was so mad so I thought it would teach him a lesson." I gulp getting even more panicked about it, Tyler stays silent for a moment and neither of us make a move to get out the car. Suddenly he startles me by chuckling though, "So after everything that happens you decide the best option is to kiss me in front of him!" We vacate the car and Tyler is still snorting as he grabs my bags, "Well I guess that means I'm free to kiss you whenever I want." He continues smirking, not even bothered or fazed in the slightest by what I've done.

"You always manage to surprise me, I thought you might be angry but you're fine." I compliment him still in shock about how casually he's taking this.

"Why would I be upset with you? It's great to have a partner in crime, I'm so used to pissing Michael off by myself and it's no fun to laugh about it alone." He replies lightly, but it does make me wonder what kind of trouble he's gotten himself into in the past. I hope because I've made a big move Tyler doesn't feel compelled into turning this into a game and making a bigger one, it wouldn't be a good idea to see who can annoy Michael the most.

It's nice to be back in Tyler's home, he leads me upstairs for the first time where there are three bedrooms. We both pause for a moment, will I be joining him or will we be separate? After a few seconds have ticked by Tyler leads me to the room furthest away from the stairs. The walls are a pale cream with a matching carpet, there is a shelf full of CDs and a posh music player in the corner of the room. A fairly big desk is on the other side of the room next to a wooden wardrobe which has a small TV placed on top. A beautiful double bed takes up the centre place of the room with a blue duvet on top, and then there's a painting of a wolf pack howling to the night sky in the snow hung above the bed which completes the room.

I turn to him and smile, "It's such a lovely room, is it yours?" I ask him and his mouth curves up into a delighted smile.

"Yes, so you like it then?" he's clearly pleased with my reaction.

"Yes definitely," I assure him as we turn to look out the window which has a wonderful view of the garden. The curtains are almost exactly the same shade of blue as the duvet, but these have swirling patterns on them. Tyler puts my bags down and I follow him back downstairs, "Are you bothered about what we eat? It's just because I don't think I really have much in at the moment." He apologises.

"No it's fine, I'll eat whatever." I answer truthfully as I'm not fussed over if a meal's fancy or not.

"I have quite a big variety of DVDs we can watch later, if you'd like?" he suggests hopefully and I smile. DVDs always make the day better and are a nice way to pass time so I agree appreciatively.

"So what do you usually do when you're home alone?" I ask intrigued as I want an insight to what his usual day is like.

"Not much," he responds, slightly embarrassed. "I have this little routine when I get home, so I flick through the TV channels, have a shower and occasionally play music and then watch a DVD before I go to bed." I can't hide my smile as it's very similar to what I do when I'm at home.

Tyler shows me where he keeps everything in the house in case I ever need anything and then I get a closer look at the music he's written, the notes are all drawn on neatly and only a few songs have lyrics that go with them.

"So how often do you compose music?" I ask him as I look at all the sheets of his work.

"I tend to do one or two songs a week," he tells me after a moments deliberation and then shows me the piece he's going to play in the assembly tomorrow. After we've finished I assist him with setting up for dinner by getting all the plates and cutlery out whilst he sorts out the fridge and pops the food in the oven. It's a relief to not be on my own, I like having the comfort of people being around me and being with Tyler is all I can wish for. He keeps me from worrying about all the sounds I hear that probably have reasonable explanations to their causes anyway. I wonder how he copes being alone every weekend, however I decide not to ask as I don't want to make myself seem utterly pathetic.

As Tyler returns to the oven to get our meal out I'm surprised to notice the smooth muscles in his arms, he isn't one of those people who look like they take the gym seriously. However he's noticeably in good shape and he never seems to tire out or find anything difficult. Also it's not like our job has any physical elements in it which could be a cause for his natural muscles which show when he flexes them and how in shape he looks. So despite the fact that I know I could be making a fuss out of nothing I decided to simply ask him, "Do you work out Tyler?". He glances at me, taken by surprise by the unexpected question.

"Not really, but for my old job you had to be fast and fairly strong. So I never worked out properly but enough to be useful." He replies as he places our dinner on the table.

"Why?" he continues as we sit down together.

"Well it's just I noticed that you look quite strong that's all," I eye his arms which look soft but are actually hard and smooth underneath, his chest also looks pretty impressive even though he's got his shirt on. Tyler simply shrugs and smiles but I think that he's secretly pleased, as we eat I can tell he's also thinking curiously of things that we don't know about the other. We both are stunned when we notice how fast our time together is passing unlike when you're alone. We select a couple of DVDs to watch and then get comfortable on the sofa, we sit snuggled up together and watch the films which are thrillers with comedy randomly added in as well.

By the time we both have finished it's half eleven and we go upstairs after locking up and turning all the lights out, I get changed into my pyjamas in the bathroom and brush my teeth before joining Tyler who has used the en suite from one of the other bedrooms. He's already tucked under the duvet so I switch off the light and blindly climb into the other side of the bed. The duvet is thick and warm and I snuggle in beside him, we lie facing one another and our eyes are only just beginning to adjust to the dark. So when I take my eyes away from his face which is resting against a pillow and this is when I notice that he's shirtless. I blush instantly embarrassed, hopefully though it isn't obvious in the dark. His eyes however miss nothing and so he quickly picks up on my expression and the cause of it, it's stupid of me to think he wouldn't notice. His mouth curls upwards but he says nothing as we simply watch one another in the dark, I try to force myself to relax but it's increasingly difficult as we're both staring at each other. If this keeps up I'll never get any sleep and will probably end up laughing about how ridiculous our situation is.

I roll over so that I'm no longer facing him, but subtly the movement has brought me closer to him. I sense him inch closer to me; now that I'm not watching him some of the pressure has been taken off and Tyler feels more able to be near me without either of us feeling awkward about it. I feel his warmth behind me and so I move just a tiny bit more to close the distance between us and I feel my back press up against his bare chest. His warm arms then wrap around me and his cheek brushes against mine before he rests his head down next to mine on the pillow. I easily sink into a warm and restful sleep in his arms, this has to be the happiest I've been. The next sound we both hear is the piercing alarm clock on Tyler's side of the bed and we both wake with a start. It takes me a moment to realize where I am and then I feel Tyler's warmth around me and last nights events come back to me. We both groan as we realize it's time to get up, had the night really gone that fast? I really can't be bothered to get up, however when Tyler gets up he gently carries me out of bed with him before putting me down to make sure I get up.

That's when I remember that Tyler's always in later than me and this is probably why so I force myself to get a move on. I change in the bathroom and when I've finished Tyler is still in the en suite so I begin quickly dumping my possessions into the bag I've brought with me. I pull the curtains open and am greeted by glorious sunshine, good thing I put a t-shirt on then. When Tyler comes back in it's a funny sight, he is dressed in his usual smart clothes but his hair is completely messed up from sleep and he hasn't done up the buttons on his shirt yet. I approach him and then begin to do them for him, when I've finished and look up at his face he bends his head lower to meet mine and I close my eyes as our lips lock. This is the perfect wake up call for me, when we pull apart and go downstairs we prepare breakfast which Tyler surely can hardly taste due to the amount of time it takes him to eat it.

We have roughly ten minutes before we have to go, I wonder if Tyler's morning is always this hectic. I brush my hair after quickly putting away my cup and bowl in the sink. I grab my bags, we put our shoes on and then Tyler retrieves the house and car keys. After locking up we get in his car and are off to the school, I can't help but feel nerves as we're definitely not getting on with Michael any more.

Chapter Fourteen

As we arrive I can see Jess waiting at the door, she's clearly wondering why I haven't turned up yet as usually I would have been here ten minutes ago. However she then spots me and Tyler getting out of his car and we head up to the building, she greets us as normal and doesn't even question why I've gotten a lift from Tyler which I have to admit surprises me as it's not normal to be this close with another colleague. When we come into the staffroom Izzie instantly joins us, relieved we're here but none of us bring up the topic that is on the tip of all of our tongues. Another problem though is that Izzie doesn't even know what happened after she left, there's bound to be some serious punishment on the way.

Jacqueline also joins us and begins enthusiastically talking about the trip next week, next week... How can it already be nearly the summer holidays? It does mean I'll be getting paid more though and it will be my birthday too. However what am I going to do with all the weeks off? Before I head off to mine and Tyler's office it's as if Izzie has read my mind, "Do you want to go shopping in the holidays?" she asks me and Jacqueline. Well as it turns out none of us have any other plans and so we make ones together, Jacqueline also offers that after shopping we can have a sleepover at her house.

Now pleased that I actually have some arrangements for the holidays and a social life I join Tyler in our office.
"I guess we'll be going to assembly soon," Tyler reminds me, well at least it gives us a break from being stuck in here all day. Still, my mood isn't improving much as I'm beginning to lose interest in the school trip if I can't even be with Tyler. Also hanging around with Michael all day isn't my idea of fun.

We leave for the assembly early so that we'll already be waiting at the piano and set up, but it doesn't take long to get his music ready so we are left to wait.
"It was really nice to let me stay at your place," I tell him truthfully as I'd enjoyed yesterday afternoon with him. Tyler smiles and nods but I can tell he's too distracted about Michael to relax and have a conversation right now. Izzie enters the hall with her class first, after she has settled them neatly into a row at the front she joins us. We all seem as if we're mentally preparing for the rage Michael will want to unleash upon us soon. The

other teachers come with their classes soon after, but judging from previous events it doesn't look like Mrs Green and Mrs Parker are our biggest threats any more. I refuse to look at Michael when he makes an appearance, and I don't think Izzie's looking in his general direction either. After the usual waste of time comments are made Izzie informs her class that they are to meet outside the school at nine o'clock on Saturday.

Tyler plays his piece as the year groups are dismissed to go back to their lessons and then when everyone has departed from the hall I force myself to meet Michael's burning gaze, he seems unsure of what to say to us despite the fact that there's obviously a lot to be discussed. Tyler is also keeping his mouth shut, not daring to speak so I sigh and walk straight past Michael to go back to my office. I'm sure Michael won't waste the precious time he has alone with Tyler so I'm not going to bother waiting and I collect the days work by myself.

I have been working for at least half an hour before Tyler returns and Michael goes back to his own office. Tyler doesn't look impressed by whatever Michael has said, that's for sure.

"You're walking a fine line right now, and what do you think you're playing at?" Tyler mocks and imitates Michael's voice and I can't hide my smirk even though I know I probably should before I get in even more trouble. "Did he really say that?" I giggle, intrigued.

"Oh he had a lot to say, mostly about our disgraceful behaviour." Tyler grins to me; well typical, despite what happened he's enjoying himself.

"There wasn't much work to do so I've already done the work for today and tomorrow," I mention to him as there's no point pretending we have anything else to do just for Michael's sake.

"What do you think we should do about the school trip?" Tyler asks me, a more serious note entering his tone of voice now.

"I've been thinking about that as well." I haven't thought of any ideas that solve our problems about us being separated though, what can we actually do about that? "Do you think we'd be allowed to use our mobile phones?" I ask him as at least that way we'll still be able to talk to each other.

"I don't know, but it's definitely worth a try." Tyler starts writing any ideas we have down. "Also we could arrange times where we could 'need the toilet'," Tyler voices another brilliant plan which we add to the list.

By the time it is break time though our list hasn't gotten much longer, but there really isn't much we can do thanks to Michael. Izzie comes and finds us now that her class is outside, we show her our ideas on how we can be together and she seems amused but doubtful that it will get anywhere.

"Don't you think that Michael's going to be watching out for that kind of bright idea?" she points out sarcastically, I don't want our only hope of a plan to be squashed though so we keep at it. However Izzie does manage to come up with some other ways we can sneak off together which of course we obviously also add to the list. All the way up till lunchtime we discuss different strategies and I'm feeling more hopeful now as at least we've thought of ways to make this trip more enjoyable and entertaining.

Michael doesn't look pleased to see me, Tyler and Izzie all heading off outside to eat together but he doesn't say a word and leaves us to it. We try to keep our topic for conversation away from Michael but most of the questions we really want to ask each other are centred around him. We obviously want to question Izzie and I'm sure she'll have plenty to ask about us considering how Michael's more on our case than ever before, which must be some kind of record. However we know that if we ask her questions then she will in return, but to be honest it's Michael that I have the most questions for. I'll have plenty of chances on the school trip, but all the other times I've talked to him we both just lost our tempers.

I won't give up though, me and Michael have a strange bond of friendship and so I'm determined to sort this problem out eventually. Izzie departs to bring her class in, I can't think of anything to say to Tyler however it feels like there's a lot I'd like to get off my mind. Suddenly Tyler gets up though, startling me as he throws a panicked look at his watch, "I'll be back, I promised Jacqueline that I'd meet her to discuss the plans for our group on the trip," he rushes through his explanation apologetically before he races off to find her. I sigh, there's no point going back inside as there's nothing to do so I let my thoughts drift. Jacqueline's going to have a hard time organising her group with Tyler, even more so now that we have other plans I contemplate to myself with a slightly guilty smile. That's when I look up and notice Michael heading over to join me.

"Hello Violet," he greets me as he sits down beside me and he appears as if he too is trying to stay calm and not lose control in this conversation. I feel bad but I'm not going to make his life easy if he isn't prepared to do the same for me.

"I'm really sorry for what a pain I've been it's just you know that I can't -". He gently cuts me off with a wave of his hand. "It's OK, but you have to understand why I've done what I have."

I nod, I do know why and his rules are fair but I just don't like or obey them because it's hard as I understand him but it needs to be different. We both know why the other has done certain actions, but because it doesn't agree with what we want it causes this awful continuous circle of events.

"The only thing I don't understand is that you're in the same situation. If it was just me and Tyler then the rule wouldn't affect you but you won't allow it even though Izzie is the one for you." I tell him truthfully what my confusions are seeing as this is one of the only chances we have to be honest with each other. I note the pain in his eyes as I mention Izzie.

"She can do better than me" he says quietly and I look at him in shock and gasp.

"The only thing she wants is your care and love," I tell him, making sure he understands that.

"Maybe for now, but this has happened before Violet. She finds guys, thinks she loves them and then gets over them." He looks me in the eye, "I would rather not hurt myself more than necessary." His tone of voice indicates that he wants to end this particular topic quickly.

"That's why I admire your love for Tyler, you don't have to say or do anything but just from your reactions or the look in your eyes I know that he means everything to you." Michael sighs before continuing, "with Izzie I can't tell, but before you even knew you loved Tyler others could tell."

I stare at him in surprise, "Like who?" I ask bewildered.

"Well me and Izzie obviously, Jess also probably knows." He smiles at me, but Jess! She's never hinted at anything though. At least he doesn't mention Jacqueline because then at least half the members of staff would know.

"So whenever I've been angry with you I have always respected and thought well of you," he confesses to me more seriously now.

"I can find some of your decisions and choices annoying, but you are a good person and deserve to be happy." I answer and we both smile before Michael speaks up again.

"Tyler obviously loves you too, when he's not too mad at me tell him I'm sorry." Michael stands up then, neither of us is going to back down or surrender however we have got somewhere. The rules won't be changing any time soon though I guess for either of us. He walks off as soon as Tyler comes into view, clearly not wanting to make anything worse by accidentally starting an argument.

Tyler watches Michael heading off before averting his gaze onto me as he joins me, "Sorted everything out with Jacqueline," he tells me but his mind is clearly no longer set on that train of thought.

"Well that's good, the trip's so close now." I keep my voice bright and don't indicate anything about my conversation with Michael although we've obviously been speaking.

We have just one day left and then we'll be going on the school trip, so with our plans to meet up arranged and the fact that we will be sharing a room as a bonus we don't have to worry. Tyler lets it go about the fact that I've been talking to Michael considering the hell we're planning to give him soon enough, also I will have to be with Michael anyway seeing as thanks to him we're in the same group. I follow Tyler back inside so that we can get a cup of tea and chat together.

"I'll probably start packing tonight, it makes it easier if I forget anything I have a second chance of remembering it." Tyler says to me as he hands me my cup, well it's a good idea and leaves us no hassle the night before.

The main items I know I have to pack though are mostly easy to remember, "Why don't we make a list of everything to take?" I suggest as it will pass time and also it will be handy to have a check list on the way back as well. I draw out the columns for my check list section and then the items that will go next to it, it starts off simple so how many tops, jeans and socks we will need. However then we have to think about the more complicated and complex items, so our phone chargers, sun cream and any other accessories. We both seem surprised by how much we actually need to pack for this trip, the list will make sure that we don't forget the items we've already thought of which is good because I tend to do that.

We're both grateful that the day is finally drawing to an end, everyone turns up to the staff meeting as the lessons being taught before the summer holidays need to be discussed. Izzie is given more information than anyone else as she needs to prepare her class about the trips final details, and what I'm most bothered about are the payments we'll be given depending on how much we earn. However as for those of us going on the trip our total payments will be added up afterwards, I say goodbye to Tyler and Izzie, then make my way home to my flat. I put the clothes I've hidden in my bag due to staying over at Tyler's in the wash and then clean up my flat for the first time in ages, I dust over everything so it gleams to a high shine and then I even go to the effort of hoovering the carpet seeing as I'll be gone for a while.

It takes me some time to remember where I've put my suitcase as I'm not used to actually using it, but when I locate it I start going down my check list. Once I've packed my clothes I find a spare shampoo bottle, the sun cream and medicine along with all the other appliances and accessories. I'm pleased to notice that I have managed to pack everything on my list leaving me with free time, I call Izzie to see if she needs any inspiration on what else we can do for the trip but her phone goes to voice mail so I try Tyler instead. I'm delighted because he picks up on the second ring, I let him know I've already packed and he has also just finished. We chat about the trip for a while before realizing that it has actually gotten quite late, so we say goodbye to each other and that we'll see each other tomorrow.

However an hour later when I'm feeling bored and still thinking about our conversation from earlier my phone rings, "I know it's late it's just I'm really bored here on my own." Tyler has called me back, feeling the same way I do.
"It was great when I was around your house wasn't it?". It feels lonely without him here in my flat. After a while though I lose concentration of what Tyler is saying as thinking about my flat brings up a number of worries, I'm not doing a particularly good job of paying for my flat at the moment and with Michael not paying us till after the trip...

Tyler notices that I have uncharacteristically zoned out a bit, I tell him I will provide him with the reason tomorrow as it's already past midnight.

I wake up with relief now that it's Friday, finally the last day before the trip. The whole day me and Tyler discuss topics of nothing containing any significance until the conversation returns to last night.
"I really need Michael to give me a good pay soon, otherwise I'm really going to be in trouble with paying for my flat." I admit to Tyler with a sigh, Tyler however has a peculiar expression on his face that only ever appears if he's deeply considering an idea he's just had. I don't find out what it is

though as the day goes fast and I'm pleased to find out we can go home early without a staff meeting to prepare for the trip.

Chapter Fifteen

I feel a rush of excitement as I get up, it's finally the day of the school trip. I get all my bags together and ready early, I put my suitcase and backpack near the door and then hurry through my breakfast. I've been sitting around in my flat for a while with extreme impatience, so in the end I give up and leave early to go down the high street with my suitcase before the usual rush of people will be around to block my path. I instantly spot Izzie attempting to pull her suitcase along with great difficulty and I smile and force myself to go faster so that I catch up to her. I'm relieved to notice that I'm not the one who has packed the most, no wonder Izzie is having a hard time with moving.

Michael is trying to sort something out with the coach driver and Tyler's just arriving, me and Izzie load our suitcases onto the coach and then Tyler joins us. We share a glance when he sees the size of Izzie's suitcase and then an amused smirk. Jacqueline has already registered all the pupils and so we are only holding out for one who Izzie waits outside for so she can register them, Michael gets everyone else onto the coach and seated. Then Jacqueline, me and Tyler all get on after him.

Michael as the headmaster obviously sits at the front, Jacqueline however chooses the seats behind him for her and Izzie meaning me and Tyler will be at the front sideways opposite from Michael where he is able to see us. I pretend I don't notice that and sit next to the window meaning Tyler will be closer to Michael than me. Izzie and the last student finally board the coach and buckle their seatbelts, I can't remember the last time I went on a coach but it feels nice and comfortable being with Tyler.

We talk about all sorts of things endlessly and Izzie occasionally joins in with us, however I'm tired from getting up early at the weekend when I've been working all week. Everyone else has quieted down after so much chatter as well, also the journey is taking us ages as we're stuck in a traffic jam. Even Tyler appears to be worn out from the week and forgetting Michael's presence which shows how tired I must be I gently rest my head against Tyler's shoulder, I feel him smile and he rests his cheek against my head and closes his beautiful blue eyes.

We relax like that for another hour before we actually arrive, Tyler lifts his face away from mine and I raise my head off his shoulder in sudden haste as I realize how we must look to anyone else. Luckily nobody seems to have paid us any attention and our excitement picks up again for the trip now that we're here.

Michael addresses all the pupils now, "When you get off the coach I want everyone to stay together and listen to their names when they're called so that they can collect their chalet key." Michael gives us our key now and we share a look which implies that he wants us to behave ourselves, Tyler however looks like he's already thinking of other plans. We guide the class off the coach and away from the road, the whole process of handing out keys only takes ten minutes though so now we have free time until lunch.

We all have separate chalets and me and Tyler head off to find ours, we have to walk quite far but at least this means we aren't near anyone else. We unlock the door and I am genuinely surprised by what I see, I had expected it not to be very clean as school trips never usually are. However the small bathroom is decent and there are no stains or unpleasant smells anywhere. There's one thing though, obviously it won't matter to me or Tyler but Michael should probably not find out that there is only a double bed so we won't be sleeping separately. Neither of us mention it as we make the bed by putting all the sheets and duvets on but I bite my lip to hide my amusement.

We start unpacking our clothes into the small wardrobe opposite the bed, "I don't think we should tell Michael about the bed," I grin to Tyler who is also eyeing the bed with a satisfied smirk.

"That can be our little secret," he replies smiling away clearly pleased about the way things have worked out.

By the time we finish we still have an hour of free time together left, I don't want to be separated from Tyler but it will be worse when we're separated the whole day. Today there are hardly any activities as we have only just arrived so we can't miss out on each others company for too long. We lie side by side on the bed, relaxing whilst thinking about what the rest of the day will bring. Oh well, Michael can't annoy me that much today surely? But after lunch I will be alone with him with our group for the rest of the day and Tyler will have his group with Jacqueline.

Then we hear a knock on the door, we instantly get up and as Tyler answers the door he manages to block the view of the bed and it is a good thing too as it's Michael.

"Just thought I would check on you, is everything OK with your room?" he asks us and we nod praying silently he won't see past Tyler. He also reminds us that we will be going to lunch in a few minutes, once we reassure him that everything's fine he leaves. The greatest look of relief washes through us as he doesn't see the bed, just in case he comes back though I grab my bag and the chalet key. We then leave to go to the meeting point. Izzie and Jacqueline are already there and Michael is coming with the majority of the year group behind him.

Tyler's impatient as he's starving, he is looking desperately at Michael to say the word that we can go eat. I have to admit though that I am also really hungry as well, why can't we just go and eat now? After everyone arrives we rush down to the cafeteria which can be better described as a restaurant. I get me and Tyler a seat whilst he pretty much gets us everything that's available. I stare at the amount of food in front of us and look at him in bewilderment, I know he's hungry but isn't that going too far? As we eat together I worry about how it will probably be boring without Tyler, but it won't be for too long I keep telling myself. When we finish Tyler picks up on my thoughts, sometimes I swear he knows my feelings like their his own. He starts to get slightly panicky about me not being by his side later, I have noticed this a few times before. It's always like he wants to protect me and if possible always keep me in sight, it's probably one of the reasons I feel so secure in his presence because he knows how anxious I get and his anxiety comes from worrying over me.

Michael comes over and delivers us the words we've both been dreading; that we have to split up into our groups now. I inwardly sigh and get up to join him and Tyler wishes me luck before he walks off to join Jacqueline. Luckily we don't have a particularly big group, also there will be the people who run the actual activity to help us out anyway. We will be going to do Archery for the afternoon, well it's a good thing that teachers don't have to join in or that would be humiliating. Michael makes me nervous enough as it is and on top of that he's taken away my security, my partner in crime Tyler.

I walk unwillingly beside Michael feeling my nerves twist into a knot as I feel my heart beat pick up the pace as it only does when I'm nervous or I'm with Tyler due to a completely different reason.

"Will you be joining in?" he asks me, despite noticing my lack of motivation.

"Probably not, I don't do sport." Besides Archery, that has to be one of the most dangerous ones going, knowing me I'll probably accidentally make myself the target so there's no way I'm joining in. Michael smiles, probably picturing the same thing I am.

"There's no 'I' in team." That has to be one of the most irritating phrases, true though there is no 'I' in team but there are three in 'I don't give a shit'. However I don't dare voice my private joke to him.

I remember doing Archery when I was on a school trip, I had missed every single target and to this day I still don't know what all the fancy terms are such as the 'tilling point'. So instead I watch our group fail, pleased it's no longer me making a fool of myself, when I turn around though I'm surprised that Michael's no longer at my side. Then I'm stunned to notice that he's actually giving it a try. I watch him and he isn't half bad either, he beckons for me to join him as he catches me watching him from a distance. I don't join in, but I do enjoy watching him as it makes me realize I don't know anything about him or his hobbies. He can only be a few years older than the rest of us and yet he seems more capable than everyone else. The wind has no effect on his short almost curly brown hair, quite unlike Tyler's neat and slightly darker brown hair.

Tyler's more of the typically handsome and charming type, whereas Michael's face is soft, open and friendly and with his curls looks typically cute and his gentle brown eyes and smile. However as the afternoon drags on my thoughts keep returning to Tyler and what he's doing right now, as much as I like Michael as he's my friend but with authority his presence isn't quite enough to distract me from Tyler. I check my phone but I don't have any messages, Michael notices my not with-it behaviour.

"You can see him later," he promises me in his usual kind, thoughtful voice which sounds like his words have been brushed over with sandpaper but in a nice way. Michael's always been a slightly awkward person but you know he cares by the way he looks you in the eye to make sure you've understood him and that you're OK before backing off. I know I won't be able to see Tyler for long though, but imagining Tyler is with me and what he might say does improve my mood.

No one will ever be able to replace Tyler, I can think of other people like Michael who are good looking, kind and have that thoughtful sensitive side which I'm attracted to but no one else can have Tyler's blue eyes that seem to smile when his lips do. His soft, fluid and smooth alluring voice that sounds like music on its own and his amazing patience, the way he always listens to me and looks at me as I speak making me feel special and important. It strikes me again how much I actually love Tyler, I can't bear getting through even a few hours without him, I've fallen for him hard. I can't help it though, I'm attracted to him in every way possible and my heart belongs to him completely. How I'm going to cope with only a few dates in the holidays I have no idea.

When Michael finally declares we can go back to our chalets until dinner time I am deeply relieved that the day is basically over and I can be with Tyler. Tyler hasn't gotten back yet and seeing as I have a couple of hours before dinner I decide to have a shower in his absence. By the time he gets back I've finished and dried my hair as well.
"That took forever!" he complains to me, clearly he's had a worse day than me. He kicks his shoes off and slings his jacket on the floor, before lying down next to me on the bed. His anger quickly subsides as I lie my head on his chest, he holds me in his arms and my warmth radiates into him making him warmer as his face had been freezing but my lips have solved that problem. We kiss passionately until it's time for dinner, I sigh satisfied as we pull apart and he holds my hand in his warm and firm grasp all the way to the restaurant.
    The others are all sitting together despite the fact that Izzie and Michael aren't talking. However I'm pleased when me and Tyler sit on our own together like lunchtime, he's the only one I want to be with. We talk loads about what we've done today but mostly about how much we've missed one another's company. The evenings however are for year activities and so not in groups, also meaning we cannot be separated for now.

As we eat we forget about everyone else, it feels like a date as we enjoy our meal together and the stresses of being apart earlier evaporate. He jokes with me and we discuss our feelings for one another.
    "Violet, I love you and I have to admit this trip worries me, being away from you for so long. I don't think I can do it," he confesses to me. "You said you're having troubles with your flat right?" he asks me suddenly. "Yeah, I am." But what does that have to do with our feelings for each other?

"Live with me Violet, I love you more than anything. We'll be great together, I promise I'll look after you." It comes out in a rush, but he's clearly been thinking of this since I told him about my flat, he wants to live with me. My breathing stops, my heart's thumping in my chest as I reply "Of course I'll live with you, I love you and I need you, you're the only person I have to live for." We get up, rush out the building and he embraces me there to celebrate.

"So we can be a proper couple now, I can move in with you!" He kisses me as his answer, I feel like my life is finally beginning. I have found my soul mate, and we can finally live our lives as one. Long after we've stopped kissing he holds me there in his arms, we try desperately to pull apart when Izzie opens the door, however she turns around and sees us. She smiles though and comes to join us, "Michael wanted to know if you're all right as you rushed off." She explains to us, "I wanted a reason to leave his company anyway." She sighs now, being near Michael is clearly taking it's toll on her. I do my best to comfort her, but I don't think she really wants me to, it seems like she would rather endure the pain.

"By the way, it's fine to be a couple in front of me. It's only everyone else you need to worry about," Izzie grins, taking the topic into a lighter one whilst deflecting the problems off her. We both feel slightly embarrassed as we've always hidden it from Izzie despite the fact she knows, but it will be easier if there's one less person we need to worry about. So Tyler takes my hand and the three of us wonder off to be somewhere more private, Izzie doesn't bother going to inform Michael if we're OK so that in a way will be his answer.

"On this trip can you please never leave me alone with Michael, it's just I don't think I can handle it." Izzie tells us, making sure we agree. However I think the best solution is if they actually talk, but I don't say that as it will annoy her. It's a shame her love story isn't as easy as ours, however we still aren't technically allowed to be together.

"Maybe Michael's only worried because of what happened with your other boyfriends." Tyler comments, I flinch remembering the conversation I've had with Michael before. Izzie however looks appalled by the suggestion. "But you know that I never got serious with them, I have never felt like this for anyone in my life!" she snaps now at Tyler, judging from the look that's just formed on his face they've had arguments similar before I had arrived.

I step in front, shielding Tyler from Izzie with a look of pure defence on my face. I'm not going to let her speak to him like that, no matter how much pain she's in. Tyler puts his hand on my arm though trying to stop me from probably making her worse.

Chapter Sixteen

Before I can say anything though Michael discovers our private spot and to say he doesn't look happy would be an understatement, "I would like an explanation for why you all decided to disappear." He begins, glaring at all of us in turn. Izzie casts me a sour look and with great effort I manage to force myself to not storm off which would only escalate the problem.

"Well is anyone going to speak?" Michael continues, clearly getting infuriated with us as each second ticks by in silence.

"Well I think it's Izzie's place to answer seeing as you sent her here to check on us," I reply frostily out of extreme agitation. Izzie however remains silent leaving Michael to have to visibly do his best efforts to calm himself in front of us; Tyler's lips form a smirk in amusement despite the fact that we're all probably doomed now.

Tyler's so lucky that he's with Jacqueline for this trip as she's oblivious to what's going on between everyone.

"All right, Izzie you go and join Jacqueline, she shouldn't have been left on her own because of this." Michael orders and Izzie hurries off in relief to escape the situation, great so now we're going to get all the blame as per usual.

I bite my lip hard, I really don't want to cry in front of Michael but I'm so angry and upset right now that I don't know how long I'll last until traitor tears will spill over. The whole situation is unjust, clearly this trip is going to be a disaster.

"I'll find out what's wrong with her later, however in the mean time I think you should both stay in your chalet. It would be best if you're not near each other for a while," Michael speaks gently stunning us both. Returning to our chalet alone together is the best gift Michael can have possibly given us, after having a proper moan about the whole trip when it's only day one I erase my anger through kissing Tyler. His lips are like a cure to my inner pain and I feel him calm down and relax with me.

Not bothered any more about the rest of the evening activities we change into our pyjamas and slip underneath the warm duvet of our bed, seeing Tyler shirtless again reminds me of when I stayed around his house and fell asleep in his arms. There's no embarrassment this time though and we simply snuggle up together, the steady beat of his heart against me is soothing as I think about how I can always be with him from now on.

So although it's absurdly early to go to sleep Tyler's lips send me straight into a peaceful and dreamless slumber, we're briefly woken by a knock on the door but when neither of us bother answering it whoever it is goes away and we sleep undisturbed for the rest of the night.

I wake comforted by Tyler's warm arms, we rest for a while before deciding we have to get up or we'll probably be late. We've literally only just gotten ready when Michael knocks on our door, we all seem to be reasonably calm considering everything that happened last night. However that's probably because Izzie isn't here with us.

"I'll be talking to Izzie later on today, but before I do I want your opinions first." Michael tells us and yet again me and Tyler are shocked by this outcome, I thought as we're always in trouble that he won't even bother asking our opinion never mind first.

I don't really know how to start as the whole reason Izzie's upset is because of him in the first place.

"..." I attempt to speak but nothing comes out, I never know how to talk to people. Michael has realized this for a while, it's exactly why he tries to keep me out of these kind of situations. He turns to Tyler instead to spare me from any further embarrassment I feel whenever I'm too afraid to speak. When this gets really bad I feel claustrophobic as if there's a pressure or tightness around my neck making it hard to breathe, this often leads to me having an anxiety attack which usually occurs twice a day. This has gotten considerably worse since I'd lost both my parents, however that's still one detail Michael doesn't know.

"She only lashed out at us because she was already upset, Violet made it slightly worse as she stepped in front of me but it's no big deal between us." Tyler replies smoothly, however I feel slightly put out. That last comment stung as it suggests I'm not allowed to defend him. Also the next time I see Izzie I'm waiting for an apology first, Tyler's only been trying to help but it doesn't matter to Izzie if Michael gets in our way. I keep quiet and don't say anything, when nobody comments on what Tyler's said everyone knows that nobody is going to say what really happened and why. However Michael gives me that look which means he'll be questioning me alone later.

For now though we are forced to walk with Michael to get breakfast, to be honest though I think I've well and truly lost my appetite. Izzie and Jacqueline haven't turned up yet so we all sit together, I can just feel the gloom and doom of the upcoming events.

"We have a lot of activities to do today Violet so I suggest that if you're not going to eat now you should take snacks for later." Michael advises me, concern and sympathy evident on his face. However even Tyler isn't eating much, it seems he's also dwelling over the fact that we'll be separated all day.

I refuse to even look up when they join us, Tyler greets Jacqueline as obviously he'll be with her later and Izzie also simply remains silent.

She sits as far away from me and Michael as the table physically allows, "Follow me outside after a few minutes so it doesn't look suspicious." I whisper in Tyler's ear, I linger by him for a few moments and then leave without a word. I relax as soon as I'm away from all of them, I don't think I can cope with any more tension. A couple of minutes later he comes just as I knew he would, he makes my heart stutter every time I see him. I don't need to give him any explanations, I just pull him close to me and as always he wraps his arms around me.

"Don't worry about this trip, I'll always be here for you." Tyler gently caresses me, protective and concerned. I know I will be in a panic without him though, I have become quite dependant on his company and it's unbearable being away from him for just a few hours. Tyler also gets upset and cautious when he doesn't know where I am or if he can't get to me reasonably quickly. Whenever I have had to disappear from our office for a while when I come back I will find him in a stressed state, but he will always try to cover it up as it embarrasses him.

"I'll call you when we're out doing the activities," Tyler promises. I can tell though that he really doesn't want to leave my side, I feel a faint wave of nausea creep up on me and I feel weak from not eating anything. However I can't bear to bring myself to eat and just the thought of being away from Tyler makes me ill.

When the other teachers meet up with us I notice that my reactions and awareness aren't functioning properly. I try desperately to stop myself from wobbling and force myself to breathe properly, however I walk much slower than them as my vision is blurring and I am quickly getting into a panic. It feels like everything is going in slow motion and I can't seem to move properly from feeling too weak to focus. It's like I'm not quite there, I don't feel like I have any control over my actions. Tyler's so absorbed into his own panic that he doesn't pick up on my dizziness and lack of strength.

Michael has gotten everyone back into their groups and they're heading off with their instructors, he is waiting for me as we're falling behind but then Tyler finally notices that something is really wrong. Despite the fact that Michael's there Tyler sends Jacqueline off to care for their group alone. It's only us three left and Tyler gently holds me against him but before Michael can say anything along the lines of disapproval I collapse in his arms, Tyler clutches me protectively in shock just as Michael is. I feel myself blackout and lose consciousness, there is no way of telling how long I'm like this but I awake weak and dizzy.

It takes me awhile before my brain finally processes the fact that Tyler's carrying me, Michael by his side with a look of deep concern showing on his face and in his eyes. I'm too weak to speak or even move, so I close my eyes and tried to recover in his arms. After a little while my breathing returns almost to normal and I weakly hold onto Tyler's shirt, he doesn't notice as he is too busy talking to Michael but I can't hear what they're saying as I'm pressed against Tyler's chest. I summon all the strength I have left in me to lift my head off Tyler's arm and rest it against his shoulder and chest.

"Violet?" Tyler asks, hope instantly rushing through him and colouring his tone of voice. I manage to open my eyes and the relief that washes over him and Michael would have been comical usually, but right now I just want to lie down.

Michael rushes ahead to go and find someone as I can't even speak to refuse or protest.

"I was so worried about you, you really gave me a fright but this is exactly why I need to be with you." Tyler's voice comforts me and I quietly listen to his little rants and concerns feeling reassured by being in his arms. I don't know how I'm going to cope with the rest of the day though when I'm in such a state. A few people come rushing over to us and so when we are inside Tyler gently lays me down, but he holds onto my hand to make sure I'm all right. After I have been checked multiple times I am just advised to not do much for the rest of the day, I've recovered quite a lot but because of how long it has taken me to reach this stage it's recommended that someone is to be with me at all times.

Tyler and Michael escort me back to the chalet and Tyler is allowed to be with me much to both our relief. Michael goes back to our group leaving us alone and we rest on the bed for an hour which helps gain some strength back. Tyler forces me to eat something and then we head outside for some air, I still can't get over how he managed to carry me with such ease earlier though.

There's a bench that overlooks the most beautiful and spectacular scenery which Tyler selects for us to sit at, "Are you all right?" he asks me, his handsome face frowning with worry.

"Yes I'm fine now, but it was quite scary." I admit and Tyler shudders slightly in agreement, I know I scared the life out of him earlier.

"Maybe Michael won't separate us now," Tyler voices his thoughts and both of our hopes. However I have my doubts, on the plus side I know Michael will let us see each other more frequently after this surprising episode.

When I've convinced Tyler enough times that I'm going to be OK he takes my hand in his and we walk down a cobbled path together. It's amazing the contrast between the views here and where the activities are placed, each activity has been spaced far apart from each other on wide plain open green fields. Whereas now me and Tyler are walking through some of the most vibrant and pretty plants and flowers I've ever seen, on either side of the path are small woodlands with butterflies surrounding us. Everything is eye catching and fascinating in its own way, I feel captivated by all the natural beauty around us.

"It's like walking on one of those trails isn't it, where you follow the coloured post?" Tyler asks reminiscently, he looks completely at peace with the environment and his confidence makes me wonder if he does this often.

"I love walking on those trails, they usually are in woods as well." I reply, it pleases me that Tyler also has a keen interest for nature, it's just one of the many things we have in common.

I don't expect it when Tyler halts suddenly in the middle of the path, our hands still linked. He smiles, his blue eyes shining as he surprises me with a kiss but when I get over the shock I gladly invite it. My heart always beats doubly fast when I think about how me and Tyler are a proper couple now, especially as I'll be moving in with him. No matter how much I like and respect Michael that little detail will be kept secret if at all possible. We pull apart satisfied, maybe this trip won't be so bad after all as everything is looking positive now and I still have my birthday to enjoy.

We walk past streams and wide varieties of other wildlife features before Tyler turns to me, something seems to be on his mind.

"I was just wondering that at some point during the holidays, if you would like to meet my mother?" he asks me, his voice curious and holding hope. Tyler's never mentioned his mother before, but it will be intriguing to see her and I guess I will meet her some point in the future anyway.

"Sure, that would be nice." I reply glad that he feels comfortable to introduce me to his family and that he wants me to be part of it.

"It's just that I've told her a lot about you and she really wants to meet you," Tyler admits embarrassed but I smile as it's nice to know he likes to tell others about me.

We has walked quite far when we realize that it's already lunchtime, "Do you fancy a picnic?" Tyler asks, his sea blue eyes gleam with satisfaction when I nod. Luckily there is a food shop nearby selling many goods at rather extraordinary prices. We buy sandwiches, snacks, strawberries and grapes and Tyler adds a rather fine bottle of champagne which I've only tried a few times before.

He leads me out to the edge of one of the grass fields, we can't see any of the activities from here but it means that we can enjoy ourselves alone. The grass is dry so we have no problem sitting down and spreading the food out between us, "Have you ever been in a relationship before?" Tyler's sudden question surprises me.

"No, I've never loved anyone like this before. Obviously I've fancied people but I've gone off them in that way because it was never real," I answer truthfully and he seems appeased with my answer so I ask him the same question back.

"I had a girlfriend once, but to be honest we only went out because everyone else had a partner. So I only did it to fit in because before you I've never had a real and serious relationship, I never even kissed her because I didn't love her like I love you." Relief washes through me that we share our love only with each other as the first and for forever, I think it would have hurt a lot if he'd ever been this close to someone else.

"Shall we?" he gestures towards our picnic, we both look relaxed to know that we've only ever belonged to the other.

Once we've finished our sandwiches an idea forms in my mind as I pick one of the grapes from the vine that limply holds them, I gently toss the grape at him in an attempt to keep the mood playful. Naturally I was expecting to take him by surprise but instead he neatly catches it in his teeth and then gulps it down leaving me in astonishment.

"Thanks for that Violet, I didn't even need to pick it up myself." Tyler comments sarcastically, however he grins and we both grab handfuls of the grapes ready to bombard the other with. At first we play fair; he threw one and then I did. However as he catches them every time and I don't I decide to cheat by throwing three at once, which only results in him somehow catching all three. This quickly leads to lobbing them at one another until there are none left, I am laughing so hard that when my phone rings and it turns out to be Michael I can't even answer.

"I just called to check on you both, but clearly you're doing fine." Michael remarks but by his tone of voice I know he isn't being mean.

"Honestly Violet, so immature." Tyler tuts at me in a ridiculously posh voice which only makes me worse.

"You're both immature, so don't enjoy yourselves too much and we'll be meeting up later." Michael laughs and then hangs up, there's no chance he's convinced that we won't get up to no good.

"Well I have no idea what he was talking about, I am very sophisticated and mature." Tyler continues in the posh voice and I scoff at him, him being mature is the stupidest suggestion I've ever heard. We both chuckle to ourselves though as Michael is definitely going to want proof that we haven't been doing anything too stupid.

Tyler pours the champagne out into two very fine, elegant looking glasses, if anyone had been watching they would have thought that we were rich. It has to be the most romantic gesture I have ever done or seen, we help ourselves to the strawberries and take small sips of the champagne.

"Well I think this is an appropriate moment, don't you?" Tyler asks before leaning towards me and we kiss yet again, surely we're going to break some kind of record this week. I let myself get lost in the moment with him, the only thought on my mind is about how much I love him and the passion we share.

Chapter Seventeen

The second we hear voices heading our way I instinctively pull away from him, in a desperate attempt to hide what we'd been doing. Tyler doesn't seem at all bothered, he is perfectly relaxed whenever somebody walks past us.

"What's the matter?" he voices openly unfazed and I shake my head in disbelief at his lack of concern.

"Are you not at all bothered that another teacher or student could possibly walk past?" I question him, trying to see if he actually cares or has thought that far ahead. Tyler shrugs, smiling and shaking his head doubting that that would happen.

"I don't think you need to worry," he reassures me but if anything that makes me more worried as when has Tyler ever got away with anything before?

He lies on his back, his blue eyes gazing up at me and his face utterly untroubled with his perfect smile. I give in and lie on my side next to him, I rest my head on his chest and drape my arm over him so I'm gently holding him around the waist. He closes his eyes peaceful as he has his arm around me, we can only have embraced each other like this for a short while before my fears prove correct and we both spot Michael a small distance away. "No need to worry, huh." I comment sarcastically as we jump up in a hurry and quickly pack everything up, and bin the unneeded packaging. Tyler hides the champagne behind him and we subtly try to sneak past.

"Ah, there you are." Great, Michael has seen us instantly, so much for subtly.

"This is the only food shop nearby, so I left my group behind to get something." He smiles at us however it doesn't take him long to realize Tyler's hiding something behind him. Knowing there's no point in pretending Tyler sighs and shows Michael the champagne bottle, bracing himself for the worst reaction seeing as you shouldn't technically be allowed to drink at work.

To our amazement though he laughs, "Well don't drink the whole thing today, we'll meet up at five o'clock so I guess I'll see you then." Michael walks off, not at all bothered about what we have been doing with our time.

I smirk at Tyler now that Michael has gone, he had looked so shame faced when he'd shown Michael the bottle that his face had been a picture which was priceless.

"Shut up," Tyler grins noticing my obvious amusement.

"I didn't say anything," I comment but I giggle and he gently shoves me playfully with his arm.

"So what do you want to do with the rest of our time?" he says to me as we link arms.

"Do you think we'd be able to do an activity by ourselves?" I ask him, it hadn't been particularly fun with Michael but I was more than happy to give it a go with Tyler.

"You've already done the Archery haven't you?" he responds.

"Yeah," I'm not sure if I really want to go back.

"Would you mind doing it again if I taught you?" Tyler suggests eagerly, I don't want to disappoint him so I agree but I have my doubts about Archery. When we get there none of the groups are using the range so the instructor sets up for us and then stands a small distance away.

Tyler skilfully positions himself, his eye focuses on the target and then lets the arrow loose. It flies perfectly straight and then hits the centre target. Tyler flashes his teeth at me, "I've done this before." He confirms what I had obviously been thinking, I swear I've never met someone so gifted at so many things.

"What haven't you already done?" I ask as he really does seem talented at everything he does.

He smiles, "It's because I've attended every club I see on advertisement, when I was in school I hated the lessons so I wanted to find some good points about attending." Well he has a good point, I had been the complete opposite though at school and had never joined in anything.

Tyler helps me position myself and hold my arm correctly, he does his best to show me how to aim and see the target in the right way and then he assists me with letting the arrow loose. It hits the target, just underneath the arrow he's already let fly.

I smile and then high-five Tyler, "You know there's being good at something and there's being amazing." Tyler smiles at the compliment, but as always he doesn't boast which is one of the many qualities I like about him. This time I attempt to do it by myself, Tyler's teaching techniques clearly work as I only miss the target by an inch. Once we've practised and competed together for awhile we both get surprised by the time, we only have a couple of hours until we'll be meeting up with Michael later.

"Do you want to head back?" I ask him and he wraps his arm around my waist and after thanking the instructor we return to our chalet.

We still have an hour to kill before meeting up with Michael and there's nothing to do in this area, we don't bother shutting the door of our chalet so we can get some air in the room.

"Well I suppose we could always play a game," Tyler suggests to me his lips fighting with the effort to hide his devious smile. I raise an eyebrow at him, I can see where this is going and I know I'll regret it.

"Depends on what type of game," I answer him carefully knowing I should be very worried.

"Well we could play truth or dare," Tyler's eyes glint deep with humour as I silently shudder at the thought and try to keep the absolute horror of his suggestion from showing on my face.

"That game tends to work better with more people," I try to worm my way out of it without seeming like a spoil sport or scaredy-cat.

He is not deterred by my evasion "Fine then, we'll play that later." Tyler promises holding me to that one and foiling the only hope I'd had. "If you won't play truth or dare with just me, then would you do prank calls?" He 's enjoying this, it's like he knows the best forms of torture as this is only getting worse.

"Depends on who it is," I claim, trying to veil my panic and disguise it as interest instead, inside though I silently curse.

Tyler smirks at me but he is pleased that I am planning on participating, "OK we will between us have to prank call Michael and some other people." Aww crap, I should I have known better than to even agree to any of this. Tyler's lips twitch at my reaction and then he withholds his number before tapping in Michael's into his phone, it doesn't take long before the ringing stops and Michael answers. I cover my mouth with my hands to prevent myself from laughing as I don't want to give him away.

"Hello, this is James coach driver from coach 264." Tyler puts on the accent the coach driver had had, and I can't believe that he's actually pretending to be someone we know.

"I am calling to discuss the fact that it isn't possible for you to be driven back on Saturday," Tyler continues and I stare and gape at him in shock, we're going to be in unbelievable trouble when Michael finds out. I don't even want to imagine the consequences for this... There's a lot of talking from the other end of the phone before Tyler manages to speak again. "There's no need to involve your members of staff," Tyler practically chokes the words out from trying to stop having a laughing fit. I on the other hand can't hold it in any more as the situation has gone beyond hilarious, I rush outside so I won't make Tyler laugh however my giggle cuts short. Michael's heading over and when he sees me he appears to be getting more aggressive in the conversation. I hurry back inside and desperately try to warn Tyler to hang up, however he doesn't understand my sign language so I point to Michael through the window who thankfully isn't looking in our direction.

"Shit!" Tyler curses forgetting the accent and the fact entirely that he 's still on the phone before he hangs up. Michael stands outside fuming for a moment before heading over, despite the fact that the situation we've gotten ourselves into is appalling we both erupt into uncontrollable laughter. My sides hurt by the time Michael knocks on the door which I'd closed on my hurried entrance back in, I push Tyler forward to be the one to open the door and after a quick squabble with me he finally relents and opens the door, to an unimpressed Michael who appears to have entirely lost it this time.

"What have you two been up to?" he asks in an irritated tone of voice and the frustration is so evident on his face that I bite my tongue hard to distract me from laughing.

"Nothing much, we just thought we'd be here early." Tyler tries to cover up for us but it's a pretty lame attempt, we already know we're damned and done for.

"Well I've just had a rather unpleasant phone call," he continues not convinced by Tyler's cover up at all but he is too furious to care. I gently elbow Tyler so that he will say something which doesn't go unnoticed by Michael.

"Well that's a shame, who was it you were talking to?" Tyler puts on a picture of perfect innocence and I can't believe the amount of nerve he has to do that, I have to look away as I can't bear it and I know I'll explode into a fit of giggles if I so much as glance at Tyler.

"That bloody bus driver causing a whole load of trouble, and if I ever have to hear his accent again..." Michael trails off full of rage, this time neither of us can contain it any longer. I feel it tremble through me and shake my shoulders until both of us are crying with hysterical laughter.

"I don't see what's so funny, if you knew what he said you wouldn't be laughing yourself silly!" Michael snaps at the pair of us, I crack up harder and Tyler practically roars with laughter, clutching his sides.

"He said not to involve your members of staff," Tyler gulps out trying to breathe in between each chuckle.

"And that we couldn't be driven back on Saturday," I continue and because we're officially busted now we high-five and carry on laughing at him.

I see the realization dawn on his face as he understands what we have done, "Right who's bright idea was this practical joke?" he thunders at us, not finding it at all amusing. I point at Tyler who doesn't deny it, proud of the fact that he had thought of it.

"Well why am I not surprised?" Michael states sarcastically and Tyler simply shrugs nonchalantly which only escalates the problem.

"Don't shrug at me, I thought that was a serious situation I was going to have to deal with!" Michael shouts losing the plot, I don't think he could have been more pissed off if he'd tried.

"What's going on?" Izzie asks from behind us, we'd been so absorbed in the problem we'd not even seen her approach.

"These two thought it would be funny if they prank called me," Michael reluctantly explains still fuming.

Despite herself even Izzie looks amused, "What did you say?" she quizzes us getting intrigued which only pushes Michael even further over the edge.

"Tyler pretended to be the coach driver and that the bus on Saturday was cancelled," I giggle and Izzie cracks up giving us both high-fives.

Michael is seriously displeased and disgusted by the lot of us, "Well it's nice to know that you all find it so funny and don't realize the severity of the situation." He retorts before striding off, sick of the sight of us although we're supposed to be meeting up now anyway.

Now that Michael's gone though it only leaves us and Izzie, I turn to her hoping that everything's going to be all right.

"I'm sorry about earlier, I was just so upset about Michael and obviously you didn't like me talking to Tyler like that". She looks as hopeful and desperate as I feel, I smile and then she gives me a quick hug to show she means it.

"I really hope that you sort something out with Michael," I tell her truthfully as both of them deserve that.

We walk together to catch up with Michael as there's no point hanging around here, "What do you think we'll be doing?" I ask as I don't fancy going to a disastrous activity completely unprepared. However it immediately becomes clear that neither of them have given this a thought before and so we all mentally prepare for whatever form of hell this activity might consist of. Much to all of our relief though it turns out that we don't have to take part, it's impossible to describe the immense feeling of peace I feel that we don't have to do it. I do notice that a large portion of the class however are scowling and don't enjoy the idea of the team based activity.

I have to admit that somewhere at the back of my mind I do feel guilty that we are leaving Jacqueline and Michael to do all the work, but it's been so long since I have got to talk to Izzie that we spend our time having a catch up.

"When do you think you're going to try to have a proper talk with Michael?" I ask her as obviously she can't now but maybe later on today.

"I don't know, but I'm going to wait for the right moment because it might be awkward or inappropriate otherwise." Izzie informs me and I have to agree, sometimes you can say everything you want to but if the timings not right then it's not worth saying.

I can see that Izzie really does care about Michael, it's just a shame that he can't see that as otherwise everything might be different.

"Do you want me to talk to Michael for you, just so that there's more chance he'll listen?" I offer as the hardest part of making amends with someone is talking to them for the first time after falling out with them.

As I expect though she declines, "I should probably do it myself because he might not take me seriously otherwise." She has a valid point but I hope she talks to him soon as I don't know how much either of them can take.

We sit down on one of the long wooden benches leant up against the wall and watch Izzie's class suffer. Although we're glad it isn't us Tyler's trying to control and contain his boredom and fails immediately, he fidgets every two seconds which only heightens my awareness of my own boredom that seems to hang in my head like a dark rain cloud. I sigh willing time to move faster so that we can have dinner and go back to our chalet.

The second Michael dismisses the class he signals to me, Tyler and Izzie that we are to stay behind whilst Jacqueline leaves.
"I would appreciate an explanation for why you three were under the impression that you could leave everything to me and Jacqueline," Michael prompts us displeased. Uh-oh.
"You seemed to have everything in order and didn't ask for help so we simply supervised." Tyler responds, but even he is weary this time that we've overdone Michael's patience in the space of a couple of hours. When Michael sighs it occurs to me again how much older he seems than all of us when in truth there's only a few years difference.

Izzie can only be two years older than me, Tyler's three years older and I don't know how old Michael actually is but I'm guessing that he's twenty seven. That would make him and Izzie have the same age gap I have with Tyler. Michael catches me having one of my deep thinking moments; it quickly becomes apparent that I'm not really focusing on the situation actually occurring.
"Just don't let it happen again," Michael doesn't press the matter any further; probably knowing it's not worth the hassle. "Come on, lets go to dinner." Michael gestures for us to go ahead but I match my pace to his.

"I'm sorry about earlier," I apologise feeling it to be necessary as we really had wound him up before.
However his lips twitch upwards, "Don't worry about it Violet, I guess I shouldn't have been surprised something like that would happen at some point." Well that's true, I can't deny that me and Tyler are always in trouble. So for now everything feels peaceful, getting on with Michael and Izzie, Jacqueline and obviously Tyler. It better not be the calm before the storm as at the moment the jig-saw puzzle fits into place perfectly.

Chapter Eighteen

Dinner has been a quiet event, however it's not been an uncomfortable silence. I don't want to jinx it but it seems that everything can only be better from now on. The next few days pass the same; everyone trying to maintain some form of peace between each other. I have to admit I am concerned as Izzie still hasn't attempted talking to Michael yet, despite how much they need to discuss.

I won't let anything drag me down today though, not on a special occasion like this that I get to share with my friends. So of course, today is finally my birthday. I get myself ready for the day with anticipation whilst Tyler has a shower, however I hear him select a few curse words of specific choice as the power of the water keeps going off.
"I'm just going to see Izzie, I'll be back soon!" I call out to him so that he will hear me.
"Yeah, OK." He replies, not sounding thrilled with his current situation as I vacate the scene.
    It doesn't take long to get to her chalet and as Jacqueline doesn't seem to be around I am able to speak to her alone.
 "Izzie you really need to talk to Michael," I remind her pointedly as I know she's trying to delay it.
"I know, I will." She says to me but she doesn't sound very convincing at all.
"Preferably before the end of the trip, also you're both my friends so I don't want things to be awkward today." I prompt gently and she grimaces apologetically as she knows I've seen through her delaying tactics.
"It's hard because I do want to talk to him, but at the same time I really don't." Izzie finally admits and I sigh but with understanding, she fears his rejection which could hurt in so many ways.
"The longer you leave it though the harder it'll be," I warn her before I turn to leave.

"Where's Tyler?" Izzie asks me, only just clocking the fact that normally we're inseparable and he's not here.
"Having a fight with the shower and losing," I laugh.
"Oh ours is rubbish as well," Izzie agrees but she also laughs when I mention Tyler's stupidity and choice of words.

"OK, I'll talk to Michael at some point today." Izzie promises, on a more serious note now before I leave to go back and see how Tyler's coping.

Well he's dressed, however his hair is so soaked that it's dripping water all over his clothes leaving millions of diamond droplets scattered over him, making him look like a mess but to be honest I still find it really attractive. I desperately try to hide my amusement as I seize a towel off the metal rack and begin rubbing it through his hair. He seems too annoyed to even speak so I comb and dry his hair whilst he tries to dry his clothes. I like having the excuse to gently run my fingers through his soft, almost silky hair as I help him, I've always loved playing with the hair at the back of his neck when I kiss him or holding his face close to me. I bite my lip when I see the sheer volume of water soaking the floor in a huge puddle, clearly the shower has gone from having no power to too much.

As I leave the door half open Michael comes in to see if we're ready for breakfast, the first thing he does is observe the chaotic state of our room. I give a small shake of my head so that Michael won't say anything, he looks at Tyler's probably grumpy expression and then quickly catches on.
"Will you be ready to go down to breakfast in five minutes?" he asks us, his eyes bright as he enthusiastically anticipates the new day.
"Yeah probably," I answer and my smile can no longer be hidden and so Michael exits to prevent me from laughing and irritating Tyler further.

When I fix Tyler's tie for him I sense his blue eyes watching my face, his pale warm hand gently brushes across my cheek leaving a tingling feeling as his lips follow after. Then, breaking me out of the spell of being locked in place by his eyes he takes my hand in his before we go to meet everyone else. The class eat in a separate section to the staff so as we pick our choice from the options of food and drink available we don't bother worrying about the fact that we are holding hands.

However we both make the vital mistake of forgetting that Jacqueline doesn't know about us, I only realize when we have already walked all the way over to them and sat down what we've stupidly done. I feel an immediate rush of embarrassment which doubles when Izzie smirks and elbows me under the table, Michael however notices and so quickly tries to steer the conversation onto the fact that it's my birthday to lighten the mood.

I still have to be with Michael throughout the day but I've been allowed to call Tyler, also we're able to take breaks and see one another which makes the day worthwhile. It turns out that our group is doing rock climbing today, there's literally no way in hell that I'm going to take part. Ever since the Archery I have made myself participate to appease Michael, this would be a step too far over the line though and as it's my birthday maybe that'll work to my advantage. Protesting turns out to be unnecessary though as Michael also declines on the offer to take part, much to my relief.

Tyler's doing zip wire today and so is excited about doing his activity, I can understand why though as it's kind of thrilling and me and Michael have done it twice. However as a great coincidence the climbing wall and the zip wire belong to the same tower, just on opposite sides of it. Me and Tyler share a grin when we realize we will be able to stay together, I really must have luck on my side for today. Michael's eyes trail after Izzie as she leads her group away in a different direction, oh well he shouldn't have to wait too much longer and then she'll talk to him.

Tyler volunteers to demonstrate for his group how zip wire is supposed to be done, when really anyone can do it.
"Let him show off, he's used to doing zip wire professionally quite a lot." Michael tells me, reading my face with ease again. That is actually quite impressive though, I wonder where he learnt to do that? To prove his point though Tyler does look like a natural and skilled when he speeds across the length of the wire, and jumps expertly down with no assistance needed. His group all look stunned and when he comes back over we all gave him a mini round of applause, he looks unbearably handsome anyway but that just turns me on.

"Showing off?" I tease him but he has a right to when he can do it like that.
"Just a bit, but I've done it many times before." Tyler confirms what Michael has already informed me on earlier, simply being with him when he gets so enthusiastic is cute and makes my heart pound.
"Well your group is never going to live up to that level of expertise," I laugh and we watch my group attempt the perilous rock climbing.
"Are you not going to join in?" he asks me, his eyes still shining from the thrill of his own activity and they warm my heart as they gaze at me.
"Not rock climbing, I hate it," I tell him truthfully.

"I have to agree, it isn't exactly my idea of fun." So that leads to a discussion of what activities we like and dislike, unsurprisingly Tyler seems to be talented at nearly everything however we do share one that I match him for. We both have our eyes sparkling at the challenge of competing at ice skating; I don't know if we actually will do this but I'd love to go with him.

"Well when the school trip is over we should book an ice rink and have a go together," Tyler suggests pleased that we can enjoy an activity of our choice together.

"I've done ice skating ever since I was little," I tell him looking forward to it as I haven't gone recently as I haven't been able to afford it. However now that I have this job and will be selling my flat so that I can live with Tyler we can do whatever takes our fancy.

"Yeah, I haven't done it recently either which is a shame." Tyler agrees, also excited by the idea of going together.

"It will be really exciting when I live with you, won't it?" I ask and an instant smile softens the features of his face as a confirmation.

"When we live together we can always be together, home and at work." Tyler says and we both like the sound of that.

"Yeah, when this trip is over we can't be separated. It will always be me and you, maybe you can write a song about that." I suggest and he smiles.

"That's not a bad idea actually," Tyler considers quietly.

"I can always play you our other song as well," he reminds me and I already want to welcome my life to the dramatic change Tyler will bring. I'll be able to live my life more to the full when I'm properly with Tyler, for once I'll be able to see the glass as half full instead of half empty.

I have a special connection with Tyler, our love goes extremely deep and as I have thought before on many occasions our silent communication and shared desire makes us soul mates. It's hard to say whether I believe in fate or not, but me and Tyler must have been made for each other. It's like I was destined to get that job at Bank croft primary school, to become Tyler's assistant and find a purpose and point in life, something to live for.

This summer is definitely going to be the best one yet, also I have the shopping trip with Izzie and Jacqueline to look forward to. I'm nervous about meeting Tyler's mother, but at the same time I'm curious and anticipating it.

We chat all the way until lunchtime, but then Michael and Jacqueline join us to eat and we swiftly change topic.

"Aren't you going to have a go at the zip wire?" Tyler queries of Jacqueline as their group has almost finished meaning they'll be moving on soon.

"Well I want to, but it's awfully high up." She responds as she glances up at the tower which I have to admit does look like it's looming over us, so if you're already nervous it's no surprise that it almost looks threatening.

"Once you've gotten over that though it's really fun," I let her know, hoping to convince her that if I can do it then she definitely can as she'll be missing out otherwise.

"Maybe you could go up the tower and see how it feels," Tyler encourages, eager to make Jacqueline join in and share his favourite activity with him.

" I can always go with you," he continues gently. In some ways it's probably good that I'm not with Tyler for every activity. Michael knows not to push it if I insist on not doing something, but Tyler's enthusiasm is hard to fight and not influence you.

I talk to Michael whilst Tyler tries to win Jacqueline over, and let's face it I get the sense that he'll probably succeed sooner or later.

"So have you got any plans for the holidays?" I ask Michael, curious to know whether he's the travelling time or prefers to stay at home with family.

"I'll be going to Cornwall for a week to see my family, but other than that I'm not doing anything in particular." He replies and seems glad that I want to make the effort and get to know him better, like me it doesn't take a lot to make Michael happy. All I need in a day is for Tyler to smile or talk to me even for the briefest amount of time and that makes my day, just seeing him happy is calming and almost therapeutic so the more I see him even if it's from a distance the better everything seems.

"So did you used to live there?" I ask him intrigued as Cornwall is one of the many places I've never visited but always wanted to.

"Yes, my family moved there when I was seven, but as an adult I decided the lifestyle would suit me better here." He tells me, he talks about it like it had to be some of the best days of his life.

"So what about you, have you got anything planned for the summer?" he asks, also interested in what I'll be getting up to.

"Nothing much, but I'll be meeting up with Izzie and Jacqueline for a shopping trip and I'll be seeing Tyler as well." I might as well admit the truth seeing as there's no point hiding what he can already guess.

Michael smiles at my plans though instead of showing any disapproval, "You know Violet, you've settled in here really well." He compliments me and I suppose he's right; it's weird to think that I've only worked at the school for such a short time though as it feels like ages.

"That's probably because I was welcomed really nicely," I answer simply as although there's been a few blips along the way, it has been great getting involved with the school so much already. I can tell he's thinking back to the day that I arrived.

"This school has really benefited from having you Violet, nothing was organised or functioned correctly but more importantly you're a great friend, no matter what life throws at you you fight through it walking out stronger than before." He smiles, speech over and walks off back to the activity whilst I think over all his comments in depth.

It's true I guess, I don't let anything like my anxiety and depression beat me, I've been knocked down many times but I'll never be broken and I have a strong will despite the weakness I suffer even at the best of times. Being isolated and alone never solves anything, confronting problems when you feel ready is the only way forward and confiding in somebody you love. Naturally this isn't always possible, but when you can confide in someone you have to make the most of the rare moment and seize opportunities until it becomes a natural occurrence. Until then my only friend has been the lyrics of songs that you can relate to every word of, I feel distant from everyone else. Other people will say they feel like they're on a different page of the book to everyone else whereas I feel like I'm in a completely different book altogether. You can never truly let those feelings go, but you can move forward, it never does any good to live in the past which until I met Tyler I've constantly been doing. It never brings any good to dwell on all the what ifs, but sometimes the past isn't finished with us even if we want to be finished with it.

Tyler and Jacqueline's conversation ends when they see Michael walk off leaving me alone, "After I've got Jacqueline to do the zip wire I'll be right back, I promise." Tyler tells me and I smile, it's been a long time since I truly believed somebody to keep their promises for me, but my trust in him goes miles.

"OK, good luck Jacqueline." I try again to convince her it will be fun before they head off to go up the tower. I envy Jacqueline at being able to spend the day with Tyler, however she doesn't feel the same way about him that I do much to my relief. So nobody really gets a bonus of who they are paired up with, but at least it's brought us all closer together.

I seat myself down on the grass which gently sways due to the gentle mild breeze, I've chosen a spot where I will get a decent view of Jacqueline when she gets past her nerves to do the zip wire. They have both just reached the top and I can see their faces looking very small and far away from this distance. I wave up at them, knowing that I must look like an ant to them down here. Tyler's encouragement must have paid off as then Jacqueline does it, she goes speeding down the zip wire screaming with joy and the shocking thrill of it the whole way. Tyler follows after, doing it for the second time before they come back over to join me.

Both of them are smiling, Jacqueline can't get over the adrenaline shock and how amazing it had felt.

"We told you it was worth it," I tease her but I'm glad she's done it and enjoyed it as she might have spent the rest of the day regretting it otherwise.

"I can't believe I actually did it," She grins feeling proud that she has achieved her goal of trying it out.

However as everyone has done it now, that means their group will be moving on to a new activity. Whereas mine and Michael's group are nowhere near finished yet. Jacqueline heads off to tell Michael that they will be moving on meaning leaving me alone with Tyler for a few moments.

"Take care of yourself Violet," he whispers to me making my heart ache when we aren't even separated yet.

"I will, I guess I'll see you later." I sigh whilst taking his hand in mine.

"I love you," I tell him whilst I have him here with me alone.

"I love you too," He instantly replies and we share one of those moments, but then Jacqueline and Michael head over making us pull apart.

"OK, well you'll be off now. So have fun and we'll meet up later," Michael basically gives the order for them to leave in a subtle way as we need to go back and tend to our own group. I wave Tyler off and then me and Michael go back to see how the rock climbing is going. It turns out that some of the pupils are stuck at the top and the instructors are trying to advise them down and failing.

"If you put your foot on the red rock and then the yellow one you can start to make your way down," I call out to one of them and begin guiding them down until they reach the bottom safely.

"Thanks Miss!" they shout in relief before rejoining their friends.

"Well done Violet, that was quite impressive." Michael compliments me, then when the last pupil makes their way down we head off to the next activity.

We have two options, we can either go cycling with our group or be left behind on a picnic bench for an hour and a half waiting for them to come back. I know which option I would have preferred, however I'd promised Michael that I would make an effort and of all the activities cycling definitely isn't the hardest or most horrendous. Luckily for us we are going to be at the back and the instructors will obviously be leading, so we can go as slow as need be without anyone criticising.

However it turns out to be nowhere near as bad as I'd originally thought, the route we take is very picturesque and as there are so many of us we travel at a comfortable speed, meaning not too much effort is required. Me and Michael stay side by side most of the time, only the occasional hill or bump in the path force us to go single file. As we ride all you can hear is the quiet crunching of the gravel on the path and the sound of birdsong filling the air. We don't need to switch gears regularly so there aren't many hold ups of someone failing to switch on time, I like being able to see all the trees rushing by like when you're in a car and everything seems as if it's on fast forward.

We have been going for nearly an hour when a break is allowed, I glance at my watch and realise that as soon as this ride is over we will have to head off to the meeting immediately as that is how fast time has gone by. Yet I often wonder how Izzie and Tyler are doing, I want to know when she's finally going to get the courage today to discuss everything with Michael that really needs to be said. However I can't tell Michael in warning that Izzie is going to speak to him later as I don't want to accidentally ruin it for her.

"Enjoying the ride?" Michael asks, giving me a distraction from my thoughts.

"I am actually, it's not as bad as I first thought." I confess before continuing with, "I just can't talk when I ride as it's harder to breathe." I apologise as I would have had a conversation otherwise.

He smiles, "It's OK I know, before the trip I had to check everyone's medical background." He informs me, I guess I shouldn't be surprised.

"Well I probably have a weirder medical history than most," I comment as to an outsider the amount of problems I have must appear rather bizarre. "Not necessarily true, but it certainly is interesting." Michael says possibly trying to reassure me instead of simply saying it's abnormal. However he doesn't give the impression of just being polite, so I wonder who else has a strange medical background.

We finish the bike ride quickly so that we will get back to the meeting on time, Michael leaves our group in the instructors' care so that we can go and catch up with everyone else. Tyler and Jacqueline are already there and Izzie's just arriving like us.

"Sorry about that, it's been a bit of a rush to get here." Michael reluctantly admits, slightly out of breath still. It doesn't take long to discuss our plans, so when we're all dismissed until later me, Tyler and Jacqueline walk away. That is when I notice Izzie staying behind as she finally gets her chance to talk to Michael alone.

I give her a thumbs up behind Michael's back to wish her luck, and then we leave to give them the chance to talk in private. Tyler also looks glad that they finally have an opportunity to sort everything out.

Chapter Nineteen

"Maybe everything will have a turn for the better after she's talked to him," Tyler comments to me positively and I have to agree that that's what I'm hoping for as well.

"Well it should, I know he's wanted to talk to Izzie for ages." I tell Tyler as I've been with Michael obviously a lot more than he has recently. We both sink into deeper thoughts about how we think their chat is really going to go. I do feel more optimistic about it going well this time though as they're both desperate and want to be able to at least talk to each other again. Still, I am hoping it will progress further than that stage but I'm not going to hold my hopes too high as I don't want to be sorely disappointed.

I can see why Michael is holding back, but I really wish he would listen to his heart over his head this time as him and Izzie would make a perfect couple. It always reminds me of how lucky I am that Tyler isn't like Michael relationship wise, I need Tyler to make me know I'm loved and that he'll protect me whereas I don't think I could cope with some of Michael's behaviour and he has a unique version of his own strong will compared to Tyler's. I have the best luck in the world having someone like Tyler, he'll do anything for me and I would for him as well.

We get back to our chalet exhausted, I collapse down on the bed and rest my aching legs. Tyler lies beside me, lighting the passion and uncontrollable urge I feel whenever I cannot resist him. He quickly catches on to my mood and it doesn't take him long to join in. I rest on his chest while we kiss, I have one hand on his waist and the other gently caressing his face. He also embraces me with his hands on my waist, pinning me onto him and our breathing becomes unsteady as my lips meet his and he whispers "Happy birthday Violet," in an alluring voice before continuing.

Neither one of us is bothering to keep an eye on the time, his lips press roughly against mine causing a passionate surge of heat to pass between us whilst I slowly manage to unbutton his shirt. I press my hands against the smooth muscles of his chest and arms as I hold him to me tightly. I love the feel of his cheek brushing against mine causing me to blush despite the fact there should be no reason to be embarrassed about it. As we kiss his mouth curves upwards as he realises my slight school girl moment about finding the feel of our skin brushing and causing my whole body to tingle with pleasure embarrassing.

"I'm not embarrassing you am I?" he whispers in my ear and his warm breath tickles which makes me blush even more, his gorgeous blue eyes are sparkling and shining with delight as he teases me. I look away from his gaze and rest my head against his shoulder to avoid seeing his taunting eyes.

"You're so cute," Tyler chuckles at me, enjoying the fact that this level of intimacy is causing me to blush even though I want it, however this is just as new to him as it is to me so I have no idea where his natural confidence has sprung from.

"But you were right, I should write another song for us at some point." He says to me in such an attractive and alluring voice that I have no idea how I'm going to keep up with him. He's making my heart flutter with no effort required.

"How am I meant to express my love for you though?" I ask him, slightly breathless before kissing him again and drawing in the moment by closing my eyes. He smiles at me and catches his breath for a moment, "Don't worry, this is just fine." Then he pulls me closer to him, his arm on my back as we keep kissing until neither of us fee like we can breathe unless we pull apart.

However when we do my eye catches sight of the clock leaning against the wall on the bedside table, we only have a few minutes until we're meant to be present at dinner. Technically though we're already late as we've always been ready five minutes early, so we've never been the last ones in the restaurant before. Tyler rushes to button up his shirt, we slip our shoes on and then hurry to the restaurant silently praying that the others won't already be there. Typically though, they are.

We quickly sit in our usual places and have no intention of explaining the cause for why we're late, I'll just act normal and pretend nothing what so ever happened. Yet I did notice that Izzie and Michael are sitting next to each other now, I know better than to comment on it though so instead I give her the signal to say I want all the details later. She smiles and gives me a quick high-five under the table so that Michael and Jacqueline won't see, Tyler however who's obviously picked up on it as well gently nudges me with his elbow, whilst having a smirk on his face which he's desperately trying to conceal and failing.

Izzie easily returns it though considering how late we are, I blush and look away from the pair of them. Even though Jacqueline isn't in on the secret she's very observant, and it doesn't take her long to pick up on my discomfort and Tyler's rare display of embarrassment. Also I know that it's not gone unnoticed by her how often we call one another out on activities, we sit next to each other and are in general much closer than we probably should look. It makes me wonder with growing concern how long will it take before everyone figures our secret out? Jacqueline has no reason to think much of Izzie and Michael's reunion, as she has no idea about the real meaning behind it.

Whereas I suddenly get the job as Tyler's assistant and then we're sneaking off and getting into all kinds of trouble together. I sip my drink to find something to do to take away the awkwardness of the moment, but I feel Tyler's eyes watching me as he wills me to speak and help him out of the situation.

"Should we look at the menu now?" I suggest to them, feeling self-conscious as they're all staring at me. Michael swiftly dishes the menus out to everyone whilst sharing a look and an uncontrollable smile of amusement with me. Shut up, I silently think towards him, but he can guess what I want to say and so ends up coughing to cover his laughter.

I have to bite my lip to prevent me from bursting into laughter myself at how stupid we all are about trying to keep our relationships secret, when everyone knows anyway. Mine and Izzie's shoulders shake and my sides hurt so much that I end up crying to keep myself from laughing, that does it for Tyler though who has to get up and go around the corner. We all still hear him start chuckling though and so me and Izzie practically explode, she also has to wipe away tears.

Michael pretends he has no idea what we're doing which only makes it worse, Jacqueline however is nobody's fool so Michael's performance of amazing acting skills is wasted as she just shakes her head at the lot of us. "Honestly," she tuts and Izzie is so red that it looks like she can hardly breathe. Tyler comes back and tries to sip his drink like I had earlier, but he ends up taking one look at me and as he hasn't recovered like I'd suspected he ends up spraying it. Me and Izzie are even more hysterical and Michael can't hold it in any longer either. All our laughs boom around the whole restaurant and I can't bear to look at them, the tears stream down my face causing Izzie and Jacqueline to find it harder to restrain themselves and maintain any dignity in public.

The table is covered in a scatter of droplets from Tyler and he himself has his drink splashed down his shirt. The glass itself now holds hardly any drink, much to his annoyance. He scowls at us and although I'm really thirsty I don't dare take a sip of my drink for fear of doing it myself.
"I'm getting another drink," he mutters as he gets up to go get one and escape from us, however me and Izzie can't possibly control our laughter making him give us a fake glare which causes Michael to crack up.
"Maybe you should get a cloth as well," he suggests, gesturing towards the table. Tyler just ignores the lot of us, unimpressed and then he strides off trying to maintain a scrap of dignity which he can't possibly have left after that event, in a bit of a sulk which to be honest I can't help but find adorable.

Once he has gone I try to calm myself down and for me I manage fairly quickly, probably because I'm beginning to feel slightly guilty about our reactions towards his accident even if it had been amusing. Michael places a napkin on top of the spillage on the table until Tyler returns with a cloth, I decide it would be a good idea to actually have a look at my menu before the waitress gets here. There's plenty of choice but it doesn't take me longer than a few minutes to decide what I want; a simple steak and chips. Tyler comes back with a new drink and cloth in his hands, his shirt is a lot drier and less noticeable than before so I know why he had took so long. He must have gone to the toilets and dried it under one of the automatic hand driers. He chances a glance at me and notices that I have seen through his little plan, he smiles and rolls his eyes at me whilst sitting beside me and cautiously setting his glass down, I'm glad it doesn't take him long to recover his sense of humour.

I help him clean the table up and then tell him that I've already chosen my meal and so he opens his menu to take a look, I love to watch him decide what to have for a meal, he gets so serious and his eyes will scan the choices with great scrutiny. However after such a detailed look he decides to have the same as me. The waitress comes over and takes all our orders, it always feels weird to realise how despite all of our stupidity just how grown up and in some cases mature we all are. I don't feel any different to when I was in school, the only difference is the number of your age because other than that I don't feel like or probably seem like an adult at all.

I quietly observe Tyler, although he can seem just as stupid as me sometimes there is a very experienced and mature side of him even if he does do his best to keep it hidden. I always feel secure in his presence, not just because he's protective but without realising it he is very dominant. Tyler's confident and I like the way he takes the lead in certain circumstances, I know that he never notices that he's dominant as I know that he's also a soft and sensitive guy who's quiet and always listens but I've always preferred to let him be in control and make the decisions. I like a man with quiet confidence who can take charge in an relationship as it makes me feel safe and valued that they're always looking out for you, to protect you and show their love without even realising it. Tyler is a soft, calm individual, he really makes you feel listened to and as if you're opinion is valuable.

He's a rare gentle character who would be described as an old soul, one of the reasons I love him the most is the way he sees beauty in everything and everyone whether or not any one else can see it. He's one of the only real, genuine and open mind and hearted people I've ever met, when he's quiet his eyes are watching with a soft fondness all that's good in the world. Everything about Tyler is beautiful, there's not one thing I want to change.

Izzie is my opposite, she likes to have equal control in an relationship and what she's doing. She thinks it's sweet if anyone is trying to protect her but she feels she doesn't need it, also with Michael she prefers the fact that she has a lot of confidence instead of leaving it up to him. For these reasons it's probably why me and Tyler are such a perfect match; his confidence and social skills with my quiet, listening and observing manner. Tyler attracts me in every way, his handsome looks, alluring personality and genuine heart; which captured my own.

He doesn't have to do anything but whenever I'm with him I feel special and happy inside, he makes my heart flutter and I can never bear to be away from him. Or if I am then he always catches me watching him from a distance, or whenever someone says his name I instantly snap up and pay attention. It's as if I'm extremely aware of his presence and everything he does, I literally cannot get through the day without having him in my head and aching my heart with the love I have for him.

We eat mostly in silence but I enjoy having their company anyway, it's a shame this will be over when the school trip ends. Once we've finished and stayed for a chat we all begin returning to our chalets, everyone has got me small presents for my birthday which has been really nice. Izzie and Jacqueline have gotten me jewellery and Michael has gotten me a picture frame which I don't know what I will use for yet but it looks very pretty and expensive. Tyler has bought me a beautiful dress and said again about the song he'll write for us, I really couldn't have asked for a better birthday.

The last few days pass quickly, in a way I'm glad about that as I will be moving in with Tyler and I can enjoy the rest of the holidays with him. This trip has been really inspirational and enjoyable though; it's brought everyone closer. Michael and Izzie have been talking a lot recently and I think everyone's glad that they've been making amends.

So now it's the last day of the trip, Friday. Me and Tyler have already called each other twice before our activities even started, I think everyone could feel the impatience of wanting the trip to end so we can enjoy our other plans such as ice skating with Tyler. I really want to move in with him, selling my flat will be a shame however I can't cope with the costs any more and it's pointless if me and Tyler want to be together like we do.

Michael doesn't bother with the activities any more either, I can tell he's fed up and just wants to go home like the rest of us.

"Violet, there's something I need to discuss with you and Tyler later." He suddenly says to me and by the look on his face it must be fairly important. "Don't worry, it's nothing bad." He reassures me, however it really gets me thinking about what it is he could possibly want to discuss with us if it isn't that bad. I consider warning Tyler but then I don't see the point as I have no idea what Michael is being serious about, so I'll only stress Tyler out when he might as well get on with his activity in peace.

The day couldn't be going much slower, Michael seems as if he could go to sleep as he has been tired out from the long week. I'm not tired but I just find each second to be infuriatingly long and I can't be bothered with the rest of the day. Izzie has also looked bored earlier on today as well and Jacqueline is the only reason Tyler hasn't given up as she's forcing him to carry on. So everyone is experiencing the after effect of all the previous excitement meaning that nobody is bothering to do anything as they just want to sleep and relax for awhile to make the most of time off work. I glance at my watch and scowl, it's not even lunchtime yet so we still have over half the day left.

"Come on Violet, it's the last day and then we can all look forward to going home." Michael attempts to make me more enthusiastic but as my friend he can tell there's no point, as like a child I'm trying my best not to complain whilst struggling not to from how dull the day is.

We walk sluggishly around the activities and in the end I can't take it any more and so I call Tyler for the third time, just to keep my sanity and lift myself up a bit. He answers before the first ring has even finished.

"You have no idea how long I have been waiting for your call. Jacqueline said that if you rang then I could speak to you but otherwise forget it," Tyler complains and I cannot help but laugh.

"Michael's just as bored as I am," I inform him, goes to show the difference of who we're with. Now that we can talk though I don't care how much credit it costs me, I won't be ending this life saving conversation for awhile.

"Maybe I'll tell Jacqueline that I'm going to the toilet and then sneak off to see you for lunch," Tyler suggests eager and hopeful.

"That's tempting, if you can do it then do." I tell him, finally the first bit of excitement in the day.

"I will, we've only got ten minutes and then I can put my exceptionally divine acting skills into place." Tyler chuckles and the sound of it relights my former sparks. I'm desperate for those minutes to speed up; I don't have anything else to look forward to for the rest of the day so I want to make the most of this.

"Well I won't tell Michael, so just turn up because otherwise he'll warn Jacqueline and then our plan will be screwed." I speak urgently as Michael is coming back over and then he agrees before hanging up.

I look at my watch for must be the hundredth time so I can figure out what time Tyler will be trying to escape, however then I have an even better idea and text him to meet me near the toilets so that we can sneak off together. He messages me back a smiley face to show that he approves of my plan.

So now I am counting down the minutes whilst trying to not make it obvious to Michael what I'm planning to do or he'll never let me get away with it. Finally it's time, as normally as I can manage I ask Michael if I can go to the toilet and to my great disbelief he doesn't expect me to be running away or even consider anything suspicious. I rush off a bit faster than is probably convincing but oh well, I'm just so relieved to have a break.

Tyler had left even earlier than me in a bid for freedom, so he's already waiting for me when I arrive and I can't believe our luck and that we have gotten away with it so far. He grins with delight when he sees me and our success so now all we have to do is go off and hide somewhere.

Chapter Twenty

We walk off pleased together that our little plan hasn't failed and find a nice dry patch of grass, hidden by some willow trees to settle and have our lunch at. We finish quickly and I'm already feeling the benefits of Tyler's company as I relax and chat to him, instantly erasing my previous boredom.

"I think Jacqueline's going to be annoyed when she realises I'm not coming back," Tyler chuckles, imagining her reaction which gets me thinking about how Michael won't be particularly impressed either.

Right on cue my phone starts ringing and me and Tyler share a look of panic.

"Hi Michael," I answer it preparing for doom whilst trying to think of an excuse that will sound believable.

"Hello Violet, I was wondering if you've seen Tyler as I just got called by Jacqueline that he's disappeared," Michael tells me already knowing that I know this.

"No I haven't seen him, sorry I'm taking so long I just wanted to get a drink and it's quite a walk away from the activity to get there." I lie guiltily, wondering if it will work and Tyler covers his mouth with his hand as he realises the mess I have potentially gotten us into.

"Oh well that's OK, I just thought that maybe he would have joined you so I could let Jacqueline know as she's really not pleased." Michael falls right into the trap much to my relief, this is actual proof that he's tired out from this week as usually without fail he'll see through me as for some reason everyone can read my thoughts and emotions easier than reading a book. I don't like being deceitful but mine and Tyler's plans would be ruined otherwise so I'm glad.

As soon as he hangs up I start laughing in disbelief, Tyler stares and gapes at me for a moment in shock and then grins in delight when he understood what this means; we have gotten away with it. We stand up and shielded by the security of the trees and cover they offer I begin to kiss his soft, smooth and sweet lips which instantly respond to mine and kiss me back losing me in another world momentarily. Every time he touches me or we kiss I feel like there is a song in my heart, I can never be at peace unless he's with me and he always catches my breath and brings a blush to my cheeks and it honestly feels like I'm glowing when I am with him. The best part is that I can see the happiness that I bring him too, the stunning smile that always appears whenever he sees me, the soft and tender look that he gets in his eyes whenever he says that he loves me and the way that even when he's had a bad day I can always pick him up and listen and be there for him as he has no problem letting me know facts and details about him that he wouldn't share with others which makes me feel privileged.

I let him hold my face, cupping it and tilting up towards his with his pale hands as we kiss causing my whole heart to practically burst with love and affection for him. My body trembles with a tingle of pleasure as it's truly the best feeling when you have someone who makes you feel special and valued, someone who devotes their time to you and makes promises that stay with you forever. I pity the people who don't have this as they have no idea what they're missing out on or like me before who have these feelings but despair over someone they can never have, and just how perfect some things in this world are despite all the pain, there will always be a light shining in the dark even if you cannot see it yourself you just need someone to see it for you.

When you love someone it's easier to see the individual light that shines in everyone, the side to people that makes you want to be their friend and the reason you love and value them, it's rare when people think like this so I enjoy and savour it when they do. Sometimes it can be hard to discover peoples qualities, Tyler has many qualities that I love and he shows them all the time which I like as some people hide them or you have to search for them, but it's always worth it to see the individual inner beauty that sparks within everyone. You don't always notice it but sometimes the exact things that you think you hate or that infuriates you about someone can also be the thing that attracts you to them and actually is why you've fallen in love with them, this makes you take awhile though to know that you love that person partly because you're in denial.

We pull apart for a moment and I gaze into his lovely blue eyes, I lean in to kiss him again and Tyler has closed his eyes as his hands hold my waist and his chest gently presses against me. The grass must have quieted and silenced his footsteps as when we pull apart for the second time and Tyler is whispering in my ear, a quiet cough to get our attention breaks the moment. Both our heads immediately snap around to lock gazes with Michael, the breath whipped out of me from the shock of getting caught. He stands a small distance away, his hands in his pockets and his eyes twinkling with amusement as his lips flicker upwards into an uncontrollable smile.

"Did you really think it would take me long to put the pieces of the puzzle together?" he questions us, his voice is calm and only just carries over to us. However I know it's a rhetorical question and so wait for him to continue as I fumble in my mind for an excuse which doesn't exist.

"Once I discovered that you had told both of us the toilet excuse I knew how stupid I'd been to get deceived," he tuts as if he blames himself more than us, when we have been the ones to go off and I'd lied on the phone as well.

Michael sighs but in a kind, understanding way "You know it's sweet that you're always trying to sneak off together, but you know that I'm going to have to return you to Jacqueline Tyler and Violet I need you back with me." Michael's lips are still twitching but there is a hint of authority evident behind his words showing he does mean his command. To be fair though he's taking this really well, and doesn't appear to be overly fazed by our lapse of responsibility and, as adults in general, our maturity.

I grasp Tyler's hand and he gives mine a quick squeeze before I murmur "I'll see you later," softly in his ear, kiss him lightly on the cheek and then swiftly catch up to Michael who's witnessed the whole process. Tyler waves in farewell and then he turns and is off back to his activity, leaving me behind with Michael to return to my own group. As I keep pace with Michael all I can think of is how embarrassing it is that he saw me and Tyler kissing passionately in front of him as we were unaware that he was there, also Michael still hasn't fully accepted the fact that we want to be together. I watch him cautiously out of the corner of my eye, wondering what he had thought when he'd seen us, two members of his staff like that together. His eyes meet mine, it doesn't take a genius to figure out what I'm thinking about and so his brown eyes shine with a look of distant curiosity and fascination in their depths. I can tell he's trying to suppress laughter and after that, rightly so.

"I shouldn't have been surprised that I would catch you both being so intimate one day," Michael chortles genially and it gently shakes the whole frame of his body, making him look what can only be described as quite sweet. Michael's not the way Tyler is but he shares his vulnerable softer nature, confidence and gentle approach, they also share slight nerdy moments over peculiar interests which make them cute and intriguing. For the moment though he simply influences my cheeks to burn with even deeper embarrassment.

"So how come you're taking this so well?" I ask him curiously before letting myself be relieved and he smiles.

"I already know you're together and you're in so deep that there's nothing I could do even if I wanted to." Michael answers, not bothered about getting worked up about us any more.

"What about you and Izzie?" I phrase my question uncertainly; surely they should be on the mend now?.

The way his whole face beams in response says it all and I smile with him, "We're really working everything out between us." He confides in me and happiness can be heard within every word. Neither of us make any more comments on the matter so the topic of conversation returns to me.

"Violet I understand that you're having a hard time with your flat at the moment," Michael states in a considerate voice and it's like an alarm setting off in my head. Damn it, why of all things does he have to mention that now?

I cringe away from him as I reluctantly give the weak answer of, "There's really no need to worry; I'll be fine." I try to convince him to the best of my abilities as mine and Tyler's secret rely upon my acting skills here.

"I don't think it will as I haven't paid you enough recently, so I'm sure if you calculate it properly Violet you're in more trouble than you think." Michael continues and I begin to panic, I should have realised that Michael records all the figures so I can't simply fool him with persuasive words. What should I do?

"Well whenever times get tough I usually stay with a friend for awhile," I attempt to make my voice sound casual and cool, however his extreme awareness doesn't take long to begin being suspicious of me; and for good reason.

"Oh Violet, are you seriously trying to tell me that you and Tyler are..." he trails off, unable to continue with his correct little theory as he realises yet again just how deep me and Tyler are. I am about to defend myself but really there's no possible way I can, so I resort to simply shutting my mouth and pressing my lips into line so I won't let slip anything else.

"So you're living together?" he interrogates me, his eyes fixated on my face so he can read it if I try to lie.

"Not yet, but after the trip we're arranging it." I admit, guilty and busted as he would have gotten it out of me anyway.

I can never tell what he's thinking when he looks at me like this, but I'm guessing that this is one too many steps over the line even for him. Surprisingly he just nods in understanding as if he's been expecting this to happen for awhile, it's almost like his 'only a matter of time' theory hasn't occurred as quickly as he'd anticipated either. That leaves me to ponder over what else he's waiting for to happen...

"Well I really do wish you two the best; you make the most perfect couple that I've ever seen." Michael says instead of all the points of disapproval he could have made, almost in a way of congratulations. Michael really has softened up over the whole issue of me and Tyler recently, I wonder if this has anything to do with Izzie winning him over instead of fighting it any more.

"I thought that you were dead set against mine and Tyler's feelings for each other though," I remind him confused; since day one Michael's made it perfectly clear that Tyler is my co-worker and shouldn't be anything more.

"Yes, I know. Being truthful though it doesn't make any difference to either of you which is exactly what I was testing you for, I wanted to know if you really were in love or if it was some kind of extreme phase that you would both let go of. Now I have my answer, you matter more to each other than your job does because you were under no illusion that I could get rid of one of you for distracting the other." He informs me of his well thought out plan leaving me stunned by what I'd learnt. So all this time he had been looking out for the both of us, to see if we were genuine so nobody got hurt.

My respect and admiration has always been sky high for Michael, but at this second it rises incredibly higher.

"You have no idea how much that means to me, that you would do that for us. I know you've known Tyler for awhile, but you haven't known me for very long at all and you still did that..." I tell him feeling elated and he holds my serious gaze for an immeasurable amount of time, before his lips quirk upwards and we carry on with our activity.

I have to tell Tyler about just how generous Michael has been, how he's tried to protect us all along and so now we can finally make the leap and be together.

"So me and Tyler, are we allowed to be together officially now?" I ask Michael just to verify this fact and make doubly sure that I'm hearing what I think I am.

"Yes, do you want me to tell everyone?" he offers in response, pleased.

"Oh no, it's OK I just had to make sure I wasn't imagining this as it's hard to believe it's finally allowed. Besides I'm sure everyone will figure it out anyway." I hastily explain, relieved and glad. I'd rather not have everyone gossiping about us even though it's inevitable, also I need to share the successful news with Tyler first.

"Well OK, I suppose you're right anyway most people won't need to guess for long and I think others already know." Michael chuckles and I still flush with embarrassment despite the fact that I'm delighted at the same time.

It explains so much to me now though as a lot of actions that have occurred hadn't made sense before, now it's as if everything is adding up and fitting into place.

The day passes slowly but I don't mind any more as I have one of my closest friends beside me, and I can see Tyler later in the evening. The thought of everyone being told though is too much, I'm so glad Michael has agreed to just let everyone figure it out for themselves. It won't take as long as I'd like it too though, Jess and Jacqueline have already guessed according to Michael and if I really concentrate on the past few weeks I know he's right as there have been definite signs and indications that I missed until now. They've been hinting at my relationship with Tyler for ages, Jess especially as every time she's let me in to the building in the morning she asks me about Tyler. I really haven't been very observant or quick to let the penny to drop that I've been overly obvious.

Tyler and Jacqueline turn up with their group unexpectedly as they have finished their activity, so they help us draw ours to a close so that we will be able to go off and enjoy our last dinner together. Once we get back from the trip we'll have to arrange to meet up for meals again, I for one will miss this as it has brought all of us closer than before. Izzie has already saved our usual table by the time we arrive, which leaves her to dish all the menus out as I take my usual seat next to Tyler. We're all sad that it's our last day of the trip, yet there's plenty to look forward to for the rest of this summer.

We discuss everything as we eat to prolong our time together, this naturally leads to Michael giving me a look several times across the table to see if he has permission to mention anything from our earlier conversation. I give a small and subtle shake of my head, there's no way I'm letting him announce it and I still haven't had the opportunity to tell Tyler yet anyway. Michael submissively presses his lips together and tries to avoid broadcasting his great amusement towards me, which in my honest opinion is failing on every possible existing level. To be fair he is in the position to laugh as he's seen me and Tyler kissing today, so he has every right to make fun of me. Still though, I won't miss the chance to return the favour one day as he's doing his best efforts to showcase the fact that something is going on, so I'll make his scandal equally unforgettable and he knows it. At this point in time though he doesn't appear to care as clearly I must look a priceless picture at the moment.

After we have had our final meal and dessert we continue to talk for a long time, there won't be any activities later as we need to get going early tomorrow morning, therefore this is our last real opportunity to spend time together. Before we all go off back to our chalets or anywhere else I offer to take pictures of all of them so I can savour the moment with the camera I'd brought with me, I guess it makes sense now why Michael gave me a picture frame for my birthday.

We all take it in turns to take the pictures so that everyone will be included, naturally after we have had all the group photos some people had the bright idea of individual and partner photos. I snap some of Izzie and Jacqueline, then Tyler dares to step up the mark and get a few of Izzie and Michael which they can't refuse as it would look suspicious otherwise. So after we get our laugh Michael doesn't fall far behind for returning the favour, he takes the camera so that he can get pictures of me and Tyler which we'd skill-fully avoided before. We have the same kind of pictures taken like everyone else did at first, but then Michael surpasses even Tyler on going one too many steps over the line.

He instructs us to do things such as hold hands and I can't believe how naughty and inappropriate he's being, especially if you consider the fact that nobody else knows it's official. However Tyler catches on quickly, gives me his stunning smile and decides to make the most of this by holding me to him as if we're dancing. Tyler and Michael share a long look before Tyler does something completely outrageous as Jacqueline still wasn't entirely certain before.

Letting his hands slide down my back and rest on my waist he then leans forward until our faces are only inches apart, his blue eyes silently tell me what he's planning on doing before they close and his lips touch mine. Even so my eyes widen with the shock that he's followed through, and my heart is pounding in my chest as I melt into his sweet embrace. There is an awed silence from everyone and I know that Michael's taking plenty of pictures, I know now that this is going to be an unforgettable moment in time on this trip. We smile as we kiss, so finally the secret is well and truly out and give it some time and the whole school will know about it when we go back after the summer.

They all cheer and clap when we pull apart and all I can do is smile, being with Tyler has made my life perfect.

"So in case you couldn't tell or haven't already figured it out, me and Violet are a couple." Tyler grins proudly, his delight projecting out to the others as he gazes at me.

"Mr Crowther and Miss Spring," Jacqueline comments quietly before beaming with joy.

"You make the most perfect couple ever!" she tells us excitedly before continuing with, "I always knew there was something going on between you though. No offence, but it was really obvious!" Me and Michael exchange a glance, so he was right; she had known all along.

"Well you've not even been his assistant for very long, but you're made for each other as I think this has been going on since day one." Michael states his review of the whole time I've been at the school, well it would be easier for him to tell as apparently I'm easy to read and he's known Tyler's usual behaviour for awhile. Michael and Izzie smile at each other then which can only mean one thing, they can't hide it from me that they're in a relationship too.

Jacqueline however much to their luck is too busy focusing on us to notice, I'm watching Tyler as I always do and then his eyes meet mine. His mouth curves up at the corners and I know that I couldn't ask for a better wish than Tyler, he's like my own personal star shining brightly in the sky. He grips my hand in his, then after wishing everyone a good nights sleep we stroll off together back to our chalet. I love walking beside Tyler, my pace matching his in perfect harmony and being able to look up at his handsome face. His soft features relax and his blue eyes are looking ahead, unaware of my intense green gaze, however as he's said before green is his favourite colour. I like being able to stare at him and all his perfections, but there's rarely ever a time that he doesn't catch me and it always sparks his curiosity of what I'm thinking about as I gaze at him with quiet happiness.

Tyler flicks the lights on and we swiftly get ready for bed; brushing our teeth and changing into our night clothes. When the usual procedure of Tyler organising all the pillows to his liking has finished I switch the light off and then get myself into the bed, the duvet is warm and I make myself comfortable. Tyler then clambers in next to me, shirtless like he's been all week and yet it gets me every time how attractive and tormentingly tempting he is for me.

As I lie there in the dark in his warm embrace it gets me thinking that this will be my life from now on, in many respects that's a reassuring thought as I'm making more steps closer to leaving my tiresome gloomy life behind. I've lived with the silent, unseen illness of anxiety and depression for a few years now as many people are unaware of the effects and control these have over you and if it wasn't for Tyler I'd still be in the place where there's no light in the dark and no end in sight, whereas Tyler has seen it for me and is bringing me back to life. It's a shame that I can't see my parents any more to help me through it, to never be able to introduce them to Tyler or share anything special with them again. I would have nearly no regrets about leaving everything behind if it weren't for them, it gets me every time how unjust it seems and how it should never have happened. Luckily Tyler distracts me from taking these dark intrusive and foreboding thoughts any further, usually this kind of negativity won't leave me for days however it's always there, carefully concealed and hidden behind thin and frail surfaces.

"From now on we can be together, I will love you always." His soft voice murmurs in my ear causing my cheeks to burn and him to smile in response, he still finds it amusing how embarrassed I get but his peaceful distraction means I drift off in his arms, feeling complete.

Chapter Twenty One

We wake early and for once neither of us has to go to the effort of forcing the other to get up and ready for the day.

"Good morning," Tyler's pleasant voice greets me now that we are both up and dressed.

"Hello Tyler," I reply and we both smile, I'm getting a good vibe off of him today so I'm guessing that he's just as pleased as I am about going home today. As I brush my hair I spot that Tyler has deliberately refused to put his tie on, it always irritates him that he can't put it on properly and so he has tried to evade the fuss by packing it when he wasn't supposed to.

It doesn't take me long to uproot it from his suitcase, and I go up behind him so that I'll stand a chance of getting anywhere near him with it in my hands. I kiss his cheek to distract him and take him off guard from what I am trying to do, I have accomplished getting it around his neck but when I want to fit it around his collar he instantly jerks away from me.

"You sneaky so and so," he exclaims in shock and then we both start laughing.

"You're the sneaky one; hiding it away in your suitcase." I giggle as he begins tickling me as payback so I have to quickly surrender, I'm laughing so much my sides hurt. Tyler stops and allows me to recover but keeps his arms around me, he is still chuckling over how quickly I've given in to his attack.

"Stop it, we need to get ready and go to breakfast." I mockingly scold him and brush him gently aside.

We leave our chalet in a rush determined not to be late, Michael's already seated and Izzie and Jacqueline have just arrived with us. Despite my best efforts Tyler yanks his tie off from around his neck and carelessly screws it up in his hands, this earns a smirk from Michael who wears his tie very neatly and knows that Tyler avoids wearing a tie at every possible opportunity. Tyler scowls and ignores him turning to Izzie instead, she however is too busy giggling at his stubborn behaviour so he looks to Jacqueline as I am also teasing him.

"I suppose we should be loading our suitcases onto the coach now if we want to leave on time," Michael's remark sends us all heading back to our chalets to collect everything. The chalet looks bland and empty now that all of our belongings have been cleared out, we take one last look of the place and then vacate the premises locking the door behind us for the last time. Once everything has been loaded and all the pupils have been gathered, registered and seated onto the coach it's time to go. Me and Tyler sit next to each other again and I am glad to get the window seat. Izzie and Jacqueline sit on the other side and Michael was in front again, they also are excited about going home.

Nobody talks much due to how fatigued everyone is, I rest on Tyler's shoulder as I watch the scenery flash by and he reclines his head back against the seat. However when it is lunchtime everyone perks up a bit and begin complaining that it's time to eat, thankfully the restaurant has provided food for us to take with us on the journey so we don't need to make any stops. We eat ravenously because of we have had such an early start and so have been awake many hours. Tyler has taken parts of other lunches and added it to his own and I can't hold back a sigh, how it is possible to eat that much I'll never know.

Once I've finished I remain quiet so I can enjoy the tranquil views out of the window, then I recall the fact that I have my phone in my bag so I start listening to my music. Tyler notices my anti-social behaviour and so I give him one of the ear plugs so he can listen too. He doesn't seem surprised by my calming music tastes even though he has never asked what I listen to, I guess he's probably figured a lot out about me without needing to ask though.

Tyler has a way of sensing things sometimes as he has said things before that he should have no knowledge of, I have never mentioned it to him because I'm curious if he'll realise that I never actually told him certain things. I guess he just knows me really well despite the fact that in truth we haven't even known each other for that long, sometimes you just know when something is right. I don't think I'll ever stop wondering how he can go from being so incredibly normal and in the moment to being distant, thoughtful and as if he's somewhere else; a place of extreme knowledge and agonizing pain. This is also something I don't question him about in fear of causing him any further discomfort and distress, if he doesn't want to relive the traumas of his past in the vivid way I sometimes do then I don't want to pry and trigger anything.

We don't speak for the majority of the coach journey, however when we only have a twenty minute ride left Tyler strikes up an important conversation.

"Should we go to your flat first so we can transfer some of your belongings over to my house?" he asks me enthusiastically, anticipating the event already.

"That's a good idea, we can probably pack most of it in one trip anyway." I admit with a shy smile as I really don't have much belongings, so it should be easy.

I feel an unusual thrill spark in me at the thought of finally moving in with Tyler, we'll have so much to do when we get back that I just want to get started and stuck in now. Everyone chats, gaining the energy we have all previously lost back as we're all ready to feel the benefits of the summer break. I share a smirk with Tyler when we overhear Michael and Izzie discussing having dinner together tonight, but we're both pleased that those two are finally making progress.

The coach turns around the final corner and Tyler practically leaps out of his seat in his haste to get on with our arrangements for the afternoon. The parents of the class are already awaiting the arrival of their children to collect them, so once we have made sure everyone is on their way home Michael dismisses us to go and enjoy our holiday.

We retrieve our suitcases and then I follow Tyler off to his car, he opens up the boot and then I begin helping him load them up and into the car. With a bit of effort he manages to force them both in and close the boot again, which is now completely full. Being the charming gentleman that he is Tyler then holds my door open for me, waits till I'm safely in and then closes it before walking around the side of the car to get in himself. We wave our goodbyes to everyone else and then we're off, on our way to my flat. Tyler drives almost as fast as the speed limit allows, so it doesn't take too long before he pulls up the car in front of the block of flats where I've lived for the past two years.

I fish my key out from my pocket and then we make our way up the flights of stairs and to my door, which I unlock with ease. That's when it hits me that I don't think Tyler's ever seen the inside of my flat before, as always though he appears perfectly at ease in his new surroundings and just gets on with it. We grab plastic carrier bags off the sofa so that we can pack items into them and make it easier to carry everything down back to the car.

I start off packing simple items, wrapping up ornaments and picking up necessities and essentials before piling them carefully into the bags. Tyler however is naturally seeing only the bigger picture and begins taking down my stacks of books and DVDs, which inhabit an entire corner of the room. I continue taking items down which mainly consist of sentimental objects whilst Tyler starts clearing space by picking up the already full bags and taking them down to his car, so he can assess how much will fit into his car before we have to give up for the day. We end up working non-stop for an hour before Tyler's car can't possibly hold anything else; my flat looks plain and bare now as almost all of my possessions have been loaded into his car, much like how we'd left the chalet looking bleak after we'd left this morning.

After locking up we head back to Tyler's now cramped car and Tyler drives us to his home which I can now call mine as well. We don't bother with unpacking my bags today as it's too much hassle, and so instead we dump them into one of the guest rooms along the same corridor as our bedroom. Despite how long we have taken at my flat, much to both of our surprise we still have most of the day remaining to enjoy.

"Maybe we should unpack our suitcases, I don't think I'll have any clean clothes unless I wash them now." I suggest a reasonable offer to Tyler whilst implying that really it needs to be done and we may as well do something useful with our time.

He gives a fake exasperated sigh before getting up and we bring our suitcases upstairs to unpack. I begin by taking out everything that can stay upstairs so that I won't have to make loads of pointless trips up and down the stairs. I put all my bathroom items and lotions away first as I haven't got many of them, so it takes a short amount of time to organise them in Tyler's neat cupboards. Tyler being the opposite of me is practically ransacking his entire suitcase just to take out all of his upstairs items, I try to hide my amusement as I grab all my laundry and leave him. When I pile all my clothes into the washing machine it amazes me how whenever I look for something in the cupboards everything is neatly arranged and belongs in helpful places. I have to admit that after what I've observed of Tyler, I didn't expect to see the cutlery near the table in a drawer and the washing and cleaning powder above the machine.

Tyler's going to have to wait to wash his clothes as mine fill the whole washing machine, I turn it all on and adjust the settings before heading back upstairs to see how Tyler's doing. Apart from his clothes; everything has been put back into its usual place and is no longer covering the entire bed. He has separated his clothes into two piles, the ones that need washing and the ones that don't, he tells me proud of his out of character organisation.

"Violet," Tyler stresses my name in a guilty voice which immediately makes me sigh as my mind races through all the possibilities about what he could have done, before I turn to face him.
"Yes?" I question him whilst mentally preparing myself for whatever bomb he's about to potentially drop on me.
"You don't mind if I have to go out for a bit do you? It's just I haven't got any meals left in the fridge because of the trip." He informs me apologetically and it's so ridiculous that I smile; of all the things that I'd been thinking of something that small hadn't even occurred to me as it's hardly a disaster.
"Honestly, I thought you meant something serious. Of course you can go and get us something," I laugh at him. I suppose having no food in the house really is a catastrophe for him.
"I won't be long," Tyler tells me, gently kisses me on the cheek and then he goes downstairs and I hear the gentle click of the door as it shuts behind him.
　　Whilst he's gone I may as well sort all of his clothes out to save him the hassle later, I smooth them all out before finding hangers to slip them into so I can hang his clothes up in order. I like to keep certain clothes together, so as I tend to do with my own I hang up all his shirts in a row and then his jumpers and suits.

Once I have finished I accidentally stumble upon something rather fascinating just by chance. Hanging up next to Tyler's other clothes is a uniform of some kind; he must take good care of it as it's very neat and not a single part of it looks like it's fading or is very worn. I gently run my hand over the material and marvel at the texture of it, the uniform is a dark blue jacket with pockets and white embroidery in specific places. At the bottom of the wardrobe I spot black, outdoor shoes next to a matching black and professional looking torch. There's also a smart belt draped over the black trousers, what kind of uniform is this? I'm awestruck by what I'm looking at as this is obviously a proper uniform and not some kind of dressing up item, it doesn't look like it's anything to do with the police but it's clearly linked to some kind of authority. I have a very strong feeling in my gut that this has to be involved with Tyler's previous job, well whatever job it was it's evident that it must have been a good one.

I close the wardrobe and go downstairs to wait for Tyler, I wonder if he will be sensitive about me asking about the uniform and anything towards or related to his past. He knows that I have to find out eventually, but what can be so bad about what he did anyway? I won't force him to tell me though if it really makes him so uncomfortable, there's no need to put him through something he'd rather leave behind in the past.

The door then opens, snapping me awake from my reverie. He smiles his dazzling smile as soon as he sees me, I take in the admirable sight of him as he stands there in the doorway.

"Hope I wasn't gone too long, did you miss my amazing presence?" he asks me, grinning as I help him take all the bags into the kitchen.

"Hardly noticed you were gone," I giggle knowing it will annoy him.

"I know a lie when I hear one," Tyler whispers in an attractive voice in my ear. I let him embrace me at first, his lips trailing down my neck which is extremely distracting but then I notice that I never unloaded my clothes from the washing machine. I leap out of his arms in a desperate hurry to to get everything out into the laundry basket.

"Oh Violet, are you really so incapable without me that you can't even sort out your own washing?" Tyler teases me, amused by my out of character lapse in organisation. I cast him a fake scowl as I make my way outside with the basket to hang everything up onto the line to dry in the warm summer breeze.

"Wait, let me help you." Tyler follows me outside and then using the brightly coloured yellow pegs we begin hanging each individual piece up onto the line. Once we have finished Tyler takes my hand so that I will automatically turn towards him and he can claim my full attention.

"Will you forgive me?" he asks, his mouth curving upwards as he speaks. Despite my best efforts I can't resist smiling with him, I don't even try to refuse as he wraps me into his protective arms and places his lips on mine.

"How easy I surrender," I murmur softly to him and he smiles but says nothing as he takes in his effortless victory.

"We have nothing in our way now, I can kiss you whenever I wish." Tyler tells me and his satisfaction and delight about this fact can be heard within every word.

"Come on, we should probably make a start on dinner." I say to him as I take his hand in mine and gently pull him along after me.
"Luckily it will only take thirty minutes," Tyler tells me as he holds up the packet. Oh well, at least it's an easy meal and we won't be kept waiting.
"Oh I still need to put my clothes away upstairs," Tyler suddenly recalls which reminds me that I still need to ask him about his uniform.
"No worries, I already put them away whilst you were out shopping." I inform him as I put our meal in the oven.
He pauses for a brief moment, "Oh thanks, you didn't have to do that." Tyler begins but I shake my head.
"I wanted to help," I reassure him and we sit opposite each other at the table while we wait for the food to be ready.
"Tyler... can I ask you something?" I approach him hesitantly, worried that he might not want me to pry or he could become upset and not open up. He holds my gaze and by silent communication through reading my eyes he understands that whatever it is I have to say is serious.
"Sure, you can ask me anything you want, you know that right?" His response is positive but I see him bracing himself. I nod in answer to his question and then take a deep breath as I prepare carefully how to word my question.
"The uniform you have upstairs, does that hold any relevance to your old job?" I ask him in a quiet, nervous voice. He doesn't seem at all surprised by my question, probably because he guessed when I saw him stiffen at the fact that I'd sorted his clothes out.
"I thought you'd probably seen it when you told me that you had put my clothes away," he replies in an even quieter voice than my own, however it is soft to show he's not angry with me.
"The uniform was for the job I used to do," Tyler confirms for me, his eyes holding mine, witnessing my reaction.
"Now let me make this clear, it wasn't my job that was the problem to me, it was what happened on a particular shift in that job." Tyler spoke slowly, making sure that I definitely understand that somehow vital detail.
  We both pause for a moment, before I finally break the dramatic silence and ask the question I've always wanted to.

"So what was your old job Tyler?"

He watches me for a moment before answering with, "I used to be a security guard, in places that needed maximum protection and contained many rarities and expensive valuables."

Chapter Twenty Two

It takes me awhile before that fully sinks in, but it definitely explains the reason for his uniform and other items.

"So why didn't you want people to know?" I ask him, confused with what's wrong with being a security guard, it sounds quite admirable to me.

"I really liked my job; protecting certain buildings and making sure nothing was being stolen." Tyler begins, thinking carefully before continuing.

"I never wanted anyone to know about my job though, that would lead to the inevitable questions about what happened one night." Tyler admits to me and I hold my breath, what could possibly have happened to shake him up like this?

"I quit my job soon after, it was a difficult decision but I wanted to move on meaning I'd have to leave my action packed life behind." Tyler continues without me needing to pry.

"That was the reason I had to be in good shape, if you ever have to catch a criminal or run for backup. My zip wire skills came from the training centre we had to attend twice a week, we used it to get from building to building." He tells me and I listen in an awestruck silence, a lot of things are beginning to make sense to me now that didn't before.

"That's amazing, that you used to do all that. I never would have guessed or even thought that I'd know someone who had an extraordinary job like that." I confess to him, practically gushing over what it must have been like for him. Tyler smiles slightly, appreciative of my comments.

"It was hard work, but I enjoyed it." Tyler says, but his voice indicates that the topic is now closed so if I want to discover what happened to him, it would have to be another day. I'm content enough by just knowing that I'm one of the only people who knows what his job was, grateful that he's showing his trust in me. I'm so lost in thought that it surprises me when Tyler gets up to retrieve the food from the oven, we start off eating in silence as we both mull over everything from our conversation. It does not take long though before I think we both decide to put it behind us for later reference and simply make the most of our evening.

"When do you think we should book an ice rink?" Tyler ponders once we've finished eating. I smile as I remember his promise that we will go ice skating together at some point in the duration of this summer.

"I don't know, soon though as I'm really looking forward to it." I enthuse with him and he also smiles in agreement.

"Good thing it's the summer holidays, more people will want to go swimming so if we're lucky we can get a rink with less people." Tyler mentions a good point, ice rinks aren't the in season place to be at the moment so we stand a decent chance of having less people around.

"I have a friend who works at one of those places, I can easily get us booked in for next week if you fancy to do it soon." Tyler suggests to me and he is so eager to please that I feel my heart skip, I smile glad that his desires are in sync with mine.

"Yeah, I can't wait." I tell him as I ponder over what else we should plan for this holiday.

"So I know that we already have a few plans, but do you think there's anything else we should definitely do?" I ask as otherwise we'll have weeks of free time that should be filled at least a bit.

He answers with a smile and a flirtatious look gleams in his lovely blue eyes, making me prepared for the teasing that will come next.

"Yes, I have thought of something that needs to be done." Tyler grins, tormenting me as he holds me to him and I lie my hands on his chest, and gently clutch his shirt.

"Not the kind of plans I was thinking of, but you knew that didn't you?" I whisper and move my hands so that I can hold his face close to mine and run my fingers through his hair. I cherish the level of intimacy and closeness we have, I never thought I'd be able to have this so soon and all because I aced my interview all that time ago. I still like to remember the first time I met Tyler, if I had known then what we would become now I would have thought it was a joke, not possible as how could you get so deep with someone in such a short period of time? However meeting Tyler Crowther, the deputy head of Bank Croft primary school has to be the best miracle that's ever happened to me.

"So what would you like to do with the rest of the evening?" Tyler asks, his hands now stroking my long black hair.

"Maybe we could see if there's anything good on TV?" I suggest to him, I gaze into the depths of his blue eyes before releasing him and taking only his hand as we enter the living room. Tyler gets the remote control off the coffee table and then he snuggles up to me on the sofa. It quickly becomes obvious though as he flicks through countless channels, that we aren't going to find anything to hold our particular interests.

"By the time there are any good TV programmes on, we'll probably be retired." Tyler sighs, not surprised by the lack of channels sparking his interest.

It doesn't bother me though as it gives me the chance just to enjoy his company which I now always can.

"What did you think of me, when we first met?" I ask him, intrigued as my first memories and impressions of him are what I treasure dearly because they're the marker of my future. Tyler smiles instantly as he recalls that first day of having a work partner.

"When I first saw you when I stood in the doorway, my only thoughts were that I had a new best friend, for sure." He tells me truthfully and we both smile.

"If you knew what I'd really be to you then..." I say and he grins in understanding.

"I don't think anyone could have convinced me that that would be possible at the time, but here we are." Tyler chuckles and I'm glad things have worked out the way they have.

"What was your first impression of me?" Tyler asks in an alluring voice, his lips twitching as he awaits my answer.

"You were the typically charming character, I knew as soon as I saw you that I'd fit in and you'd look after me, especially for the first few weeks." I confide in him honestly and he appears appeased with my answer.

"So your first impression wasn't of how attractive I am?" he asks in a teasing yet clarifying voice, I look away from his perfect face as I smile at that.

We have been talking for quite some time and so it isn't too long later when we we're locking the house up and heading upstairs for bed. I change quickly whilst Tyler's in the bathroom and then we swap so he can get changed. It's going to be nice having a break from work, and now the trip's over we can enjoy ourselves for the first time without having anyone like Michael interfering or getting in our way. No offence to Michael, but he really did give us a hard time. Everything will be different when we go back though as everyone will know about me and Tyler, Michael has said that I need to frame one of those pictures he took and put the others up in our office. Also whatever Izzie has said to Michael has clearly worked a treat, as near the end of the trip they were as inseparable as me and Tyler.

That will definitely peak peoples' interest when we go back after the summer.

I go back into the bedroom to find Tyler already under the covers, so I flick off the light switch and join him. I lie my head down on the pillow and gaze at Tyler quietly in the dark, his lips curve up into a smile as he lies there watching me too. It reminds me of the first night that we shared together.

"Tomorrow would you like to stay here, or is there anywhere you wish to go?" Tyler asks softly, closing his eyes as he talks.

I curl up next to him under the duvet before replying with, "I don't mind staying here tomorrow, I haven't seen the garden since the first time." I tell him, pleased that I will get the chance to have a proper look at the house too.

"It's meant to be good weather, if you like we could have a barbecue as I bought the equipment when I went out earlier." Tyler mentions and his eyes open so he can witness my reaction first hand, I can't even remember the last time I'd had a barbecue but with guaranteed good weather I'm definitely up for it.

"Sure that sounds like fun," I tell him and then I remember a conversation I've had with him before.

"What made the barbecue at the last summer fête fail?" I ask out of interest and Tyler immediately smirks.

"If you can imagine it raining and picture Michael burning the only food that the barbecue managed to cook, then you can understand exactly why it failed." Tyler snorts, clearly it had been an event that was impossible to forget.

"That's why this year was an epic improvement on every level," Tyler chuckles and I smile and shake my head, clearly a lot of disasters have occurred at that school before and after I arrived.

I inch closer to Tyler in the dark and his eyes hold mine, then he pulls himself closer to me as well. I gently press my hands against his warm chest and then snuggle right up to him, it's literally impossible for us to get any closer. His protective arms hold me against him and his warm lips press against my cheek. We embrace one another and I feel his legs brush against mine and then his hands hold my back, I roll off my side so he can hold me to him as I lie gently on his chest and his lips meet mine. On the school trip we had tried to stop ourselves from getting carried away, but there's nothing to hold us back now.

A sense of freedom and release stirs inside me at that thought, there's nothing in our way, no obstacle to prevent us. I open my eyes to see him watching me, temptation shines in them and I smile as we continue. He doesn't look as if he'll ever tire, there isn't a single moment where I get cold as he's lovely and warm, radiating his heat into me as we lie together. I rest my head upon his shoulder, my hands and arms on his chest as I press against him and this must have been the position we stayed in as I wake up like this in the morning.

Tyler's still asleep, his cheek pressing against mine and I don't dare move in fear of accidentally waking him. I listen to his gentle and slow breathing as I carefully rub the sleep from my eyes, it seems that even when Tyler's asleep he's smiling as his lips flicker up every now and then. I glance at the clock on the bedside table and decide I should probably wake him up, I gently caress his face with my hand and a few seconds later his blue eyes open in a daze. He gazes up at me for a moment and then a small smile plays upon his lips, we stay like that for awhile longer with him gazing up at me, looking vulnerable and defenceless.

"You looked so sweet asleep that I didn't want to wake you," I whisper softly, being the first to break the silence.

"You fell asleep first last night, so I had to be careful not to wake you but it gave me quality time to think about you as I watched you." Tyler spoke calmly, it's easy for him to use such bold words to express his feelings for me.

"Were you awake for long last night?" I ask him, curious as I can't remember when exactly I'd fallen asleep in his arms.

"Long enough to enjoy watching you," he answers grinning.

"What can be so interesting about watching someone sleep?" I ask him.

"You said so yourself, it's sweet." Tyler shrugs as if it's obvious before sitting up, taking my hand and pulling me off the bed and directly into his arms.

"Making a habit of this aren't we?" he voices the rhetorical question before giving me a brief shower of kisses.

"Well it's a habit I like and have no intention of changing," I admit to him.

"Yes, I agree that of all the habits I have this one has to be a favourite." Tyler chuckles lightly and we begin choosing our clothes for the day, so I make sure that I get one last glimpse of him shirtless before he heads off to get changed.

After I've gotten dressed I check my phone to see if Izzie has bothered to text me yet and keep me updated. It turns out she has and in the message she informs me that she had dinner with Michael the other night and it had gone really well. I send her one back to show my approval and that everything's going well with Tyler too. To be honest that's actually an understatement, me and Tyler are perfect together and nothing can be improved upon. By the time I get downstairs Tyler is already there; he has everything laid out ready for breakfast so I join him at the table.

"Izzie texted me; everything's working out well with Michael." I tell him after I've finished eating and as he's getting seconds he nods.

"I wonder how long it'll take before everyone figures out their little secret, especially as that will be a big deal in the staffroom." Tyler points out what I've also been thinking for quite some time.

"It's going to be weird having everybody know about us," I say as before only our friends had known and kept it quiet, so it will be strange for all the other members of staff to be gossiping about it.

"We do have the whole summer before they will know though," Tyler reminds me, still I know it's been lingering in his mind too. Also it must be harder for him as he's known everyone longer than me, which will mean they've all obviously known him since before I arrived. It really will be a big shock to everyone, he tries to reassure me that it will be fine but I still wonder how a few certain members of staff will take to the news.

"It doesn't matter what anyone else thinks, you're still my assistant but my partner too, it won't really be any different as we liked each other before anyway." Tyler eases my nerves and he's right as always, I had taken to him immediately when he'd smiled in the doorway of our office.

"You know I think you had me the moment I first saw you," I tell him truthfully and that instantly catches his attention.

"It was quite awhile later before I realized what you meant to me though," I continue glad to let him know how early on he had actually appealed to me.

"I don't know when it was that I discovered the feelings I'd developed for you, but I felt so embarrassed that I couldn't talk to you normally any more when we were friends." Tyler admits thoughtfully and his words melt my heart. When I had loved him before we were together it had been extremely difficult; trying to hide how I felt about him from him and everyone else.

"I can't believe how much everything's changed since I first worked as your assistant," I state my mind, mainly to myself but a flawless smile appears on his face and he takes my hand, leading me outside.

Glorious rays of sunshine settle on my skin as he leads me over the stream, to a bench surrounded by bluebells.

"Don't fret over everybody finding out about us, I'll be with you every step of the way and I'll protect you." Tyler spoke softly in my ear, his hand still in mine.

We remain silent for a moment and then Tyler tells me something he knows will cheer me up.

"I've booked the ice skating for tomorrow at two o'clock in the afternoon," It genuinely surprises me that he's been able to book that in not much notice.

"Really? That's great!" I exclaim excitedly, delighted that we have an amazing plan for tomorrow. We chat enthusiastically about ice skating before Tyler offers to take me out on a walk at the back of the garden, in the forest. There's a small wooden gate, with a simple latch on it which leads straight from his garden onto the single trail leading directly into the woods.

He points out many birds, rabbits and squirrels to me as we walk and there is also a black wild pony which we see from a distance. He naturally impresses me by knowing the majority of the names of the trees, flowers and plants that grow out here. This is why that day out on the school trip had made him feel so at home.

"Do you walk out here often?" I ask enjoying the splendid views and tranquillity that this calming, almost magical environment and atmosphere holds.

"Can you tell?" Tyler teases, knowing it's probably obvious how much he knows about it and enjoys this place. "Whenever the weather's nice I guess," Tyler gives me a proper answer now and it makes me happy to hear that, because walking through the woods is one of my favourite things to do.

We stroll together for awhile longer before he suggests heading back, as we've already spent an hour out here but it's hard to tell when you're having a good time.

"I think it's quite romantic walking out here," Tyler raises an eyebrow at me and grins as we near the small wooden gate again leading back into his beautiful garden. Him saying that reminds me of how my mother had told me that my father had proposed to her when they'd been out on a walk together. Me and Tyler have our whole future ahead of us, so anything can happen I guess.

Chapter Twenty Three

He locks it behind us and then after glancing at his watch, decides that we should get the barbecue out considering it will need time to get going.

"Would you like to play chess?" he asks me, eager so I don't want to dampen the mood and disappoint him. Last time we played though Tyler turned out to be a pro, so I'm not going to get my hopes up for standing a chance of winning.

To be fair he lets me have the white pieces so that I am able to go first, I doubt it will really make any difference though. It starts off simple and I'm doing OK, but as I watch Tyler knowing him as well as I do I know that there's already a plan formulating in his mind for the best strategy to use against me. It doesn't take long, for every one of his pieces I manage to get and satisfactorily knock off the board he ends up taking three of mine.

"How do you do that?" I scowl slightly, why does he have to be an expert at everything? The most irritating part is that Tyler can always point out my mistakes and where I've gone wrong, it makes me feel like a fool and so naturally I want to give up. Tyler however insists that we keep playing so he can teach me, I carry on reluctantly just for his sake as I'm losing interest in the game that is only infuriating me anyway.

Whilst Tyler completes a move which results in taking out one of my best pieces, I check on the barbecue to see if it has heated up yet and calls him over to distract him from the game. We gather all the food up and then go back outside to put it on the barbecue. Tyler looks briefly back at the game, but this time he doesn't press on the matter as he's guessed that I'd only played for him in the first place. Being the gentleman that he is, he returns the favour by abandoning the game.

I place my hand on his shoulder making him instinctively turn towards me, then I kiss his unexpectant face. I sense his surprise but he swiftly recovers himself and his soft lips kiss me back.

"What brought this on?" he asks me in a gentle murmur, his eyes gazing down into mine.

"To apologise," I tell him and confusion surfaces on his perfect features.

"For what?" he quizzes me, his handsome face puzzled. I play with his hair, running my hands through it before answering him.

"About the chess, I did try." I admit to him and his face instantly smooths, relaxing and I can see the tender softness of his features so I gently caress his cheek with my hand and feel the warmth radiate underneath it.

"No worries, I was just glad that you played with me even though you didn't want to." Tyler whispers in my ear and raises his pale hand to brush a lock of my hair out of my face and behind my ear. Then his pale eyelids close and I lean closer to kiss him again and he responds passionately, nibbling my lower lip.

"You're giving me another hunger compared to the food, one that is overly tempting." Tyler spoke softly before drawing me nearer to him.

"Am I satisfying your desires then?" I ask of him, feeling allured and turned on by his attractive choice of words.

"Very much so," he replies before he grabs my hand and I let my other one rest upon his shoulder whilst Tyler embraces me. He gently pins me to him, so that I belong in his arms as always.

"Maybe we should check on the food, it wouldn't be good if it burned." I remind him.

"You distracted me," Tyler accuses but his eyes glimmer, his hands leave my waist after lingering there for a moment before he turns away from me to go to the barbecue. It turns out the food is fine so when Tyler begins serving it up, I pour us both a glass of lemonade. My mind travels back to last night; I wonder if Tyler will be open to the idea of a repeat but far more intimate if the kissing reaches another level. We've probably exhausted every technique that actually exists though.

He hands me my plate and I snuggle closer to him on the bench, feeling the warm rays of sunshine soak into my ivory skin. Tyler is thoughtful as he eats making him demolish his food a tiny bit slower than usual.

"Something up?" I ask him and he shakes his head and swallows before replying.

"Just wondering when we would meet up with my mother," he voices his thoughts and my curiosity returns as I imagine what she'd be like.

"Any time I suppose, there's plenty of weeks so we can see her a few times." I suggest, pleased that I can meet her as it will be nice especially as I no longer have my own mother.

He notices my distraction but doesn't question it, guessing what I am thinking about and not wanting to upset me. I don't need his comfort though, in some ways I'm slowly beginning to heal from my tragedies. I don't think I'd be doing this well though if it weren't for Tyler.

"We could always see her after the ice skating or the day after," I suggest to him and breaking him out of his own reverie.

"So you wouldn't mind, if she met us at the end of the ice skating?" Tyler asks me for confirmation, his eyes eager.

"That's fine, you can tell her now if you want." I remark and he pulls his phone out of his pocket; so he can do just that.

It doesn't take him long to dial the number before there is a short pause and then he immediately greets her. He discusses our plans and how we want to meet up, awhile later he says goodbye and hangs up.

"She's more than happy to come and meet you tomorrow," Tyler informs me and he's delighted that our plans will be successfully taking place. It's nice to see how much Tyler wants me to meet his mother, also how highly he clearly thinks of her as some people take their parents for granted and forget how much they do for you.

"Do you call her often?" I say curiously as I had always called my mum for a chat and some support. Tyler nods as he slips his phone back into his pocket.

"She's lonely since she split up with my father," Tyler explains and I nod in understanding. It's a shame when relationships don't work out, my parents had always been together so I can't empathise but I can sympathise.

"I'm so glad that I'm no longer alone," I say quietly and he looks at me, it's evident that he wishes to receive an explanation.

"I hated being alone in my flat, unable to call anyone." I admit to him in a small voice and understanding lights his wise gaze.

"I never really enjoyed working at the school that much before because apart from Michael everyone else had to teach, I was on my own with a lot of work to do." He sighs, his mind taking him back to the time I hadn't been at the school and it must have been hard on him.

"Also I've been living alone as well, when you agreed to move in with me I must have been the happiest person." Tyler pauses for a moment before continuing with, "just like when I realized what feelings I had for you, except I didn't know what to do as I didn't want to accidentally reveal them and ruin everything."

"That's exactly what I was trying not to do, I thought if you knew I was in love with you and you didn't share those feelings then it would ruin everything as well." I confess to him, shocked that he'd felt the same way.

"I thought my feelings were really obvious though, which is why Michael kept giving me warnings." I admit to him and he listens curiously and then in surprise.

"At first I tried to deny my feelings even to myself, I didn't want to think about what would happen if you found out..." I trail off, remembering how hard it had been before.

"Well you never have to worry any more, Michael dropped us both in on each others secrets." Tyler points out; it's true if it hadn't been for Michael we would never have gotten together this quickly. My affections for Tyler have reached an even higher dramatic level when I'd found out he shared them, if it was even possible to like him even more.

We spend the rest of the evening hours outside talking and watching the sun, which is now beginning to go down and set as an orange glow in the distance. Silently we head back inside and I watch Tyler, glad that I have him and he has me. Sometimes I often wonder if we were actually designed for each other as we're so in sync, it's like we were meant to be. I go upstairs leaving Tyler to turn all the lights off and lock up before joining me.

I slip underneath the soft and warm duvet, which is in fact the same one from when I stayed over before. Now is the first time I feel some nerves set in place for tomorrow, what if I end up disappointing Tyler's mother? Tyler might have described me better than he probably should have, which would mean she might not like the fact I know part of Tyler's secret and she may disapprove of me. This is probably natural to feel anxious as you anticipate meeting your other half's family, but still Tyler won't have to go through the stages of approval and having anxiety as an actual condition just intensifies my problems.

I try to quiet my worries when Tyler comes back in the room, his quick eyes will pick up on it with concern otherwise and there's no need to let him know that I'm fretting over something so trivial. He flicks our bedroom light off in one swift motion with his pale skilled, slender pianists fingers and it takes me a moment to get my eyes to adjust to the dark.

His warm hands reach for me within the sea of darkness and I gently press up against his side, letting him embrace me in his protective and secure arms. I let my mind take me to thoughts of the ice skating tomorrow and I relax, allowing my former tension to leave my body as ice skating is familiar and something I've enjoyed for years. I actually have a talent for ice skating, I've attended every class of it I could and therefore I can do all the lifts, dances and any other techniques. I can easily imagine Tyler being an expert on ice, let's face it he can basically do everything. This time though we will be equals, can't let him guide and shield me forever.

"Have you seen 'Dancing on ice', that television programme?" Tyler suddenly asks me and I realise his lovely blue eyes have been focused on me the entire time.
"Yes when I watched that it inspired me to not only learn the skills, but to dance too as it looked so exciting." I answer him and he seems pleased with my dedicated to the subject answer.
"Well it won't just be me showing off tomorrow then," Tyler teases and I smile and roll my eyes, honestly I know my world practically revolves around him but that doesn't mean he should make use of that.
"Afraid not, I do possess my fair share of talents you know." I tease him now and he chuckles quietly near my ear, he enjoys it when I attempt to get my own comments across directed at him seeing as it makes the insults flow and keeps things amusing, we often laugh at some of the ridiculous back chatting talks we've had.
  We don't speak afterwards, I simply run my fingers through the locks of his hair and his eyes hold mine as they always do, shining and sparkling with what I can only guess to be amusement or pleasure. His arms loosen slightly before we both sink into a restful and calming sleep, I see his blue eyes drift shut and his mouth flicks up at the edges into a smile before my eyes close too.

I wake drowsily in the morning, Tyler has gently woken me as I was in his arms it would be impossible for him to move me and get up otherwise. We still have plenty of time until the ice skating at two o'clock so I don't rush to get up. He's ready before me and therefore makes his way downstairs to prepare us some breakfast while I start getting changed for the day. I decide to go for light clothing as then when we go ice skating it will make it easier and Tyler also puts a shirt on. Then I see my white dress, the one I'd danced with Tyler in and seeing as Tyler always somehow manages to dress well and quite smart I may as well do the same for this occasion.

When I come downstairs and enter the kitchen where Tyler already was he turns around and his eyes appraise me.

"You're wearing your dress," he compliments me, a slight look of awe gleamed in his eyes and I smile. As I'd predicted Tyler also looks smart, he 's wearing a white shirt and black trousers and a stunning smile which wins me over every time. I kiss him lightly on the lips before pulling away to sit at the table and join him for breakfast which he's already served.

"Are you looking forward to this afternoon?" Tyler asks and I can hear the excitement tingling in his voice and it quickly becomes tangible because of his enthusiasm which I also share.

"Yes, I really can't wait, it's going to be great!" I exclaim happily as we eat as it's pretty much all I've been thinking about recently. I begin cleaning up my plate whilst wondering what we should do before we would have to set off to go.

"Oh, I forgot to mention we have the rink to ourselves except from one other couple" Tyler tells me cheerily, happy about this fact and I have to admit it is a bonus I wasn't expecting we would get.

"So who's your friend that got this sorted for us?" I ask curiously.

"I'll introduce you to him when we get there," Tyler promises and I'm excited to meet one of his friends.

"Seeing as we can't do this later, I think it's only appropriate we do it now". Tyler spoke softly despite his obvious energy and before I can ask what he means his hands find my waist. I place my hands on his shoulders and then he presses his lips against mine varying from being gentle to a clear desire as they press slightly rougher. He has a point, there is no way we can do this later on the ice rink and then when Tyler's mother shows up so we may as well make the most of our time now.

If you ever imagine how the perfect kiss should be then being with Tyler is like multiplying it by a thousand, he takes me to a different world every time he embraces me. Naturally my hands travel from his shoulders, up his neck and back into his dark brown hair and Tyler gladly accepts, not ready to give up yet. However I don't notice how much time has already passed and when he pulls away from me for a breather we are both surprised that we should start getting ready to go.

I quickly fetch my bags and Tyler collects his keys before we go out the front door and Tyler quickly locks up before we head to the car. He opens the passenger door for me and then walks around the car so he can get in. I relax in the comfortable seat as Tyler puts the wheels in motion and we begin to drive off to the place. Tyler is a skilled driver, so despite how fast the scenery is flashing by the window I know there is nothing to worry about. I watch him carefully, his face is so intent on the road and his hands firmly on the wheel, that is when his eyes flicker in my direction and meet mine.

His mouth twitches up in amusement but he says nothing and I don't want to distract him from the road. We are nearing the place now as much more signs are appearing indicating which way we have to go. Tyler's visibly calmer now that there is a definite chance of getting there on time.

Then as he turns the corner the place is suddenly right in front of us, the building itself looks massive with advertisements for the activities available shown all over it. There's a man waiting outside and when he sees Tyler he waves, so he must be his friend that he was talking about. There are plenty of parking spaces so Tyler quickly pulls into one and parks the car in one swift move.

"Tyler", the man greets him, he's the same height as Tyler but has blond hair which flops slightly into his eyes. Tyler grins and answers with "Daniel", they shake hands and then Daniels' brown eyes appraise me and my hand holding Tyler's.

"You must be Violet Spring", he pronounces in an intrigued voice and a warm smile. His greeting reminds me of how I'd met Tyler as well, the same kind and charming manner.

Chapter Twenty four

After I return the greeting his eyes linger on me for a moment with curiosity, he grins at Tyler and then gestures for us to go with him and enter the building. As Tyler had predicted, all the people inside are waiting to go to the swimming pool and so we quickly dodge around them to get to the ice rink.

"There will be one other couple joining you later on, you can get the skates over there and if you need anything I'll be around" Daniel informs us, gesturing where to go and then he leaves us to get on with it in peace. The skates are black and very nice, probably new and have an elegant shine to them making them look presentable and professional. We quickly slip them on and tie up the laces, then we head off down the rubber path and up to the rink.

Tyler walks onto the ice first, confident and well balanced. He offers me his hand which I accept, but this time do not need. We both start simple, skating slowly away from the edge so we can only support ourselves. However Tyler begins picking up the speed and skating effortlessly across the entire rink, his eyes taunting me to join in the competition. Well I may as well prove myself, I can't let him soak up all the limelight forever.

We both look beautiful and like experts in our fine clothes and as I skate I give him a twirl in my dress before joining him. A smile immediately forms on his lips and he takes my hands in his and we begin to skate together.

"Fancy doing 'Dancing on ice'?" Tyler suggests to me as we glide along.

"Should be interesting as long as you don't drop me" I tell him.

"How could you say such a thing?" Tyler pretends to be offended, but I simply smile to purposefully annoy him.

He places his hands on my waist and stays right behind me as we skate, then I take his arm and twirl underneath it. Both of us however stop as we notice what must be the other couple arrive and join us on the ice with Daniel who assists them before leaving again. They seem to be roughly the same age as us and we both quickly pick up on the fact that they instantly clung to the sides for support. Tyler bites his lip to hide his smirk and then I know he's panning to show off, and show off a great deal as well so now I have to hide my smile.

Tyler whispers in my ear and then bows to me as I curtsey to him. I take his hand and then we begin, we start off with fancy footwork and a few simple dance moves that can easily be performed normally and not only on ice. Then we skate backwards, glide, twirl and finally we're going to do lifts where my trust in Tyler will be very clear.

At first he takes my waist and lifts me up in his arms and I position myself like a star as he skates with me, then he twirls me above his head before he places me down so my legs wrap around his waist to support me as I lie my head back and Tyler spins around, then he grasps my hand and lifts me up so that we spin around together. Me wrapped around his waist, his hands holding mine and we glide together oblivious for a moment of everyone else. Then he gracefully sets me down without interrupting the flow of the movements and we perform a lot of skills that I've seen on 'Dancing on ice', we both must look like professionals. I have no worry about being on the ice, everything feels completely natural and there would have been no need for a rehearsal as we both skate and dance like we do it for a living.
The other couples' awed gasps break the spellbound silence which had captured us in that moment. Tyler from his professional black skates, black trousers and white shirt can only be described as well dressed and handsome and I fit perfectly in his arms with my white dress so we really make a statement, his eyes are bright and pale skin glowing; slightly flushed now from the lifts. I feel the heat in my own cheeks as I smile at him.

When we both look away from each other, the couple seem amazed, Daniel has come back and also appears to be very impressed. Then at the outside of the rink I spot a woman who is probably almost fifty watching us both with curiosity, she's dressed simply and has dark brown hair which stops at her shoulders. She looks at me with evident interest before raising her arm and waving at Tyler, her face open and friendly as she smiles at us across the rink. This must be Tyler's mother, their hair is the same shade of brown and they share the same beautiful blue eyes which sparkle and say as much as their mouth does.
Tyler releases me from his arms and take my hand instead, then we skate over to the woman who now stands with her hands on the side of the barrier which the other couple are clinging to.
"Hello," Tyler greets her instantly, pleased that she is here.

"Hello Tyler," she responds with before looking back at me.

"Mother this is Violet Spring, my partner". Tyler informs her what she clearly already had guessed.

"Violet, this is my mother Emily" Tyler continues for my benefit. It seems to me that Tyler's quite formal when speaking to her.

"Pleased to meet you," I smile and greet her, she also looks very happy about meeting me and responds with the same greeting.

We have almost finished our skating session anyway so we leave early to go spend time with his mother. We say goodbye to Daniel after returning the skates and it feels weird to be wearing normal shoes again now.

As Tyler fumbles around with his car keys Emily turns to me, "So have you also done ice skating before?" she asks, breaking the ice and starting a warm conversation in her open and pleasant voice.

"Yeah, it's one of the only clubs I did do and I really enjoy it." I answer happily and she seems appeased with my answer.

Once Tyler has unlocked the car, I start to go in the back as I expect his mother will want to be in the front with him.

"Oh don't worry Violet, you go in the front. I prefer the back anyway," Emily reassures me, but she seems to appreciate my manners and consideration all the same. I still feel unsure, but for her sake I get in the front next to Tyler who is ready and waiting for me. He clips my seat belt in for me and then starts up the car.

"Would you mind going to a café?" Tyler asks us, thinking of a suggestion for what we should do.

"That's fine," Emily replies, clearly it's the ordinary thing that they do together anyway. I simply nod in agreement, curious to which one we will be going to as there are so many in the area.

We don't talk much as Tyler drives, so I take the chance to look out the window at all the places we pass. It must be close by as we don't pass any fields or go down any different lanes leading off to other places. That is when Tyler pulls the car up and parks outside a small café which doesn't look too busy, but clearly has enough people to create an atmosphere.

When I get out the car Tyler takes my hand and Emily matches our pace to the café. Tyler holds the door open for us and a woman appears gesturing the selection of tables which we can choose from. We decide on one tucked slightly around the corner from everyone else so we can enjoy our own private conversation. Tyler is impossible and constantly being the gentleman by pulling my chair out for me and offering to buy us drinks first.

Once Tyler has got up to get them though it gives Emily a chance to talk to me alone.

"So you're happy with Tyler?" she asks, she seems to be double checking what she's already observed.

"Yes of course, I love him" I tell her, blushing slightly at the end and she smiles.

"I just want to make sure you're both happy, and Tyler's always talking about you when I call him. I quickly picked up on it when you became his assistant," Emily continues, pleased and satisfied with the way things have worked out; at least she seems to approve of me anyway.

Tyler returns and places our glasses down on the table, however he gives me a quick knowing look about the fact that we've been talking about him in his short absence. I simply bite my lip and return a look of 'I'll tell you later' back and he seems glad about that.

"What have you been doing today mother?" Tyler asks, not letting on that he knew we'd been talking about him earlier to her.

"I've just stayed at the house today, this is the first time I've been out for a while actually" she confesses to us and I feel pity that she's mostly alone. I wonder why she and Tyler's father did separate though, I suppose I could always ask him later but it might be a sensitive topic so then again I probably shouldn't ask.

"Have you two got any other plans for this holiday?" she asks both of us and then shares a look with Tyler, implying that he probably means to do something but hasn't actually said it.

However he gives a small shake of his head to her and guessing that I'm not meant to see this exchange, politely look away from them.

When the silence becomes a little too long though because of their face off I answer with, "Well at some point I'm meeting up with Izzie and Jacqueline, also we could meet up with some other people if you have anyone in mind?" I then suggest to Tyler at the end to draw him back into the conversation.

That is when I notice that none of us have touched our drinks, so I begin to quietly sip mine while I wait for Tyler to respond. He pulls his gaze away from his mother and then turns to me, swallowing before answering me. "Yes of course, and it's good that you're meeting up with them as well."

His voice sounds nervous, he's trying to please me whilst keeping guard and a watchful eye on his mother to make sure she doesn't say whatever it is I don't know. I begin to feel nervous myself but Emily simply nods at what we've both said, clearly not prepared to say anything else on the matter which makes me feel that I'm missing out on something big right now.

Well I'm definitely asking Tyler about this later as it seems important and even significant or essential somehow. I don't really fancy being kept in the dark about something, especially if it involves me. It's hard to think though what Tyler and Emily can be thinking about concerning plans that me and Tyler might have for the holidays, why would there be any secrets about something like that? I have to admit that if it hadn't been for Emily dropping herself in on it I would never have guessed that Tyler's hiding something from me, which to be truly honest worries me as I love and trust Tyler so I really hope that I'm getting worked up over nothing so that we can all laugh it off later.

My gut instinct doesn't believe this though, Tyler would never give a reason to get worked up about something and worry me unless it is important and meant to be a big deal. I glance at my watch now, feeling a sudden desire for the day to be at an end and to leave these troubles behind or to at least confront them alone with Tyler later.

He picks up on my unease and distress and also peeks at the time, then downs his drink in one swift moment that if I'd blinked I would have missed altogether. This only leaves Emily to finish her drink before we can even think of making an exit, also there's no doubt in my mind that we're going to have to give her a lift home. It's far too expensive to get a taxi here and back, leaving that as the only option left available.

Tyler looks very close to giving his mother a scowl as it dawns on all of us that as the day has progressed our time together has become more strained and uncomfortable due to unspoken events and thoughts. I want to get to know Emily more, but at this current time I think it would be wise if we part ways and hope for better chances to see each other again. As soon as she goes I need to discuss this with Tyler as I want to make sure everything's out in the open and I want him to understand that I'll support him about whatever as long as he stays honest and open with me, that he can depend on me but it hurts to think he might not completely feel that way anyway.

Emily finishes her drink, observes our tense faces for a moment before rising from her chair indicating it's time to go and it's our cue to get out of here. Emily's going to use the toilet first, meaning me and Tyler have a chance to be on our own.

"We'll be in the car" Tyler says smoothly, showing that he doesn't have the patience to hang around here any longer despite the fact that it could come across as being rude. She simply nods and we leave her, not bothering to hesitate or hang back first with any behind glance; we simply bolt for the car which was waiting for us.

Relief washes over me like a crashing wave when we get into Tyler's car and are away from Emilys' watchful eyes and the confrontational atmosphere, now I think I know why Tyler's so polite and mature around his mother.

Tyler lets out a long sigh, "I do love my mother but she doesn't half give me a hard time."

Well he's got that right, I want to know how we're meant to get through a whole car journey with her first though.

Tyler quickly seizes the opportunity now that Emily has gone to ask me about earlier.

"When I went to get the drinks, I'm guessing she said something about me?" Tyler assumes eager and a little annoyed in case he'd find what she had said irritating.

"She just asked if we were happy and said that you told her a lot about me over the phone when I became your assistant" I answer truthfully, watching his face so I can witness his reaction.

"Well that's true, but isn't it obvious that we're happy together? She arrived when we were dancing for goodness sake!"

Tyler sounds exasperated and I can only agree with him as how much convincing does someone need, Michael had picked up on it immediately so whatever I've been doing must be impossibly obvious.

I start leafing through Tyler's CD collection so that the music will hide the fact that there's an awkward atmosphere when Emily returns. If music's on then that's an excuse to getting away with having nothing to say to her. Tyler has a huge variety of CDs so I'm lost for which albums I should pick, Tyler is smiling when I look up clearly enjoying the fact that there is so much choice available. I smile too, but I'm not going to let that beat me; I intend to pick a nice album to listen to seeing as I'd discovered earlier it's an hour drive to Emily's.

When I consider giving up though, I stumble across one of my most favourite albums ever. Tyler has 'The very best of Keane', and there's no way I'm going to miss out on an opportunity like that. I caress the case softly with my fingers and then slip it out of the collection so Tyler can see what I've chosen, before Emily comes back.

Chapter Twenty five

He isn't at all surprised, I'd listened to Keane before but he seems to appreciate what I've chosen for us anyway. When Emily gets in she notices the relaxed environment we've created in her absence, hopefully she will go along with it and not ask any questions which will annoy Tyler.

We are off on the road within a matter of seconds and instead of immediately looking out the window my gaze rests on Tyler who is relaxing to the music already. His blue eyes are fixed on the road ahead, his pale cream face show no hints of a frown any longer and his lips no longer press into a line but are set slightly open. He has undone the first few buttons of his shirt, obviously feeling the heat as his arms also look slightly flushed and pink. He must have sensed my eyes on his face and so looks up to meet them with a small, smooth smile, his lips twitching upwards. My lips also curve up into a smile and he lifts me out of my previous mood with ease.

So afterwards he keeps one hand on the wheel and the other holds mine as his eyes focus ahead again on the road. It's only when I notice that we've already gone through half the album we will almost be there and we can drop Emily off at her home. The sun isn't as high in the sky any more, but by the time we get there and back it shouldn't be dark.

"Have you had a good day out?" Tyler asks his mother in an attempt to at least leave the day on a good note with her.

"Yes, it's been very interesting as well" she replies, which implies there is more to be said but she holds her tongue which is probably wise.

"I think it's been a good day, and it's nice to have finally met you Emily," I say to her in my own attempt to brighten the mood and make sure that I come across to her in a good light. Still, doesn't mean I didn't find it hard to talk to someone even Tyler finds difficult to deal with and so uses formality to get around it.

"Yes, I've been looking forward to meeting you for a while. Tyler's said so much about you, so naturally I've been curious."

She spoke in a voice that makes me unsure if I've passed her expectations or not.

I squeeze and hold Tyler's hand a little harder so I can release my anxiety and be comforted by his warm touch. He clutches my hand firmly for a moment and then takes his back placing it onto the wheel, however before I can feel rejected his eyes flicker to the window and I realise that we have stopped outside a fairly big house. Tyler gets out of the car so he can go and help Emily.

"Well it's been nice meeting you Violet," she tells me and holds my gaze.

"Yes, I hope to see you again some time" I tell her, not overly convinced if this is true or not but I'm not going to let it show on my face.

Tyler opens her door and then walks her up to the house, only once she is inside does he turn around and begin heading back to me. The relief on his face can't be disguised or described, I feel a wave of sympathy for him as clearly he's struggled through parts of today but at least the ice skating has been enjoyable. He gets in next to me again and simply grins, pleased that now we can be spending our time only with each other, I'll ask my questions for him later when we get home but for now let's just enjoy our privacy.

The drive back seems to go a lot faster as me and Tyler simply talk and discuss everything until there's nothing else left to say. We've gotten back to the house at a good and reasonable time, however as neither of us can be bothered to cook we raid everything in the cupboards to have snacks instead of a proper meal. We don't bother with the table either and so sink into the sofa in the living room to eat side by side. Now might be a good time to broach the topics I'd wanted to discuss earlier on with him.

"Tyler," I say to make sure I definitely have his full attention seeing as I want an answer to these questions, and therefore must show him that I'm being serious. He looks at me instantly, probably hearing the edge in my voice and waits quietly and patiently for me to continue.

"When we were at the café earlier, something seemed to be going on between you and your mother about plans for the holidays. I just wanted to know if you'd tell me what it was, if there was a problem or something," I query with him, desperate for him to explain it to me and tell the truth.

He remains silent for a moment, hesitant as well would have described his immediate response to what I'd said to him just now.

"I think she was referring to when I'm planning on telling you the full story about my past, and what happened on that particular shift one night."

He spoke softly but in a quiet and almost authoritative voice. I hold my breath slightly as this is something I'd wanted to know practically since day one, however I've never wanted to force Tyler into telling me until he's ready.

"Have you decided when you'll feel comfortable about telling me?" I ask gently, trying to be sensitive for him.

"I think it's gone on long enough and I'll never really want to say it but it would be unfair if I don't say and in some ways I do want to tell you. You're the only person I'll ever want to know about it so I've decided to tell you now, if that's OK?" he tells me, preparing himself.

In answer to his question I say "That's OK, I'm ready to hear it."

He takes a few deep breaths, and his eyes will no longer look at me whilst his fingers keep interlocking with each other and twisting and I notice the palms of his hands already appear to have small beads of sweat forming on them. He begins chewing his lip slightly and then he sits forward and up straight, positioning himself in a more presentable manner to indicate the significance and severity of what he's about to say before raising his head slightly higher and then the secret I've never known begins to slowly spill through his lips.

"As you know, I used to be a security guard working at very important paces which needed protecting at all times. So this particular shift was at night," he pauses for a moment before continuing, "I was in a team that night so two of us would patrol around the place whilst the others stand by all the doors and ways of entrance."His voice drops a little lower now.

"I was well respected and a second in command."

This surprises me as I hadn't realised how high up he was in his job.

"That night me and someone who was my junior were the ones patrolling the grounds of a very important place, some of the items inside probably cost millions."

I listen in awe, not daring to make a single interruption.

"That was when we spotted a couple of some sorts trying to break in by climbing over the gates leading up to the main building."

Tyler's eyes show that he's reliving that night as he speaks about it.

"Naturally we rushed over to confront them, understanding that we'd probably have to use force," his voice holds an edge to it now.

"However they had more weapons than I could possibly have anticipated, before we could say anything I had one man down and I'd also been injured."

I hold my breath at this and he visibly flinches as he talks about it.

"That left me to deal with the situation alone, with no help and it was my hand that I'd held the gun in they'd managed to damage."

He gently flexes the fingers of his right hand which makes me suddenly understand why sometimes he has great difficulty writing for long periods of time.

"I managed to call my team for back up and set off the loudest alarm I had on me at the time, we had personal alarms for emergencies you see" he elaborates to me after noting my confusion.

"They tried again to get a decent shot at me, but luckily I had my protective vest on along with other protective gear."

Tyler looks discomforted by his last words and I simply feel horrified.

"If it wasn't for my team arriving at the last minute, there was no way they would've been caught and I would've been alive."

His voice openly shakes now and I take his trembling hand in mine.

"They managed to get them arrested and kept for questioning whilst me and my other man were taken away in an ambulance."

He takes a deep breath before continuing, "It was too late for him though but it didn't take too long to fix up me, well physically anyway I don't think my mind will ever heal."

I wait patiently, still in disbelief about what had happened to him.

"When I was well enough I returned to state everything that happened and be there for the questioning."

A hint of determination and fierceness enters his voice now.

"I won't deny I was eager for revenge for myself and my friend who died, I wanted to know what they had to say and how long their prison sentence would be."

I feel a deep sense of understanding at this, due to my own personal experiences.

"It turned out that they openly admitted everything, what they hoped to achieve and why."

Surprise washes through me at this, why would they admit everything?

"The case turned out to be one of the worst we've had and so they were given a life sentence and so can never get out of prison for their whole life times. However because of the depth and harshness of the case none of this was released to the public" Tyler informs me and that last part makes me wonder how they got away with that.

"As my friend was murdered and me injured it wasn't hard to make up a murderer for the media and cover up the truth of who they really were and what happened. This was necessary for a number of reasons and so we made it that this fake had killed the couple who was responsible in the first place due to a request they made which we carried out for them".

Now I feel compelled to interrupt him, "What was their request?" I ask.

"The couple had a daughter who believed her father to be dead as after a previous failure at stealing he'd been locked up. For her sake he didn't want her to know about it and so her mother pretended for him that he'd been murdered the night he was locked away."

I hold my breath as he continues, "So when he got out and reunited with his wife that was when they shot me and my friend."

"So when they both knew they were being locked away for life, a request was made that a fake person killed them both at different times to match their previous lies to their daughter, who they wanted to protect from the truth so she could live her life not knowing her parents crimes, but believing them to be dead."

Tyler draws a few deep breaths and sips his drink before finishing off his story.

"That's why it didn't get out to the public and everyone believes this nobody killed that couple so that when their daughter was questioned she had no idea of the truth leaving her unaware of what really happened that day."

I sit quietly and consider what he's said.

"So although it's a hassle to make fake news over the media and not be able to provide answers to their daughter, I just feel sorry for her above anything else as she believes her parents to have been murdered by the same fake and is suffering due to her parents' meaningless actions which will affect her deeply, despite the fact she doesn't even know the full story".

Tyler sighs, looking angry and sad about his story and I pity him for his past, injuries and the way it affects him to this day. Even though I don't know them I resent the couple because of what they've done to Tyler which has resulted in him quitting his job and their poor daughter left in the dark about a crime that she has no knowledge of. The only thing that I do at least half respect is that they wanted to protect her and not make her life even more disrupted than it probably already is.

"Although I'm really sorry about your past, I'm so glad that you moved to the school because otherwise I'd never of met you" I tell him truthfully in a quiet voice. I don't want to upset him as that night had ruined part of his life and cast a shadow of pain over him which usually he hides very well but I can help him with now. Finally his gorgeous blue eyes which are glistening with emotion look up and meet mine, I can't believe that after losing a friend before his eyes and nearly getting killed himself he has managed to hide away his pain from everyone. From now on I can support him and give him all the help he needs, he doesn't need to hide and pretend for me.

"You know that I'll keep your secret, and that you can rely on me" I say gently to him and then he embraces me in his arms and my hands hold his shirt and his shoulder.

"I love you Violet," he whispers in my ear and presses his face against mine and we cling to each other.

I kiss him on the cheek and take his hand in mine, "Come on, you should probably get some rest as it's already pretty late" I try to convince him as he looks tired out from the stressful elements in the day which are clearly taking their toll on him.

I lead him up the stairs and into the bedroom so he can get ready for bed and I can go in the bathroom. Some parts of Tyler's story make me feel like I'm missing out on something and all I can think of is that it's vital, however I can't put my finger on why I should feel this way because obviously I resent the couple for doing this to Tyler as it has devastated his life. Also to think he was so close to losing his life that day makes me shiver and have fearful chills just thinking about it. Yet there's something more, something that's nagging me about certain things he said but I really shouldn't look into it too much and I don't want to make Tyler relive those awful memories any more than is absolutely necessary.

Trying to push aside my worries and negative thoughts I finish brushing my teeth and rejoin Tyler in the bedroom who's already used one of the en suites so he turns off the light as I climb into bed and he quickly joins me despite the fact that neither of our eyes have adjusted to the sudden darkness yet.

"Are you OK?" I ask him softly, worried that it might have been too soon for him to admit that horrific night to me, that he might be feeling overwhelmed by everything that has happened today.

"I'll be all right, after all I have you now and I never need to worry about the fact that you don't know any more as you share my secret now." He answers quietly in a calm voice, however I decide it would be best to speak of it no more. I press up against him, to reassure and comfort him and let his worries fade away into the night and hopefully be put behind him.

Chapter Twenty six

Over the next few days neither of us mention anything about Tyler's past, but I have no doubt in my mind that that's what we're both thinking about and the nagging feeling of something wrong refuses to fade away. My worries for Tyler have deepened as I'll be going out with Jacqueline and Izzie today to do our shopping trip and have a sleepover at Jacqueline's house afterwards. That means Tyler will be on his own for quite a while and despite the fact that he's said he is fine I am monitoring his behaviour carefully.

Tyler's going to give me a lift there and will be picking me up from Jacqueline's house tomorrow. He's wearing blue jeans and a white shirt and is putting my bags in the car before we are ready to go.

His blue eyes meet my green ones, he knows I'm concerned and his eyes implore me 'Don't worry I'll be fine' but the only words that leave his soft lips are, "Are you ready for me to take you now?" in his usual charming and pleasant voice.

"Yeah, I suppose" I say and get in the passenger side of the car whilst he holds the door open for me.

When he begins driving I turn to him, "Will you promise me that you'll be OK whilst I'm gone?" I ask him desperate and fearful of having him out of my sight.

He smiles at me, "Of course I'll be OK, don't worry and enjoy your day. I'll probably start unpacking your stuff so it's part of the home," he tells me and I calm down a bit, at least he's made plans and will be at home which gives me more peace of mind by a lot. I hold his warm hand in mine as he drives down the twisted lanes which lead to Jacqueline's house.

"It will be nice to see them both again, and find out how everything's going on with Michael" I voice my thoughts as Tyler pulls into a spot outside a normal sized house which must be Jacqueline's.

"Yes, please do update me on the situation when you get back" Tyler grins and we get out of the car.

Hand in hand we walk up to the door and press the doorbell which rings out instantly and we both hear them rushing to the door. When the door opens we're greeted by their cheery smiles and welcoming 'hello's. Izzie isn't at all surprised to see me with Tyler, but Jacqueline's still getting used to having her suspicions confirmed.

"I'll see you tomorrow then Violet," Tyler says gently to me.

"Yeah, have a good day" I tell him, looking him in the eye to remind him of his promise. In answer he gently kisses me on the lips in front of them both before pulling away grinning, handing me my bags and heading off to the car. We all wave him off until the car has gone out of view.

"Come inside then, we'll take your stuff upstairs and show you the room we'll all be in" Jacqueline smiles and then closes the door behind me. Her house is fairly modern but still manages to have a homely feel to it and I warm to the place quickly. The room we are all staying in has to be the biggest one upstairs and Izzie has already claimed one of the beds leaving me to put my bag down on the other one.

"So where exactly are we going shopping?" I ask them, picking up on the excitement that is hanging in the air.

"It's a place nearby where there's clothes shops, jewellery and all sorts of accessories to get!" Izzie grins, ready to go out and blast her money now.

Jacqueline has gone downstairs to get the car ready so I seize my chance to talk to Izzie alone.

"How's everything going with Michael?" I ask her as that's our secret only between me, her and Tyler.

She smiles and even blushes slightly due to embarrassment, "We've been meeting up and I've stayed over at his place for a couple of nights" she admits happily to me.

I have to admit that surprises me, I hadn't seen that one coming.

"You've stayed over at his!" I exclaim and then we both start giggling like a couple of schoolgirls and then decide to hurry up so that we won't be keeping Jacqueline waiting.

It's a short drive before we end up in the towns' centre, like Izzie had said there is a wide range of shops with different accessories on offer. Our strategy is to look for clothes first and see if we can find anything extra to match afterwards. Izzie and Jacqueline who definitely have the most experience with where to go lead me around to all the most stylish but still affordable places in the area. We try on tops, skirts and dresses for the majority of the day whilst offering advice on each other's choices and personal style.

It turns out that we all buy tops and dresses, however Izzie is debating whether or not to get a skirt as well even though it isn't in the sale and is therefore much more expensive. However when I advise her to dress to impress Izzie catches onto my secret hint and quickly purchases it from a man that has been watching us with curiosity for a while. So as a joke we try to get him interested in Jacqueline as although she doesn't know it she's basically the only single one of us and available anyway. She blushes, makes a swift exit and we are right behind her on the way out.

"Oh my goodness, look at how much time's gone by since we started!" Jacqueline exclaims in such a posh voice that me and Izzie crack up and imitate her. She rolls her eyes at us, unimpressed but she too is trying not to laugh about it.

"Should we check out a few jewellery shops before we go?" I ask as I'm desperate to see what's on sale. They all seem up for it so we go to the cheaper shops first but it's a fruitless effort and so we decide to have a look at the real jewellery that you can only dream of ever getting.

Me and Izzie are looking at the most breathtaking rings I've ever seen in my life, the prices of them naturally are the highest in the whole shop. Jacqueline is also left mesmerised but has her heart more set on some of the necklaces on display. Izzie however succeeds in pulling us away and breaking us out of the almost hypnotic spell that had struck us back there.

It doesn't take long to track down the car and load it with our purchases. I get in the back so that I can check my phone discreetly and see if Tyler has left any messages yet for me. The only one he's sent is 'Have a good day and I'll be missing you', which makes me smile, I'll call him later before we go to bed.

"So will we be making dinner or ordering it?" I quiz them whilst waiting for my phone to turn off and then put it back in my bag.

"Honestly, do you really need to ask that? Of course we'll be ordering it, it's a sleepover after all!" Izzie mockingly tuts at me whilst Jacqueline simply smirks and shakes her head in fake disapproval at the both of us.

"Do you think I should order pizza?" Jacqueline suggests now, not taking her eyes off of the road.

"Sounds good" I say and Izzie agrees so at least we have a plan for later. My thoughts are trailing off to Tyler despite my best efforts, I wonder what he's doing right now and how he's coping being at home alone. It's also going to be weird to go back and have my stuff out around his house which I now also live in. The feeling of something missing keeps returning whenever I think about Tyler and his past, the fact is though nothing was missing from his story and so I can't understand why I feel that way about it. However something sounded naggingly familiar and it's eating away at me but I can't place what part it is for a start.

Izzie has noticed my distraction and we share one of those 'Tell me later' looks. However I can't tell her later without giving away the fact that I know Tyler's past now, so I'm in a bit of a dilemma. We arrive at Jacqueline's house fairly quickly and so we begin unpacking our shopping bags from the car and upstairs into the room we'll all be staying in. When Jacqueline announces that she'll be ringing up a pizza place we write down our orders and then Izzie seizes our chance to be alone together.
"What's up?" she questions me, looking slightly concerned. I can tell both our thoughts have flickered to Tyler as she noticed earlier my reluctance to let him go and our goodbye, even though we'd only have to wait till tomorrow to see each other again anyway.
"I'm worried about leaving Tyler alone" I sigh, my concern clear on my face and in my eyes.
"Why, what's happened?" she asks me, obviously wanting to get to the bottom of this as she knows how much I love him and he's her friend too. I hesitate for a moment, unsure but I need to talk to someone about it and Izzie's my best friend.

"A couple of days ago me and Tyler went ice skating, and we met his mother there. Afterwards though because of stuff that happened he finally told me about his past.." I trail off slightly, uncertain about how much I should say. "He was really shaken about it and I'm nervous about me not being there for him at the moment," I admit to her frowning whilst thinking about him. Izzie pauses for a moment, thinking about what I've just said carefully.
"I can understand that, but there's something more here. What about you, how do you feel about it?"
I'm surprised she noticed that it's an even bigger deal than I'd tried to let on. "There's something that just doesn't seem right to me, I can't put my finger on it but there's something familiar about what he said and it's really nagging me," I sigh slightly "but I'm not mentioning it to him as he's in enough of a state anyway" I finish, glad to have told somebody.

She doesn't know how to respond to that but I can see that she looks troubled and confused by what I've said.

"How can you feel a similarity about his past?" she finally asks me muddled by the situation and I shrug. I know there is something though, his story about the girl and the couple cling to my mind and is refusing to let go.

I have the feeling that it's something disturbing though, something I don't want to know and that's what has put me off trying to figure it out so far. I can't put it off forever though, if it's really vital then I should probably start figuring it out soon and stop delaying what must be done. For now though I can distract myself by being with Izzie and Jacqueline.

Jacqueline has joined us again, telling us the pizza is on its way here. This thankfully leads to much lighter topics of conversation which I gladly accept. So not long later the doorbell rings and Jacqueline gets up and rushes to the door whilst we clear the table before sitting down.

"Well dig in everyone, it's arrived" she announces, placing them on the table and sitting opposite me as Izzie has already claimed the seat next to me. As we eat I mostly stay silent and listened to their conversation so I can get away with not thinking about much and just enjoy the quiet. They are talking about nothing in particular when Michael suddenly gets brought into the conversation by Jacqueline which makes me regain my attention to see what Izzie is saying.

I quickly pick up on the fact that Jacqueline has pointed out that Izzie and him are pretty close, this makes me wonder if she's beginning to guess her secret as Izzie sits there not making eye contact with anyone.

"You've made up a lot after what happened on the trip," Jacqueline observes and I bite my lip, forcing myself to hold my tongue so Izzie will have to respond.

"We are getting on better now, so I suppose we are quite close" she hedges, trying to dodge around what Jacqueline has really implied.

I shoot her a look which says 'You're going to have to tell her eventually' and she returns it with an inward sigh.

However Jacqueline picks up on our exchange and understands that more is going on than anyone's actually willing to say.

"More is happening than what meets the eye here isn't it?" she asks, already knowing what her answer will be. I don't say anything as I know how it'd felt when everyone was guessing about me and Tyler before I'd hardly found out myself, it's Izzie's place to decide whether Jacqueline should know yet or not. Izzie gives a small shake of her head so I remain silent and Jacqueline accepts this by asking no further questions.

The time is passing quickly as we watch a number of DVDs and TV programmes when we get bored. We all head upstairs and change into our pyjamas in different rooms of the house, before finally getting ready to go to bed. None of us have any intention of getting any sleep though considering it's called a sleepover everyone does the opposite, usually seeing who can stay awake the longest. I grab my phone so I can call Tyler before going to bed and check up on how he's doing.

Unsurprisingly he picks up on the first ring, his voice instantly greeting me. The fact that he's glad I'm calling is evident by the relief that can be heard in his voice.

"Violet" he gently breathes out my name and I smile simply at hearing his voice as if he's near my ear.

"Have you had a good day?" I address him, hoping that he's coped all right as I've missed him even with having distractions throughout the day.

"It's been long and tiring sorting out all your possessions I'll admit, but I've finished because I went to your flat and collected all the remaining items so all you have to do is hand your keys in and sell it" Tyler tells me, he really must have had a long day to achieve all of that.

We chat for a little longer before ending the call as Izzie and Jacqueline have come back as they'd been giving us some privacy before. At least Tyler's OK and will be picking me up tomorrow, I see the pair of them smiling and shaking their heads about the call.

"What?" I ask them and Izzie simply giggles.

"It's just the fact that now I know you're together and it makes me think of all those times I should have guessed months ago," Jacqueline is also laughing about it. Especially as it's not always allowed to have a relationship with the person you work with.

We are all in bed now and conversation turns to the fact that I'm the only one who isn't single and I'm the youngest. I smirk at Izzie, wondering if she is going to drop herself in on the secret about Michael. She looks unsure whether she should say anything or not.

"Oh something is going on here that I don't know about isn't it?" Jacqueline half asks, half whines at the pair of us.

I smile, "It's about Izzie, not me" I say and Jacqueline instantly turns to her.

"Are you with somebody and haven't told me?" she continues making Izzie scowl in annoyance.

"Sort of" she reveals and then refuses to admit to anything else so we turn the light off to try and actually get some sleep considering it's already the morning now.

Chapter Twenty seven

We all wake early to get up and ready, me and Izzie shove everything into the bags we've taken with us before getting sorted in the bathroom whilst Jacqueline who doesn't need to rush prepares breakfast. I decide to wear one of the new tops I bought yesterday with a dark blue skirt I've only worn once before last summer. I make small plaits in Izzie's hair and she straightens mine to perfection with her straighteners before she packs them away.

Apart from some lip gloss I haven't put any make up on but I use that as an excuse to dominate the mirror afterwards.

"Are you seeing Michael today?" I ask seeing as it seems like she's dressing to impress.

"How did you know?" she replies in astonishment, unaware of how obvious it would be to anyone who saw her and knew the secret.

"Glamorous much,"I say, gesturing at her and she simply blushes not bothering to deny it.

We join Jacqueline downstairs and put our bags near the door for when we will be going. I eat quickly wondering when Tyler will arrive, I can't wait to see him again; even though we've hardly been apart I've still missed him a lot. Then I remember that I hadn't seen Izzie's car outside, meaning she'll be getting a lift. Is she really daring to get a lift with Michael from here? Then I notice she's picked up on the fact that I've figured it out and seen through her plan, she mouths the words "Don't say anything" to me so that I won't give it away to Jacqueline who is oblivious to our private conversation.

I bite my lip to hide the smile which is fighting its way onto my face, Izzie will kill me if I give it away but how she's going to get picked up without Jacqueline seeing I don't know.

The doorbell rings then and me and Izzie leap up to fight towards the door and see whose guy it is there waiting. We both stop in surprise though, both our hearts momentarily faltering as we open the door. Michael and Tyler are standing side by side, Tyler wearing jeans and a light blue shirt which has the first few buttons undone which leaves me gaping at his perfectness. Michael is wearing black trousers and a white shirt, Tyler's blue eyes meet mine and a flawless smile spreads across his face and Izzie and Michael blush and grin when they see each other.

We all rush towards our partners, Tyler taking me in his arms and I hold him to me and we kiss each other in the process. Michael and Izzie smirk, but don't repeat our greeting as it would be embarrassing and plus Jacqueline is on her way over. Surprise washes over her face to see us all there greeting each other, especially when she registers Michael standing next to Tyler, the pair of them grinning as they hold our hands. She isn't surprised to see Tyler though, after greeting them both we collect our bags and say goodbye to Jacqueline, she doesn't ask but watches Izzie go and get into Michael's car.

Tyler takes my bags and puts them in the boot of the car whilst I get in, glad to be back with him. He climbs in and I take in the sight of him, he looks well and rested which I'm pleased about as I really had worried about him and if he'd be OK in my absence.

"Did you have a good time?" he questions me as he puts the radio on and the wheels in motion.

I smile, "Yeah we all managed to buy some clothes and accessories" I tell him and he smiles in response.

"So what you're wearing now is new?" he asks, his eyes appraising my outfit.

"The top is, but I got the skirt a while ago."

He seems surprised but doesn't question the fact that he's never seen me wear it before.

"So how did it go, sorting out my possessions?" I query, intrigued to hear how he managed to get everything sorted and from my flat as well.

"It took me quite a long time, but I've got all your belongings out and around the house" he announces to me and I can tell he feels proud of himself as he says it. It will be weird selling my flat as I haven't really had it for that long but obviously it's something that has to be done and it would be silly to keep it when I live with Tyler now anyway. Also it'll be helpful to get the money for it and no longer have to be paying its bills.

We arrive quickly and it feels nice to be back home with Tyler. Now I get to see where he has put everything in the house and if it all fits in nicely with the rooms. I get my bags from the car and go inside, eager to find where he has put everything, some things are noticeable such as my ornaments whereas my books or photo albums are placed neatly in different places.

"So were you OK, without me?" I ask him, turning to face him realising that he has been watching me.

"I'm fine, actually. I'm more worried about you" he answers me, completely serious.

"You're worried about me?" I ask in surprise, it wasn't me that had suffered a near death experience.

"Ever since I told you about my past, you've acted differently, like something's not right."

He's said exactly what I've been thinking, he really never does fail to pick up on everything. He waits patiently for me to answer him, but I am able to see the panic and worry in his eyes.

"I feel like I'm missing out on something big, something obvious but I can't figure out what it is. All I know is that there's something familiar about what you said." As I speak I see that my words unsettle him.

"Why would you feel familiarity with a past like mine?" Tyler asks, his voice sounds on edge and slightly tense. In that one moment Tyler has phrased the question in such a way that the pieces of the puzzle fall together. It isn't exactly his past that's familiar, but the person mentioned in his past, someone he has never met for safety precautions. The girl, the young daughter in his story of the couple who had committed those crimes. It's about her and it's vital, the similarities between her story and mine; there are too many which is very disconcerting and is making me think of something I really wish I hadn't, but the more I think about it the truer it seems.

I feel the blood leave my face rapidly and Tyler quickly draws me to him.

"The girl in your story, she believes her parents were killed by the same person at different times and doesn't know the truth doesn't she?" I ask him in a weak voice, beginning to feel light headed. I feel the surprise ripple through him at my question.

"Yes, but what's that got to do with it?" he quizzes me, confused.

"Tell me about her", I beg him, urgency seeping into my voice.

"I've already told you everything I know" he seems unsure why it's so important.

So I'm groping at the last straw I have left now, "What was the name of the killer you created, the fake?" I whisper as I try to stay conscious.

"Andrew Woods." Tyler said the name I'd been expecting to hear, the name I've loathed for so long now and only to find out that none of it was true.

I don't lose consciousness but I feel myself slowly sink to the floor and momentarily lose my eyesight and hearing. When I regain my senses it takes me a few seconds to realise that Tyler has me in his arms on the floor. He's repeating my name in panic so when I manage to open my eyes properly and weakly hold onto him I feel the relief and confusion coming off him in waves.

"What's the matter, what's wrong?" Tyler is asking me, desperate to make sure I'm OK and confused to what brought on the incident in the first place.

I let him support me and pull me up off the floor, but he refuses to let go of me in case I haven't recovered and I'm still unstable.

"The girl that you thought you'd never met is me" I tell him in a strangely calm voice, the words not sounding like they belong to me. He freezes for a moment, neither one of us breaking the tense silence.

"How can that be?" he asks in a voice that implies he is in pain.

"We have the same days off in the year, I'm the one who keeps trying to find out any information I can on the case, the one who believed my father died years ago and then my mother too. I've been living a lie without realising it," I murmur to him quietly.

Tears stream down my face as I realise that Tyler's the man I was never allowed to speak to, I'd been made to believe my parents were dead. How can I honestly cope now I know that we share a different version of the same past, I've fallen in love with the man who I thought had helped heal me from my past but who has actually torn it back to the surface.

We spend the next few days weary of one another, hardly speaking, frightened of the truth and what the other might do. I feel guilty whenever I see Tyler's dejected face, we have both caught the other crying on numerous occasions. My feelings have changed dramatically though since I first found out. I've always loved my parents, thought they were good people but now I can't help resent them. They've let me believe they were dead, they've committed crimes, killed Tyler's friend, tried to kill him and have ended up devastating both of our lives and leaving us damaged. Tyler thinks I'm blaming him, but really I've wanted space as I've had to deal with the biggest betrayal you could ever know from people you'd never expect it from. I just can't believe my parents, the people I've always respected are the people who've ruined mine and Tyler's lives, who have caused us to suffer and panic more than others and lose the people closest to us.

I spot Tyler on the bench in the garden, he looks like the most unhappy person in the world and I can't bear to see him like that when it's neither of our fault and both of our sufferings should be finally put to an end. I walk outside quietly so he won't hear my approach, only when I sit beside him does he notice that I'm there. He won't look at me at first and I feel ashamed for making him suffer for so long but I take his hand in my trembling one. He holds it tightly and slowly looks up to meet my gaze.

"Violet, if I'd known-" Tyler begins but I cut him off.

"Don't blame yourself, you did nothing wrong, I just needed space to deal with it" I confide in him truthfully and he looks like he's about to say something and then decides against it and stays quiet. I let him hold me in his arms and I hold onto him firmly, I'm not going to let him go.

"So what do you think we should do about it?" Tyler asks me eventually.

"There's not much we can do" I admit to him, however I do have an idea. I just hope Tyler agrees as I can't do it by myself.

"I do have an idea though that I think is necessary to help us leave the past behind and never go back to it again," I state in an unsure voice as I don't know how Tyler's going to react to this. His eyes flick up to meet mine, cautious and yet eager; we want to leave this behind us.

"I want to go see them, my parents so they know what they've done and I want to know why they did it. I'm not going without you though," I voice my idea and as I expected he looks very nervous.

However I don't expect his next words, "Fine I'll go with you, but for obvious reasons Violet I hate them." His voice is harsh and unforgiving.

"That's the reason I'm going, they ruined our lives" I say, I can feel the anger on the tip of my tongue. Tyler nods, so we're in agreement then, thank goodness for that.

"I don't know about you, but I'd rather get this out of the way now if possible" Tyler decides and I have to agree, the sooner we can leave everything behind the better. Tyler whips his mobile out of his pocket ready to make any calls which will guarantee our entry. He speaks in a fast voice to someone explaining that we want access to see them now, when he gets off the phone he nods at me and we go inside to get the car keys.

I glance at my watch, we have plenty of the day left to do this so it doesn't matter how long it takes.

Tyler pauses for a moment, "Do you think I need to wear my uniform?" he asks me. He has a good point, it could help us enter and make him recognisable.

"Yeah probably, you won't have to show any ID at least" I tell him.

"That's in my uniform anyway, I'll just put the shirt and jacket on" he says before going upstairs and I head outside to the car.

Nerves flow through me now, in many ways I really don't want to do this, but me and Tyler are going through this together and I'll gain strength from that. As I watch him walk out the door and look up my heart aches, it's unbearable to think I'd never have met him if my parents had managed to do to him what they did to his friend that day. I don't know how he's managed to keep his face calm and his hands steady, I'm completely shaking and I'm failing at hiding that fact. As we start driving one of his hands grab mine for reassurance and I feel the chill of sweat as his slippery hand firmly holds mine.

It has taken us an hour before signs for the prison even come in sight. Once we arrive though we have many routes to drive down before the main gates loom ahead with two guards waiting on either side of them. Tyler stops, confirms our phone call and we drive through and park in the nearly empty car park which makes me feel isolated from everything I've ever known simply by being here. We both take deep breaths and then let go of each other's hands to get out the car.

Tyler leads me inside and down quite a few corridors before there are a few men wearing the same uniform as Tyler ahead of us. One man's eyes widen in surprise at our approach.

"Tyler!" he exclaims, unable to contain himself.

"Ralph" Tyler greets him and shakes his hand, it's evident that nobody thought Tyler would ever return to this place. Ralph's eyes observe me with interest for a couple of seconds before nodding in understanding and pulling a set of keys out of his pocket.

We follow him down one final corridor before there is a barred gate which is from the ceiling to the floor and room length to guarantee maximum security.

"The last cell on the left hand side" Ralph informs us quietly as he unlocks the main gate. As we enter I notice there is a white stripe along the floor, it is to prevent you from getting too close to the cells for obvious safety reasons.

Tyler takes my hand in his again and we slowly make our way down, as we walk past everyone I don't dare to meet the eyes of the other criminals. However I sense their eyes burn into me and Tyler wraps his arm around me instead detecting my extreme fear and discomfort. We pause before the last cell, Tyler shares a look with me, checking I'm going to be OK with this. As it was my idea in the first place I am definitely going to go through with it, and Tyler's hatred fuels me to go forwards with him by my side.

"You can do this" Tyler whispers and then we take the last few steps forward and we turn to face the people who have changed everything.

Chapter Twenty eight

At first I simply stare at the people I'd once called my parents, they don't look up obviously not expecting us to be anyone other than the usual security guards. The first time I'd seen my father in years and my mother for months, I feel no sympathy for these people and know in my heart I'll miss them no longer. Tyler's blue eyes look like they have flames within them, his other hand clenches into a fist and his posture is unnaturally straight, he holds his head high above them. Finally their familiar faces look up and their eyes rest on me and Tyler, and when they notice us they appear to be in a daze and in shock at the sight of us.

"Violet" they say my name in unison, disbelief showing on their faces at the fact I'm here. I don't reply to either of them and they quickly realise why. To be here means I know everything about what they did, of course I wouldn't be happy to see them, they just don't know to what extent. They look at Tyler now, I can see a mix of shame and embarrassment coming from them but I detect no signs of regret which makes me so angry I have to grit my teeth together to prevent me from hurling all sorts of insults at them. They also note his arm around me, Tyler simply glares at them and refuses to speak.

"Why did you do it, what were you trying to achieve?" I demand of them in a cold, unforgiving voice. My parents know I've always been one to give mercy but there is no trace of it now to be detected. They don't even try to beg me first, they know it's best to just come out and say it.

"We were in unbelievable debt, and needed to get the money from somewhere" they admit, knowing it is no excuse for what they've done.

"So you ended up killing an innocent man and nearly another" I say in disgust and Tyler openly flinches.

"We needed that money or you have no idea what would have happened to us, it got so bad we were prepared to do anything. We wanted to protect you Violet" my father claims.

"Don't spout that crap to me, you let me believe you were dead and had both been murdered. You uprooted my life and his, and all it was for was because of debt!" I shout at them, tears of rage pouring down my cheeks. Everyone remains silent for a moment, then "You have no idea how much that ruined and affected my life, and then when I finally think I'm coping because of Tyler I found out what you did to him. Nearly killed him and devastated his life too". It comes out as a whisper.

They can no longer look at me, but they both stare at Tyler.
"How did you find our daughter, why did you tell her?" they ask in bitter voices.
"I didn't know who she was, I ended up getting a new job after what happened. She became my assistant.." Tyler trails off, he didn't like answering to them.
"You became his assistant, assistant to the man who's responsible for us being here?" my mother declares in shock.
"You're responsible for you being here, yes I'm his assistant, assistant to the man you nearly murdered and who did nothing wrong" I snap at her, appalled by what she'd said.
"You're not the people I always believed you to be and that's what sickens me the most; so now you've got what you wanted. You're dead to me now, I'll never be seeing you again" I tell them in the fiercest voice I can muster. They are both left in a devastatingly fearful silence at my last words, Tyler hugs me to him letting my tears soak his shirt and they simply watch. Neither one of them stating the obvious that we are in love with each other, it doesn't matter Tyler has hardly spoken; he doesn't need to and is as shaken by the experience as me.

Without another word or glance at them Tyler leads me away and back past the cells and out of the gate. They don't try to stop us and when we are in the corridor I run back the way we'd come, Tyler hard on my heels behind me to catch up. I become oblivious to everyone around us, Tyler leads me out the building as fast as possible and speaks to nobody including Ralph who notices us. I can't actually believe what has just happened, it's as if time's slowed down now and nothing can make it speed back to a normal reality.
    Tyler gets me in the car and buckles my seatbelt for me as I just sit there in a daze. When he drives, he travels slowly and cautiously as he seems to be trying to focus which is difficult obviously after both our minds are now racing from everything that has happened. My tears dry on my face and no

more are left in my eyes, it's over now. I never have to go back to this, I know the truth, I've seen them and there's nothing worth salvaging from this so I can move on once and for all now.

We get home and the rest of that day was mostly quiet, me and Tyler discuss a few issues but I think we both have realised that although there has been pain today, there's only brighter days ahead. There are no secrets now, no past issues that the other doesn't know about and we're on the same page.

To be honest we've been closer than ever afterwards and our relationship has progressed and we've been planning other things to do in our holiday.

*

It's been three weeks since that all happened and I've never felt so happy, everything has fit into place and I'm enjoying the day but it's nearly the evening now. Normally I would be enjoying the day with Tyler but he's been making a lot of phone calls and recently a strange thing I've picked up on is the fact that he keeps his hand constantly glued into his pocket. I haven't asked him about it but he does it all the time, we'll be holding hands but his other hand will be in his pocket as if he's got something in it. I have the feeling Tyler's arranging something behind my back, he's been calling and texting people all the time but today he must be setting a record.

Let's face it, Tyler hardly ever goes on his phone normally and seeing as we'll be returning to work next week I want to enjoy my time with him. He comes back outside, his face a mix of nerves and excitement which instantly grasps my attention.

"Violet" he utters my name in an out of breath voice from all the talking he's been doing.

"Yeah, what is it? What's going on?" I ask him, I would appreciate an insight into what the hell is happening.

He smiles, "We're going out to one of the best restaurants I know, so we should get dressed up smart and go" he tells me, his excitement evident in every way possible.

"What, are you serious? That's amazing!" I gasp in astonishment, we then rush inside to get changed.

I pick out a dark blue dress which is the best one I own and quickly change into it. I brush my long black hair and then straighten it. After applying some pink lipstick, I put on my only pair of high heels and then go downstairs to find Tyler. He has polished black shoes on, black trousers, a neat white shirt and the collar shows nicely against his smart black jacket and tie. He smiles when his blue eyes look up and see me, then we head out to the car and get on our way.

When we arrive and climb out the car though I gape, when Tyler had said we were going to one of the best restaurants he knew he wasn't joking. It has to be the most famous restaurant I've ever heard of, we link arms and walk up to the doors. A man who is as suited and booted as Tyler opens the doors for us and leads Tyler over to confirm our booking.

"Ah yes, just follow me" he ushers us around a few corners to something I wasn't expecting. Standing beside a rather grand table are Izzie, Michael, Jacqueline and Jess. They're all dressed up and instantly smile as soon as they see us.

We rush towards them.

"So you didn't tell me where we were going and I can't believe you didn't tell me we would all be meeting up!" I exclaim to Tyler and the others all laugh.

"It was a surprise," Tyler smiles and we begin greeting and hugging each other before we sit down. It's so nice to see them all like this before we go back to work next week, I just wonder why Tyler kept me in the dark about it when everyone else was in on it. We talk about everything as we make it through our starter, main and many drinks before we decide to have a break before dessert. I notice that everyone is watching Tyler, obviously expectant of something that hasn't happened yet and looking at me with excitement.

So when everyone has returned from the toilet or wherever they'd gone I ask Tyler the question that has been on my mind.

"Tyler, what is the actual reason we're here for, because I'm getting the impression there's more to this than a simple get together?"

Everyone held their breath now, waiting for some kind of big event to happen I'm guessing.

"Yes you're right, there is a specific reason I organised this get together," Tyler spoke slowly, choosing his words carefully and his hand returns to his pocket as he stands up.

He takes my hand so that I stand up as well in front of him and everyone else. His gorgeous blue eyes hold mine as he draws in a deep breath and then bends down on one knee before me. That is when he produces a small black box from his pocket and opens it so I can see the most beautiful ring it has inside it.

"Violet Spring, will you marry me?" Tyler asks the question I've always wanted to hear from him and obviously there's only one answer I'm going to give.

"Yes," I whisper in shock, still unable to believe what is happening and we both break into wide smiles and he slips the beautiful ring on my finger which I admire.

He stands up and then his lips meet mine and my hands hold his face as his wrap round my waist. We both hear the awed applause and cheering and clapping but we don't pull apart. I am his and he is mine, I am his assistant and now his fiancé and nothing will change that. All that matters is that ring on my finger and his lips on mine, the marker of our future.

Acknowledgements

Thank you to all my friends and family that have supported me throughout the time I wrote this book and encouraged me to get this published so that others can enjoy it.

Thank you to Matthew Klimcke who encouraged my writing throughout primary school

Thank you to Mrs Lancaster who believed in my work in year 9

Thank you to Jess Walker for helping me improve my writing skills whether he knows it or not, also for all his generous support when I've been struggling

Finally thank you to all my teachers who have been supportive and helped me believe in myself, I appreciate all the help and chats I've had over the years considering many different problems from Jess Walker, Gregory Coughlin, Matthew Klimcke, Mrs Lancaster and Jane Fry.

Authors note

I have written this book at the age of 15 when I'm currently battling anxiety and depression, I hope this can be an inspiration to others with this silent illness and that anything is possible if you don't give up. If like me you enjoy reading books to find an escape from the real world then I hope my book satisfies you and brings enjoyment to all those who read it.